Bad Vibrations

Dan Anderson

ISBN 978-1-60145-543-7

Library of Congress Control Number 2008906024

Printed in the United States of America.

Murder, Mayhem & Malice Press, P. O. Box 616869, Orlando, FL 32861-6869
2008

Dedication

To Virginia—*Je t'aime plus q'hier, moins que demain.*

To Dan—as he navigates his way through the threshold of a happy and successful life.

To Misha—a loving and gentle soul that happens to reside in a canine.

Acknowledgments

There are several people to whom I am indebted for inspiring, encouraging, and bringing to fruition the escapades of Chauncey and his coterie. Although some may be reluctant to have their association with this tome revealed because of its outré nature, I must nevertheless thank them for their substantive and meaningful contributions. First, are Sandra Cantrell and Dawn Cantrell, indefatigable readers, who served as sounding boards to provide ongoing feedback on character and plot development. Next is my wife, Virginia, whom I took advantage of to provide the Spanish text since that is her first language. Next is Stephen Evans, editor extraordinaire, whose disciplined approach produced order out of chaos. Finally, I am grateful to my dog, Misha, who encouraged me to persevere and edit. When I would fall asleep in front of my PC in the wee hours of the morning with the manuscript flickering on the screen, he would hump my leg to wake me up and get me back on track. Additionally, he convinced me of the need for extensive revision by relieving himself on my first draft.

All people, places, and events in this book are fictitious even though they may have a namesake in reality. Any resemblance to an actual living or non-living entity of any sort is purely coincidental and much too vague for anyone to take implied offense.

Chapter 1

"Woman Murdered With Vibrator."

As macabre as it sounded, the headline was not a figment of someone's perverse imagination. There it was, on page one of the Metro section in the *Los Angeles Times*. My attention captured, I folded the newspaper to the article in question. It was uncomfortably warm in the small bathroom of my private detective agency and I fanned myself for a minute before reading on.

In the lurid style of crime journalism, the article proceeded to describe how one "Boom Boom" Saperstein, an exotic dancer at one of North Hollywood's "gentlemen's clubs," had been found dead, floating in her bathtub, the murder weapon still inside her. Electrocution was given as the cause of death, in spite of the fact that the vibrator's electrical cord had been unplugged from the wall and lay innocently on the floor. Also noted in the story was the fact that Ms. Saperstein was the five-hundredth homicide of 1980.

I was just beginning to get into the more graphic forensic details of the article when the bell over the door of my office jingled, indicating the arrival of company. I finished my business and opened the bathroom door a crack to preview my visitor. A soft whistle nearly escaped my pursed lips. Standing in my office, looking out the window, was a stunning creature, the kind I thought only existed in the celluloid world of aerobic workout tapes. She was tall, about five ten, and wore skin-tight designer jeans with a yellow halter that was under considerable stress. Her hair was several shades lighter than her halter and cascaded down her back, terminating in tawny curls midway between her shoulder blades and waist. Her stiletto heals clicked nervously as she began pacing back and forth across my chipped parquet floor.

I quietly closed the door and took a few extra minutes to tuck in my shirt, straighten my clip-on bow tie, and brush the wide lapels of my green plaid jacket. After putting on my broadest smile, I stepped into the room with my hand extended. To my surprise, the statuesque vision had vanished, leaving no evidence of her presence except the lingering fragrance of her perfume. In her place, almost swallowed up by an old armchair in the corner, sat another woman.

This lady was a far cry from her predecessor. She was diminutive, elderly, and plain; surrounded by a nimbus of withered and wrinkled weariness. Her dull, gray hair was drawn tightly into a bun, its simplicity matched by her dark gabardine frock. Her most salient attribute was her drabness. She spoke in an indistinctive, cracked voice.

"Mr. McFadden?"

"Yes," I replied before asking, "Did you happen to see a young woman in here only a moment ago?"

"No, but I saw one jump into a car by the curb as I was entering the building."

"I wonder what she wanted," I mused. "Well, probably not important. What may I do for you, madam?"

She looked around the sparsely furnished room purposefully. In addition to the chair in which she was submerged, the room contained only a folding chair, a used metal desk purchased at a garage sale, a telephone and answering machine, an appointment book, and a two-drawer file cabinet.

Sensing her disapproval, I offered a pseudo-apology. "Please pardon the appearance of this room, madam. It's a recently opened branch office and the decorators are in the process of sketching some layouts for my review." I had been tempted to tell her that, like the poet Phillip Larkin, deprivation was to me what daffodils were to Wordsworth but I refrained.

She took another look around and sniffed audibly. "Mr. McFadden, I may have a job for you. It could involve some danger. Do you have a pistol?"

That was a loaded question. Somewhere in my possession I did have a revolver. However, infrequent use had eroded its value since most of my cases involved rather mundane fare such as matrimonial infidelity, missing persons, background checks for pre-nups and child custody, insurance fraud, evidence procurement, and surveillance. Truth be known, I was more at home with a camera than a firearm.

"A private investigator's license in California doesn't allow me to carry a concealed weapon. However, I can 'pack a piece' if the situation warrants it. Incidentally, may I have the pleasure of an introduction?"

"I'm Rubella Saperstein."

"Saperstein . . . Saperstein . . . that name sounds familiar." I rubbed my chin and studied her thoughtfully.

"It was in all the papers this morning. My niece was murdered night before last. Poor Cleotha."

"Was she the strip . . . uh . . . dancer who was found murdered with a vib . . . uh . . . who was electrocuted in the bathtub?"

"Yes." Her answer was sandwiched between sighs.

"How can I help you, Mrs. Saperstein?"

"I want you to find her killer. My niece worked a couple of miles from here so I know the area. I picked you out of the yellow pages because of your address. I don't have much money, but I figured that anyone setting up shop in this part of town couldn't be charging very much."

I could see that getting her to speak with candor was not going to be difficult.

"Have you been to the authorities?" I asked.

"I just got back from the police station," she said.

"What did they say?"

"They weren't very encouraging," she confided.

I sat down and leaned back in my chair, brimming with confidence gained from five years of exposure to police personnel and procedure. "Let me guess. They said they wouldn't be able to launch an investigation anytime soon because of budget cutbacks."

"No, that's not it," she replied.

"Then they said they couldn't do anything because of a manpower shortage due to the current crime wave."

"No, that's not it, either."

My confidence eroding, I leaned forward and said, "Then they told you that since your niece was not a prominent citizen whose demise had provoked a public outcry, her murder had been shoved to the back burner?"

"No, that's still not it."

Crestfallen, I surrendered. "So, what did they say?"

"They said they didn't give a shit."

I sighed and leaned back in my chair. "I'm afraid that's pretty much the lowest rung on the crime investigation ladder. Don't hold your breath waiting for an arrest."

She nodded her head twice in defeated agreement. "It's clear that if justice is to be had, it will have to be bought and paid for. I don't have much in the way of savings, but I'd like to see poor Cleotha's death avenged, if the price is right." She cocked her head and looked down her nose at me with suspicion. "And, just how much *do* you charge, Mr. McFadden?"

"My normal rates are $100 a day plus expenses, but you're in luck. Since your niece was in the entertainment industry, I can extend a professional courtesy discount, which would amount to $49.95 per day plus expenses."

After a moment of eyebrow-scrunched reflection, she replied, "I guess that's reasonable enough. Do I pay you now?"

"Two days in advance for a couple of reasons. First, consideration such as money is necessary to validate an offer and its acceptance and to form a binding contract of mutual assent. Second, such consideration officially establishes a principal and agent relationship between us which authorizes me to act on your behalf in all matters within the sphere of my appointment."

She absorbed this information for a moment before accepting my offer. "All right, Mr. McFadden . . ." She leaned forward, reached into her canvas satchel, and pulled out a roll of money. I watched as she removed some rubber bands that compressed the currency into a tight cylinder. Then, I watched as she slowly peeled off a one-hundred-dollar bill—I thought I saw Ben Franklin blink, probably dazzled by the rare exposure to light—and I watched as she rubbed it vigorously between her thumb and forefinger to ensure that two bills were not stuck together. Satisfied that only one had been successfully extricated from its colleagues, she resecured the roll and stashed it back into the satchel. ". . . Here you are." Finally, this mesmerizing vignette mercifully ended and she handed me the payment.

Even at an arm's distance, the bill exuded the smells of arthritis ointment and mattress mold—the aromas of the old and frugal—but I quickly accepted it and slipped it into my pocket.

"Can you start on the case right away?"

"Let me check my calendar and see." I picked up the appointment book, hoping she hadn't noticed how dusty it was, and licked my index finger before thumbing through the nearly blank pages. Other than a few paper lice that were unaccustomed to disturbance, I found no conflicts, which I well knew.

"You're in luck, Mrs. Saperstein," I said. "There *does* appear to be an opening into which I can squeeze you."

"Thank you, Mr. McFadden. I'm very pleased." The wrinkles around her mouth softened into what I assumed to be a smile. Her voice went up a note and she touched her hands together. That was probably as close to frenzy as she ever got. I reached into a desk drawer and pulled out a small spiral notebook.

"I'd like to get some information from you, Mrs. Saperstein, if I may. First off, what do you do for a living?"

"I'm a housekeeper for a wealthy man in San Marino. I live in the servants' quarters."

I flipped a few pages and jotted the information down. "Thank you. Now, tell me about your niece."

"I raised Cleotha from infancy," she said wistfully. "Her parents were killed when she was a baby, and I'm all the family she's ever known."

"How did her parents die?"

"They were trampled to death years ago in an after-Christmas bargain basement sale at Blaufelt's department store. Their battered bodies were found beneath a pile of fluorescent Nehru jackets by the cleaning staff the next day. It was horrible. Thank God, Cleotha was too young to remember."

"I'm sorry. Please, go on," I urged.

"Cleotha was such a good girl when she was growing up—Girl Scouts, good grades, honor society, you know; all the right friends. However, when she got to be fourteen or so, she started running around with a fast crowd and I began to lose control of her. She wouldn't listen to me anymore and became rebellious and disobedient." Mrs. Saperstein paused, absorbed in recollection.

"She was a well-developed girl. In fact, that was the cause of her problems: her body matured faster than her judgment. She began flirting with boys and leading them on. I'll never forget the first time I had to put up bail for her: she'd surrendered her virginity in the end zone during halftime at a Rams game. Five men were arrested for contributing to the delinquency of a minor, including the place kicker and free safety."

"She certainly sounds precocious."

"As soon as Cleotha graduated from high school, she ran away from home. She got a job at the Glad Gland, a seedy strip joint in North Hollywood."

"Is that when she adopted the stage name, Boom Boom?" I asked.

"No," Mrs. Saperstein replied. "She'd picked that nickname up earlier in high school. After football games, she used to do the dirty boogie with the starting players on top of the wooden planks in the bleachers. I was told that the noise made by these loose boards as they rhythmically slapped her bouncing booty sounded like 'boom-boom-boom-boom' and the nickname stuck. Her yearbook has more athletes' autographs than the Pro Football Hall of Fame." Mrs. Saperstein stopped to recompose herself and blink away a painful memory.

"I'm beginning to see a pattern," I said, briefly basking in the visual of her explanation.

"Yes, well, at the Glad Gland, she danced and stripped, danced and stripped. By the time her act was over, all she had on was two sequins and a boa constrictor named Mohammed Al-Said. The snake's name used to be Jefferson or Jackson or something, but Cleotha changed it when Muslim names became trendy in the black community."

"When was the last time you saw your niece?"

"Yesterday." Mrs. Saperstein dabbed gingerly in the corners of her eyes. "She was laid out stark naked on a slab at the morgue. They called me in to identify the body."

"Actually, I meant . . . while she was alive."

"Hmmm. Three or four months ago, I'd say. Cleotha rarely called or came to see me. She led her own life and did as she pleased."

"Did she have any friends or acquaintances with whom I could talk?"

"She shared an expensive house with a girl named Wanda Latouche, another dancer at the Glad Gland. I never met the girl, though."

"Was your niece having problems with anyone?" I observed Mrs. Saperstein knotting and twisting a well-worn handkerchief.

"Not that I know of. As I said earlier, I haven't seen her much since she left home. But if she was in some kind of trouble, she would have come to see me. She knew I was always there for her."

"All right, Mrs. Saperstein. I'll see what I can do. If the police do deem this crime to be of little significance, they may allow me to ferret around." I tore a page out of the notebook and slid it, with my pen, across the table. "Please write down your address and telephone number so I'll know where to reach you."

She reached in her pocket and removed some wire-frame glasses that were held together by a paper clip. Then, after obliging my request, she deftly slipped my pen into her satchel. She looked up sweetly. "Is there anything else you need?"

I nodded my head while wondering: why do I always get these clients? "Do you have a picture of Cleotha that I might borrow?"

"Yes," she replied. She rummaged inside her satchel and handed me a snapshot. "This picture was taken more recently than the one they used in the papers."

I slipped the picture into my desk drawer. "That should conclude our business for now, Mrs. Saperstein. I'll contact you as soon as I have something to report."

She didn't budge.

"I believe I have ten cents coming."

"I beg your pardon?" I asked.

"I paid for two days in advance at $49.95, which comes to a total of $99.90. I gave you $100.00; that means I should receive ten cents back."

I excused myself, walked out to the vending machine in the hall and gave it a swift, well-placed kick. A couple of nickels trickled down into the coin return, and I returned to my office to give Mrs. Saperstein her change. She then used my pen to record the transaction in a black ledger, resumed her death grip on the satchel, and left as silently as she had arrived.

Chapter 2

Flush with funds and a renewed purpose, I thumbtacked a hastily scribbled "Gone for the Day" sign on my office door and walked down the dark hallway of my building. Only one other tenant was presently renting space in the building, an attorney named Melkoff. As I neared it, I saw that the door to his single-room office was still open due to a malfunctioning thermostat. It was doubtful he would catch a breeze from the corridor, but without air conditioning, he'd been forced to keep his office door open and hope.

I glanced inside. He was all smiles, handing a pen and what appeared to be a legal document to an elderly dowager who was squinting and rubbing her eyes. I paused momentarily, out of curiosity, just past the door. "I'm *so* sorry I stepped on your reading glasses, Mrs. Swenson. I'll have them repaired and delivered to your home. However, to avoid delay, you should sign this form today—that's right, on the line at the bottom. This document is a mere formality; it's called a 'durable power of attorney,' and simply allows me to assist you in the stewardship of your assets. It's a wise precaution on your part."

I shook my head sadly. If the old lady was turning over the management of her estate to Melkoff, it was a sure bet she'd be buried in a potter's field. He was a master in the subtle art of "asset conversion." The only thing I admired about Melkoff was that he was a self-made man. He had taken correspondence courses on civilian and military criminal law while imprisoned at Fort Leavenworth awaiting a court-martial. With his newly acquired legal knowledge, he managed to get many of the charges dismissed as well as gain valuable preparation for his future career.

Melkoff had been a staff sergeant in the U.S. Army, in charge of a battalion mess hall, until he was apprehended selling government hams and turkeys to off-limits restaurants. While in prison, he met several JAG attorneys who were serving short terms of their own for various and sundry swindles and who inspired him to steal through the back door rather than the front. Convinced that the road to wealth was more easily traversed by bending the law as an advocate rather than breaking it as an adversary, he changed his identity through false documentation and earned his law degree. He then proceeded to set up a low-overhead practice here—a fleecing operation that had grown to be unrivaled even by professional norms.

Somehow, he managed to stay one jump ahead of any inquiries by the bar association and evade indictment. But, even if he ever was caught and disbarred, I had undaunted faith in Melkoff's consummate skills as a survivor. I had *no* doubt, in fact, that he would quickly open up another racket under another assumed name and proceed once again to separate the unwary from their valuables. With his flamboyance and low ethical threshold, I was also confident that he would eventually wander into politics, lobbying, or used-car sales. I shook my head and left Melkoff and his prey, walked down the stairs, and opened the door to the street. As the door closed behind me, I looked over the neighborhood, a former grande dame that had fallen upon hard times.

Most legitimate businesses had abandoned the area years ago in anticipation of advancing urban decay. The few surviving stores, propped up by cheap rent and free parking, hung on for dear economic life and included the usual denizens of the dump: tattoo parlors, tanning emporiums, bail bond offices, paycheck cashers, liquor stores, and pawn brokers—businesses whose clients were more likely to appear on police blotters than society pages. Even the gangs that once livened up the area had fled some years ago for better ZIP codes. The only evidence of their prior habitation was the faded graffiti that still managed to cling tenuously to cracked stuccoed walls and a few looted phone booths that dotted the sidewalks like Stonehenge monoliths.

I blinked to help ease some of the irritation in my eyes. Air quality in the area had been in a funk lately from forest fires that were burning near Bakersfield. Slowly and surely, the acrid smoke and accompanying ash had risen into the upper air currents to waft their way westward. The result was general discomfort and upper respiratory misery in the coastal cities.

Looking up, I saw that the sun had already cleared the roofs of two-story buildings and was beginning to bathe the concrete sidewalks and asphalt roads with early morning rays. A summer-long drought had wilted even the most stubborn weeds. Once sprouting defiantly in cracks and vacant lots, they now hung limply under the solar bake. They had been joined by a fresh assortment of trash whipped in by recent Santa Ana winds. Newspaper pages, in particular, wrapped themselves around the bases of telephone poles and wove themselves into fences: there, they would stay until dislodged by the wakes of passing trucks or disintegrated by winter rains.

Walking to my car, I looked up and down the block. The streets were barren except for a Chinese laundry that had managed to attract a few customers with their semi-annual auction of unclaimed shirts. The laundry catered to a rough crowd and assumed that clothing not picked up after six months meant the owner had been crammed in a barrel under the end of the San Pedro pier, buried at the bottom of some landfill, or compacted inside a junked automobile at a metal reclamation yard.

My 1952 maroon Hudson was parked next door in a deserted gas station whose faded signs still advertised petrol at 36.9 cents. As soon as I sat down in the seat, I rolled down the window and started coaxing the choke and stomping the accelerator. After several minutes, she sputtered to life, and I headed to my first stop, a convenience market, to procure some peanuts for the office mice. Their recent droppings suggested a lack of dietary fiber which I sought to address through legumes and a bit of cheddar.

As I exited the market with purchase in hand, I heard a crash and looked around to my right. Standing outside of an adjacent shop was a lady cursing at the top of her lungs, waving her arms, and stomping her feet in flamenco fashion. A mid-sixties Pontiac was speeding away from the parking lot, after leaving behind a bent fender on a pale yellow Rolls Royce Corniche. Acting on instinct, I memorized the license plate number of the departing car and approached the animated lady jauntily.

"Good afternoon, madam. You appear to be in need of assistance."

"That greaseball backed into my Rolls and took off," she fumed.

"Unfortunately, in this neighborhood, many people don't leave their names and phone numbers under the windshield wipers of cars they damage. However, I may be able to obtain the identity of the irresponsible driver for you." I smiled confidently; the license number of the Pontiac securely tucked away in my memory banks.

She looked at me quizzically. "Who are you, little man? And, how could you possibly help with this?"

"Private investigator," I replied. I smiled while holding my breath and unsuccessfully trying to button my jacket.

"Do you have a business card?"

I reached into my jacket pocket and handed her one.

"McFadden Investigations," she read before cocking her head back and sizing me up.

While she was looking me over, I looked her over—a much more pleasant undertaking. She was a striking brunette, a head taller than I was, with dark brown eyes and an hourglass figure that had more sand in the top than the bottom.

"And *you're* McFadden?"

"Chauncey McFadden, at your service." I bowed slightly from what remained of my waist—it had been an early casualty to overindulgence and sloth, two traits more highly regarded in Tudor England than in anorexic Southern California.

She lowered her designer shades and viewed me with suspicion. "You don't look much like a private eye, Chauncey McFadden."

In my late thirties, I was still slightly less than five feet eight inches in height and not-so-slightly more than two hundred and fifty pounds. My poor vision had been largely corrected by black, horn-rimmed glasses; my premature baldness, on the other hand, had not been similarly blessed by any of a number of corrective antidotes. "That may be true, but my bland appearance serves me well when I work undercover," I retorted.

"What other experience have you had?"

"I've been a night watchman, museum security guard, and package checker at the super-mart exit . . . among other things, of course."

She didn't look impressed. "I thought all gumshoes were ex-detectives who got canned for insubordination or for not following police procedure—even though they usually lead the precinct in number of collars and commendations. I thought they were steady drinkers with nerves of steel who'd been dumped by ex-wives who didn't like their hours or the job stress. I thought they were lonely knights who walked the mean streets with honor and without fear."

"You certainly have a nodding acquaintance with the genre," I acknowledged. "I'm cut from a little different bolt of cloth. My application to the police academy was rejected, my only commendation in life was a penmanship award in the third grade, and I become inebriated by sniffing a bunghole; I have never been married, despite three rejected proposals, *and* I can be bought.

"However, the value I bring to the table is that I can start on your case right away, I don't charge if I don't get results, and my discretion in sensitive matters is guaranteed. You should also know that to be licensed as a private investigator in California, I have had to accrue six thousand hours of compensated experience in investigative work."

"Your honesty is refreshing," she replied. "I may have a job for you that has nothing to do with this dent. Can you come to my home this evening at seven o'clock? My name's Jill Barrington and I live at 14 Regal Place in Halcyon Hills. You'll be discussing a very important and confidential matter with my father, Alfred Barrington. I'll tell him that we met and ask him to hire you."

I was surprised at her offer since Halcyon Hills was one of the wealthiest, most prestigious residential areas in the city. Also, Alfred Barrington, better known by his previous title of Judge, had been *the* central figure in Los Angeles politics before retiring to assume a more oblique role of puppeteer to the so-called city hall marionettes.

"I'll be there." I had almost stammered as I watched her retreating derrière sway back and forth like an inverted windshield wiper. I didn't move—okay, maybe I couldn't move—and before long, the Rolls glided past me out of the parking lot and down the street. I noticed her personalized license plate as the yellow carriage and its princess receded from view: DANGER.

I hoped that wasn't a portent.

Chapter 3

Since it was late summer, the sunlight was sufficient at six-thirty to catch at least partial views of the mansions that flanked both sides of Regal Place. Each residence was ensconced on at least three acres and reflected an architectural style and quality of construction long extinct. Few, if any, of these homes had a replacement value of less than eight figures, which is why any sales price was usually met—and promptly so—on those rare occasions when a Halcyon Hills address did go on the market.

I cruised slowly past open gates, spying lawns and shrubbery that were well manicured, the recipients of meticulous care, and an occasional rainbow among the late afternoon sprinklers that whirled contentedly above serene sod. Flower beds exploded with an effulgence of color, often in stark contrast to the subdued hues of the homes themselves.

Along the road, I spotted crews of Japanese gardeners in dilapidated pickup trucks and Hispanic domestics walking to bus stops. Otherwise, the quiet of my tranquil drive was only occasionally interrupted by the hum of speeding German and Italian convertibles filled with laughing young scions of luxury, darting about with loosely tied tennis sweaters streaming from their tanned necks like the silk scarves of World War I flying aces.

The Halcyon Hills constabulary patrolled the streets in a continuous vigil for interlopers. Knowing the residents, frequent guests, and menials by sight, they approached anyone else with a cautious civility that could quickly became a brusque insistence for departure should an intrusion be unauthorized. I suppose, then, it was only natural that my rusty Hudson would attract their attention. Soon enough, with minimal fanfare, a patrol car discretely ushered me over to the curb. Two patrolmen stepped quickly from the car, each approaching a different side of my vehicle.

"What's the problem, officers? I was barely going twenty-five," I offered ingenuously.

The officer peering in my window asked, "Let me see your driver's license, pal. What's the nature of your business in Halcyon Hills?"

The other officer positioned himself on the passenger side of my car and tapped his holster, as if adding punctuation.

"I have an appointment with Judge Barrington at seven," I replied, handing over my license, "for which I shall be late if this unwarranted detainment isn't expedited."

The first officer took my license to run a check on it while the other officer propped his foot on my fender and looked inside the car. Having little else to do, I stared at his heavily starched uniform and polished brass.

In a few minutes, the first deputy returned and broke the silence. "All right, McFadden, your story's easy enough to confirm. Follow us, and we'll escort you to the Judge's place. If you're not on the level, we'll be continuing this conversation."

They climbed back into their blue and yellow patrol car and led the way. I followed in limp pursuit and we eventually arrived at a security gate, which opened after our presence was announced through an intercom. I followed the officers into the grounds of the estate on a cobblestone entrance road that was bordered by Italian cypress trees. It ended at the entrance to a transplanted English manor: a modern homage to a Buckingham forebear.

The officers parked and allowed me to proceed toward a massive oak door, where I rang the bell. A septuagenarian in butler's attire appeared momentarily and I announced myself loudly enough for my escorts to hear: "My name is Chauncey McFadden. Judge Barrington is expecting me."

As the man stepped back to allow my entrance, I turned and nodded at my escorts, then entered into a large foyer. I glanced at the butler whose slightly knocked knees, stooped carriage, twitching ears, and wispy muttonchops gave him an arresting presence.

"May I take your coat, sir?"

"Thank you, no. I'm not wearing a coat."

"May I offer you a coat?"

"I think not."

"Very well, sir. Please follow me to the Judge's study."

It was not difficult to keep pace with the dotty old seneschal. He exhibited the gait of a man afflicted with pernicious hemorrhoids or suffering the ambulatory after-effects of four decades on a rural Southern chain gang. I followed his short, shuffling steps until we reached the terminus of a long corridor: double French doors.

Once the mahogany doors were opened, I saw that the "study" was in actuality a cavernous library-museum. Besides housing what must have been thousands of books nestled in columns of never-ending open shelves, rare scholarly tomes were secured behind the leaded-glass panes of antique bookcases and brittle manuscripts were locked in glass display cabinets. The room itself was highlighted by several huge stone fireplaces with mantels of sienna marble; many brightened by Beauvais tapestries suspended above them.

The furnishings in the room were no less spectacular. As I've mentioned, in a previous life, I was a security guard at a museum. Its collection specialized in European antiques and paintings, and I picked up some knowledge on the subject as well as an eclectic appreciation. Based on that knowledge, I recognized several pieces: a grand flugel pianoforte and an eighteenth-century English harpsichord, numerous Louis XIV bronzes, console tables of carved mahogany and terra-cotta topped with verde antico marble, and commodes, or large French chests, with decorative tulipwood marquetry and gilded cast metal ormolu.

Eighteenth-century French sculpture was well represented by some thoughtfully selected works of Pigalle, Falconet, Clodion, and Houdon. Several fifteenth- and sixteenth-century Renaissance paintings were displayed against a background of Genoese velvet; featured were such Italian and Flemish masters as Marnardi, Roger van der Weyden, and Jan van Eyck. Porcelain works were much in evidence in the form of Sèvres vases, a Meissen candelabrum, and some Chelsea plates.

"This is a spectacular room," I commented in spellbound awe. After my enchantment subsided, I added, "I'll bet I can tell you the most valuable objects here."

"Indeed, sir," the butler replied with decorum and disinterest.

"The knobs of the doors we just passed through: they're the most priceless of all the collectibles."

"The door knobs?"

I thought I sensed a touch of genuine curiosity.

"Are you quite sure, sir?"

"Yes, they're the varnished balls of Charlemagne and, as you can appreciate, are virtually irreplaceable in today's market."

The butler didn't look convinced, but he furtively wiped his hands on the seat of his trousers anyway and eyed me warily. "May I get you something to eat, sir?"

"Why, thank you." I brightened. "I'd like a bologna sandwich, on a kaiser roll—heavy on the mayo."

"I'm sorry, sir, but the cook has retired for the evening and the kitchen is closed. May I bring you a cocktail instead?"

"Yes, a snifter of amontillado sherry will do quite nicely."

"I'm sorry again, sir, but the wine steward resigned this morning, and we have been unable to locate the key to the cellar. Will there be anything else?"

"I would ask for a concubine, but I'll wager that she's out of service with a yeast infection."

"Actually, sir, she's visiting her mother in Glendale."

Since this was going nowhere, I looked for a seat. Chairs, primarily English in origin, were tastefully arranged around the room and included some Chippendales, a few red velvet side chairs from the William and Mary period, and some eighteenth-century Georgian pieces. Finally, I spotted a more comfortable looking overstuffed armchair and prepared to sit down. I joked to myself that the seat had probably once been graced by the derriere of Cardinal Richelieu.

"One moment, sir—" the butler cried upon seeing my intention. He shuffled over to me as fast as his pedestrian locomotion would permit, whipped out a whisk broom from a concealed pocket in his coat, and proceeded to dust me off, grumbling each time a straw became ensnared in my synthetic threads.

A sudden draft of cold air against the back of my neck prompted me to turn around; I was face-to-face with a man, staring at me from the doorway of the study. The man was more than six feet tall and erect in carriage; his lean frame flattered the dark blue smoking jacket, white silk shirt, and burgundy ascot that he wore. He was a little older than the picture used by the newspapers, but I had no doubt of his identity: the formidable Judge Barrington.

Determined not to speak first—that was the obligation of the host—I used the opening silence to continue looking over my prospective employer. The judge was an imposing figure, a fact that had not handicapped his dominance in local politics. He had dark, wavy hair flanked with wide bands of silver that began at each temple and swept back over pointed ears to the nape of his neck. Thick, bushy eyebrows were mounted above black, piercing eyes, which could stir discomfort in the target of a prolonged stare. In his youth, he had no doubt been handsome. The passing years had muted some of this surface attractiveness, however, and given it a sinister undertone.

"Mr. McFadden, I believe."

"I'm honored to meet you, Judge Barrington. How good of you to see me."

"My daughter informed me of her meeting with you this morning and of her invitation. I hadn't really thought about hiring a private investigator, but Jill was so insistent that I finally agreed. I don't suppose it can do any harm."

He paused, and I noted that his eyes were still evaluating me.

"She also warned that you didn't look like the steel-jawed, muscle-bound, smoking-gun avenger from a film noir movie poster."

"Quite so, your honor." I had to agree. "However, I've found innocuousness to be a formidable weapon in the hands of a skilled craftsman. My feckless and fatuous appearance has allowed me to succeed in the past, where more vain predecessors have failed."

He continued the conversation, obviously not impressed. "Did Jill tell you what this was about?" he asked.

"She only mentioned that you were concerned with a family matter of utmost importance and confidentiality. Investigative matters requiring third-party tact, discretion, and efficiency are my specialty," I informed him in my most professional manner.

The judge still lacked any hint of interest, but after a short pause, he replied, "Very well, I suppose I have nothing to lose by your investigation," as he slumped into an Edwardian parlor chair and grimaced, apparently in anticipation of the painful narration to follow.

"In addition to Jill, whom you met today, I had another daughter—her twin sister, Justine."

"You used the past tense . . ." I dared to say.

"Yes." He replied, almost in a whisper. "Justine was brutally murdered two weeks ago, and her husband, Dr. Kevin Rutledge, has disappeared without a trace."

"My condolences on your loss, judge. Under these circumstances, I'm especially appreciative of you seeing me. Is Dr. Rutledge a physician?" I asked.

"No, he's a scientist. He has a couple of doctorates in computer science and engineering from MIT."

"Is he suspected of involvement in your daughter's death or is he more likely a co-victim of foul play?"

"He's just a material witness at this point. I believe the police have labeled him a 'person of interest.' No charges have been filed by the district attorney's office, but he's the subject of an intensive manhunt."

"How well do you know your son-in-law? Has he ever manifested a predisposition to violence?"

"None of which I'm aware. Kevin is a likeable young man. He drifted into Los Angeles a couple of years ago, and he and Justine were married after a whirlwind courtship. I did have reservations about their short engagement, but they were largely overcome by the hope that marriage would provide some stability to Justine's active social life."

"You had him checked out, of course . . ."

"Naturally," the judge replied. "His credentials are bona fide. He comes from a prominent family in the Hamptons, although their standard of living has become increasingly dependent upon loans and the disposition of assets rather than investment prowess."

"Then, if Dr. Rutledge *has* been kidnapped, a ransom might be a natural expectation. You, most likely, would be the recipient of that ransom note. I assume you have not received any such demand?"

"That's correct," the judge acknowledged.

"Were Justine and Kevin having any marital problems?"

The judge frowned. "No more than the usual tiffs that newlyweds have. They've been married less than a year. To be honest, I have suspected that all of this has something to do with a secret project Kevin has been working on."

"A secret project?"

"Yes. According to Kevin, and my resources inside the Department of Defense, he received a sizable grant from the federal government to build some sort of supercomputer that could accept massive amounts of data from unconventional sources and media and compute this data in trillionths of a second. In addition to the supercomputer, Kevin was to develop a number of military applications, which would give our country superiority in the fields of military intelligence and defensive and offensive weapons systems."

"How close to success was Dr. Rutledge in creating his super number-cruncher?"

"Several months ago, I got the impression that an announcement was imminent. Kevin had become increasingly excited and had dropped some comments about the vast power and wealth that would be forthcoming. Recently, though, I did notice a change in him. He showed signs of fatigue and stress. He appeared nervous and was quick to anger."

I decided to go off in a different direction for a moment. "I don't recall reading about his disappearance or Justine's murder in the newspapers."

The judge smiled wryly. "I still have some influence on what does and doesn't make the front page in this town. Justine's death was reported in a small obituary on the next-to-the-last page of the evening edition."

Penultimate journalism strikes again, I thought.

"Are there any other siblings?" I asked.

"No, just the two sisters."

"I suppose Mrs. Barrington is taking this very hard."

"My wife has been confined to institutional care for some years now because of poor mental health. She was told of Justine's death, but its impact upon her is unclear."

"I'm sorry to hear that," I said. "It must have been difficult trying to raise the girls on your own."

"Montrose, my butler, whom you just met, has been of assistance in this regard. He's functioned as a surrogate mother when asked."

There's a scary thought. "Did Justine have any coworkers or friends with whom I could talk?"

"Justine didn't work. She lived comfortably off the proceeds of a family trust administered by my bank. She's entitled to all the income from that trust and can even invade the corpus at the discretion of the trustee. As for friends, I have no knowledge of her associates. Perhaps Jill can give you the names of some of her friends," the judge replied.

"How did Justine spend her free time? Did she do any philanthropic work or participate in volunteer activities?" I asked.

"Nothing so productive or worthwhile, I'm afraid. Justine's favorite charity was herself. She passed the time at martini lunches and working on her tan."

"Had she recently asked you for any money or requested the trustee for an unusually large sum?"

"She hasn't asked me for money nor has she approached the trustee. While it's an irrevocable inter vivos trust into which I've surrendered control to get the assets out of my estate, the trustee gets his instructions from me, the grantor. Why do you ask?"

"I was just wondering about a possible blackmail scenario."

The judge reacted with a wan smile. "Justine would have laughed in a blackmailer's face."

I saw the judge glance at his watch.

"I'm afraid I have to cut this short, Mr. McFadden. I have an engagement to attend to. I've told you as much as I know, in any event.

You can get details from the police file—that is, if you're still interested in taking this case."

"Very much so. As you probably know, the spouse is usually the prime suspect in marital murders. So, unless he's been the victim of an extraterrestrial abduction, locating Dr. Rutledge will be my top priority."

"So be it. Find the killer, whoever it may be, and I'll pay you ten thousand dollars. This will have to be a handshake deal—no retainers and no contracts."

"Your word is acceptable, and I agree to your terms," I said, dollar signs bombarding my retina. "By the way, do you have a picture of Dr. Rutledge I could borrow?"

The judge crossed the room to a desk, removed a small glossy of his son-in-law from a picture frame and handed it to me.

"I'll see myself out," I offered, after pocketing the photograph. "Incidentally, how did your daughter die?"

The judge's lips tightened, distorting the hiss which passed through them. "She was found in her bathtub—electrocuted with a vibrator."

With no further discourse, we shook hands, and after leaving the room, I hustled almost blindly down the long corridor, trying to digest the shock of this latest revelation, and fumbled with the doorknob to get to fresh air. Finally, I jumped into my car and, after a drive I barely recall, arrived at my apartment. My preoccupation with the developments of this case was intense but did not prevent me from noticing the black limousine that was framed in my rearview mirror, which had followed me from the boundary of Halcyon Hills.

Chapter 4

The next morning, I drove to the corner of Buena Vista and Acosta. The attraction was a newsstand that had been operated for most of the past forty years by a colorful old Greek fellow named Jake Metakolous. Jake had staunchly manned his post since 1942, except for a couple of strokes and a coronary bypass—never a vacation, never a holiday. He had come to America from Greece as a young man during the early days of the Depression.

With the humiliating experience of Ellis Island behind him, Jake ignored the teeming, industrial melting pots of the East and sought out more open spaces. He traveled as far west as he could go and arrived in Los Angeles in 1932. With only a slight grasp of the language and no particular skills that were in demand, Jake accepted the only employment that was readily available; he became a "newsy," a job for which success only required long hours, a loud voice, boundless energy, and an ingratiating personality. Blessed with those qualities, Jake soon became the leading purveyor of the *Los Angeles Times,* and over the years, his sales multiplied and his loyal clientele expanded. Spurred on by his success and the increasing pain of premature arthritis in his legs, he opened a kiosk in the center of the city ten years later. He now manned his kiosk right in the middle of the legal district, across from the courthouse.

Jake had no family left in Greece, and he had never bothered to be distracted by marriage, so he emotionally adopted those whom society's doors had been slow to admit. And, although his income was modest, he managed to set up a curbside foundation for educational endowments. At present, some fifteen college students, primarily black and Hispanic, were receiving weekly stipends and encouragement from a man who was unknown to most of the city.

Jake was now approaching the age of seventy, but he looked at least ten years younger. His wild profusion of white hair defied combing and contrasted with his dark Mediterranean features. He wore the same red flannel shirt and gray twill work pants, rain or shine, hot or cold.

Some years before, Jake had taken a liking to me—for reasons known only to him. We had formed a warm relationship, based upon *quid pro quo:* I served as his teacher, helping him to improve his English vocabulary; he, in turn, used his location and discreet eavesdropping talents.

Free from the confines of courtrooms and judges' chambers, the power elite frequently huddled around Jake's kiosk and continued their discussions—oblivious to Jake's presence. As a result, Jake became a walking compendium of little-publicized facts about interesting people and occurrences in the city and county. My price for his aural surveillance, to be a target for any newly acquired words and linguistic skills, was well worth my time.

This morning, I could tell he was in fine form as I approached his kiosk. I was intentionally early enough to get his undivided attention.

"Chauncey!" He boomed upon seeing me. "You sesquipedalian Sherlock! You polysyllabic pundit! You crapulous crime solver!"

The fact was, fifty years in his adopted country had gradually worn away his accent until his folksy banter had just a trace of his Athenian patois. "Jake, my treasured font of municipal information. How goes it, old friend?"

"Can't complain. How about you?"

"Believe it or not, I'm working on two cases—homicides, no less, which I rarely get involved in." I leaned closer to him so I could lower my voice. "Even more astounding is that the two victims were murdered in the same way: submerged in bath water and electrocuted with a vaginal vibrator. That brings me to my first question: What can you tell me about Judge Barrington?"

"Judge Barrington? That's an easy one. He's been running the political sideshow almost as long as I've been peddlin' papers. He got his money buying real estate in the San Fernando Valley and water rights and oil leases cheap after the big war. Then he just sat on a mound and felt it grow into a mountain under his ass. Being a judge, he could fix most things through what passes for the legal system around here. The things he couldn't take care of himself, he had done by stoolies.

“He's been retired from the bench for a number of years, though, and don't make the waves he used to. Still, the bunch runnin’ the city keeps him informed and does whatever's necessary to protect him and what he's grabbed over the years. Prior to being a judge, he was a pretty sharp lawyer, as I understand it. He hushed up a lot of nasty cases for the high and mighty and built himself a big following of grateful supporters."

"Attorneys," I snorted with contempt.

"What you got against attorneys?" Jake asked.

"Nothing at all. I understand they make exemplary inmates in our penitentiary system. They usually get the soft duties, like working in the prison library or dead-heading greenhouse plants. The vast majority avoids legitimate prison life and manages to be assigned to one of the ‘Club Feds,’ those minimum security hostelries where they perfect their bridge games and strengthen their tennis backhands. Their influence in those camps for the privileged is being seriously challenged by the medical community, though."

"Doctors? Is that right?” Jake asked.

"That’s what I hear, Jake. So many physicians are being jailed for fraudulent Medicare and Medicaid billing practices, tax evasion, filing nonexistent claims, and other offenses against the Hippocratic Oath that a real power struggle for camp control is developing between the professions. I'm confident that the lawyers will prevail, however. Their training and orientation give them a clear advantage.

“It’s been said that the health of a civilization is directly related to the number of attorneys it has, and that this relationship is inversely proportional. The Ten Commandments have multiplied to more than two million laws—in this country alone. This prolific growth owes a huge debt to attorneys, those masters of treachery and trickery.”

Jake wiped his lower lip with his sleeve. "I didn’t understand half of what you just said.”

I had decided to step down from my soapbox, anyway, and get back on course. “My second question: What can you tell me about the judge's family?"

"I don't know much about them except he had his old lady committed to the state loony bin some years ago. She couldn't cope with life in the fast lane and always having to pretend she didn't hear the whispers about her husband's 'activities.' She started hittin' the sauce and acting strange, then she kept getting worse, so the judge had one of his bench buddies sign the papers and they shipped her off to never-never land at the Camino Real Sanitarium. The judge is a proud man, and he just couldn't take the embarrassment of her being the way she was. He don't visit, but he keeps her supplied with crayons, clean sheets, and three squares a day so she ain't hurtin' in that respect."

"How about children?"

"They had two daughters—twins. Street noise says their behavior helped drive their straitlaced mother crazy and put her in the sanitarium. In fact, they might as well have signed the commitment order themselves. I don't know their names, but I believe one of 'em was found dead a couple of weeks ago. Her husband either flew the coop or was snatched. It was all kept low profile—"

Jake's mouth opened to full extension, and then he tilted his head and squinted. "Wait a minute. You mean to tell me that the judge has hired you to find his daughter's killer?"

"Quite so," I confessed.

Jake released a congratulatory whistle. "You're in the big time, now, Chauncey. I'm glad to see you get a break. You deserve something better than those peephole jobs you usually get, but I hope you're not getting in over your head. You ain't handled nothing this big before, so watch yourself. I don't want to be one of your two dozen pallbearers."

"Your concern is well founded," I conceded. "My homicide experience has been limited . . . actually, non-existent . . . which does give me pause. I did do some brushing up on murder investigations in some old police procedurals last night, but I'm not sure how the information can be practically applied."

"How's that?" Jake asked.

"It said that crimes can be solved by observing two corollaries, both of which flow from the principle of motivation. The first corollary is to determine why the crime occurred. The text said that all murders are committed for one of five reasons: passion, money, insanity, power, or altruism. Determination of the reason can help limit the list of suspects to a manageable number. The second corollary was something called *cui bono,* the view that probable responsibility for an act or event lies with one who has something to gain. With this thought in mind, Jake, who do you think might have had the best reason to kill the judge's daughter?"

"Almost anybody you could think of, I would imagine," Jake said. "The judge has more enemies than a pimp has gold chains. Lots of people who've been swindled over the years would like nothin' better than to hurt or embarrass hizzoner. And, even the judge himself could be a suspect."

I leaned further over the counter. "How's that, Jake?"

"I heard that the one Barrington girl—oh, Justine, it was; that was her name," he recalled, "married her husband . . . um, Rutledge—I believe that's his name—against her father's wishes.

"Now, she and her sister were about the only people who could openly defy the judge and get away with it. She had always been known to run around a lot, and since her hubby spent a lot of time in the lab—and may have been neglecting his hearthside duties, if you get my drift—her carryings-on may have riled the judge enough to make him lose his temper and put a stop to it.

"By the same token, her fooling around may have come to Rutledge's attention. He might have taken exception to being . . ." Jake paused, looking for the appropriate term.

"—made a cuckold, the husband of an unfaithful wife," I completed.

"Yeah, that. He bought the hen but someone else was stealing the eggs. He could've come home early one night and caught her and some jackleg . . ."

Ever the gentleman, even in discussions of a sexual nature, Jake was obviously searching for a euphemism. ". . . *in flagrante delicto,*" I suggested.

"Fla-gran-te de-lic-to," Jake slowly repeated. "Yeah . . . that sounds a lot better than fuckin' around," he beamed. "Of course, since Justine was known to have a list of boyfriends longer than a Detroit unemployment line—she shuttled them in and out faster than drug overdose cases at the free clinic—one of them could've got jealous and done her in."

I agreed. "What can you tell me about her sister, Jill?"

Jake smiled. "Jill Barrington's supposed to be some kind of live wire, a real *bashi-bazouk.* She could be a suspect, too, come to think of it." Jake speculated while rubbing the faint stubble on his chin. "Jill was supposedly jealous of her sister, and they fought as only twins can over everything you can imagine. They both had plenty of money and were spoiled rotten, but neither one of them got pleasure from anything unless it had been stolen or diverted from the other one.

"Besides, with Justine dead, Jill doesn't have to split the inheritance with anyone; and Jill likes her money."

"Sibling rivalry laced with greed has been known to be a powerful motive for murder," I conceded. "How about Rutledge?"

"Don't know much about him. He's one of them workaholics whose only vice appears to be catching cards at the poker parlors in Gardena. He came to L.A. a while back, met Justine, and they tied the knot soon after. However . . . Rutledge may have played around with Jill on the side—before and after the wedding. If he did, you can bet Jill bragged to Justine about it."

"Did Rutledge have any enemies?"

"Not that I ever heard, but he did have some people interested in what he was doing. I overheard a couple of contract attorneys discussing some advanced funding that Rutledge had received from the government to build a fancy computer," Jake said.

"Then he may have been abducted by those wanting the results of his research," I said. "On the other hand, perhaps he was attempting to auction the results of his breakthrough to the highest bidder. Based upon what the judge said, such a discovery could have profound international military and political significance."

"Beats me, I don't know nothing about computers. But, there's something else you should be aware of. There's scuttlebutt around that Armand Duvalier, the crime boss, developed an interest in Rutledge. He don't play second *balalaika* to anybody when it comes to industrial espionage and getting what he wants. He keeps his own muscle on the payroll and ain't afraid to use it. Be careful if you have any dealings with him."

"Duvalier, you say. The water *is* getting deep," I said. "If it became known that Rutledge had succeeded, or that he was playing bidders against one another for his own enrichment, the number of parties interested in the physical possession of Mr. Rutledge are more than a few: our government, foreign countries with advanced weapon capabilities, unscrupulous computer manufacturers here and abroad, international terrorists, and organized crime—to name a few."

"There's a shitload of 'em all right. That may explain Rutledge skipping town, but how does it fit in with the murder of his wife? You said yourself, she was done in with one of them artificial wieners."

"You mentioned that Justine's promiscuity was not a well-guarded secret, and the abductors of Dr. Rutledge may have just taken advantage of such gossip. They may have meant only to torture Mrs. Rutledge in front of her husband in an attempt to persuade him to surrender his computer technology. Or, she may have been an unfortunate witness to her husband's kidnapping. To shut her up, a sadistic hit man may have forced her into her bedroom, seen her vibrator, and made her the shocked victim of an ingenious bit of improvisation."

"Maybe," Jake said. "There's one other angle on Rutledge you should know about."

"I'm listening."

"Although Rutledge was probably the only person who knew the whole project inside and out, he didn't work on it alone. He had this research assistant named . . . oh . . ." Jake closed his eyes and pursed his lips, calling upon his full array of facial contortions to expedite the retrieval of data from his memory. "Ka—no, no . . . Ko—no, no . . . Clover, no—Clovis! Clovis Tubinski—that's it!" Jake beamed in triumph. "Yeah, Clovis Tubinski. She helped Rutledge in his lab, on the west end of Santa Monica Boulevard. I heard she was smitten with Rutledge but wasn't getting much encouragement from him. Maybe she whacked Justine out of envy, and Rutledge because he didn't return her affection."

"E-nough," I laughed. "Jealousy and spurned love, betrayal, intrigue, revenge—too many peaks in this mountain range of motives."

The morning rush was picking up, and I motioned for Jake to wait on customers while I attempted to organize this inundation of information. But I did so to no avail. The sounds of exchanged salutations and coins being dropped into Jake's cigar box became welcomed interruptions.

"Chauncey," Jake said as he turned back toward me, "if one of the Barringtons is responsible for Justine's murder, why would they hire you to solve it?"

"A good question, and one to which I've been giving some thought. There are several possible motives. First, hiring a detective could divert attention and suspicion from themselves. Second, if the detective is unsuccessful, they've lost nothing. Third, if the detective should be killed in the process of his investigation, it might scare others from poking around in the ashes.

"Fourth, if you want to prevent a professional artist from painting a masterpiece, you let an amateur attack the canvas first. In other words, they may have hired me to muddy the trail, to render it virtually useless for more experienced trackers to follow.

"And, last, if I should be successful and confront the Barringtons with proof of their misdeed, they might have me murdered and proceed, in retrospect, to eliminate the clues that had pointed me in their direction. Since I would be an insignificant citizen challenging a significant one, my allegations, if they ever surfaced, would be dismissed and the police report filed behind year-old duty rosters."

I paused, soberly absorbing the impact of all of this.

"I have one final question, Jake. You'll recall that I mentioned I was working on two cases. Do you know a Rubella Saperstein?"

"Can't say I do."

"Perhaps her daughter, Boom Boom Saperstein?"

"Only from the article in the paper. Wasn't she the pole slider over at the Glad Gland club killed a day or two ago?" he asked. "Any connection with the Rutledge murder?"

"Only the method of murder. Know anything else about her?"

"Look up the owner of the Glad Gland, a hood by the name of Sal Valentinuzzi," Jake advised. "Also, check with your girlfriend, Girtha, when you go across the street for breakfast. I think she knew Boom Boom."

"Thank you, my friend." I eased myself up from Jake's magazine-strewn counter. "You have earned yourself double portions of *dolmas* and baklava today."

"Any time," Jake replied, "and Chauncey," he added as he put his wrinkled hand on my forearm, "be careful."

I smiled wanly. "You know me, Jake. I stay in the backcourt. I never rush the net."

"Still, this whole thing sounds dangerous to me. I don't know why you want to get involved."

His question produced a silence that drowned out the surrounding street noises. How did I say that my life had largely been a tedious downhill exercise of no special significance? How did I say that something like this challenge might offer an opportunity to slow the inevitable progression and give it some meaning?

"Perhaps . . . because I need to do something worthy of my trade," I told him.

Jake understood without me having to explain. Friends are good that way.

Chapter 5

After bidding Jake adieu, I crossed Buena Vista to a little spot called Cosmo's Diner, one of the oldest eating establishments in the city. Local wags opined that Father Junipero Serra, an eighteenth-century Franciscan and founder of a chain of California missions, had eaten his first cheeseburger and onion rings at Cosmo's.

In addition to longevity, predictability was an attribute most appreciated by Cosmo's regular clientele. The original menu, which some of those same locals say was hand-lettered in medieval script on parchment, had not changed—nor had the fry grease.

My patronage of the diner was based upon two considerations. The first was dietary preference. The breakfast special was a cornucopia of carbohydrates and fats: broiled sausage, fried eggs, hash browns, and French toast. The other was a waitress by the name of Girtha Roote, an angelic vision in her starched white uniform, white cap, and decorative red handkerchief, which peeked perkily from a small pocket above her ample left bosom. Girtha was a shade over five feet tall and a shade under one hundred and fifty pounds. The pinkish tint of her skin was the perfect backdrop for a pair of large, green eyes, long eyelashes that fluttered constantly, a mouth too small to be drawn to scale, and rosy, heavily dimpled cheeks. Her short brown locks were matted securely under a state-mandated hairnet.

"Chauncey!" she squealed as the heavy, aluminum-framed glass door closed behind me. "How's my sweetie-kins?" she greeted. "Be with you in just a minute," she yelled over her shoulder as she rushed to the kitchen to pick up some orders. Moving quickly, her animation was accentuated by the gentle swinging of the adipose tissue under her upper arms.

Waiting for her return, I looked around the diner—why, I don't know since the constituency and their seating selection never seemed to change. Toward one end, a retiree's social club of ten elderly men had pulled two tables together, as usual, and were drinking their morning coffee with unlimited refills while rehashing sports, politics, their military service, and their spouses. In the three booths closest to the door, a construction crew of roofers, painters, and carpenters fueled themselves for the rigorous day's labor ahead. A few college students, sitting by the windows for better light, were wolfing down bowls of cold cereal while doing some last-minute cramming for classes and tests. Clustered at the counter, a few corporate types in business suits toyed with their grapefruit and poached eggs while reading folded *Wall Street Journals*.

As Girtha approached, I returned her greeting. "Good morning, specter of loveliness." I saluted, removed an imaginary cavalier's hat and swept it in a wide arc, accidentally banging my forehead on the countertop at the move's conclusion.

"Chauncey, how gallant," Girtha cooed, putting emphasis upon the second syllable of *gallant.* "But, you've hurt your head. Let me get you something for it. Are you having the usual?"

I took a seat at the counter and nodded weakly while rubbing my head gingerly.

"One Pritikin's Nightmare!" she yelled over her shoulder to the harried kitchen staff. She had already seized a few cubes of ice from the under-the-counter cooler and folded them into a makeshift compress. "Hold the ice in this napkin against your head, sweetie-kins, and the swelling will go down in no time."

I groaned in appreciation.

"Chauncey, I was thinking," Girtha said, leaning over the counter and giving me a conspiratorial wink, "why don't you stop by for dinner tonight? Afterwards, we can 'get it on' as the kids say." This exchange was a normal part of our routine.

Cold water from the melting ice cubes dripped down my forehead and across my cheek. "My dear Girtha," I responded, "I would like nothing better than your companionship, but I'm working on a case at the moment and my hours are somewhat erratic."

"You're finally working?" Girtha asked.

"I'm delighted to respond in the affirmative."

"You mean I can total the tab you've been running up?" Girtha licked her pencil tip in arithmetic anticipation.

"Not so loud," I cautioned *sotto voce,* while patting her hand. "Compensation from my client is of a contingent nature. Rest assured that I shall redeem my breakfast IOUs at the earliest opportunity." My covert application for payment extension was interrupted by the arrival of my fare. "I understand . . . from Jake that . . . you knew Boom Boom . . . Saperstein," I said between bites.

Girtha looked in her compact mirror, patted her hair into place, and brushed some imaginary crumbs from her uniform. Satisfied with the results, she dropped the compact back into her pocket. "I used to see her every week at my aerobics class. Now, that girl was built—really built. The owner of the gym kept offering to hire her, as a personal trainer to the stars, but she always refused. Said she couldn't take the cut in pay.

"She told me once about this stud she was dating who was unusually well-endowed. She said the last time she saw anything that long, it was swimming up the Amazon swallowing small children on the river bank." Girtha smiled in recollection. "It's hard to believe she's dead."

"Any idea who . . . would want to see Boom Boom . . . take her act to the celestial room . . . of St. Peter's nightclub?" I was working over a piece of gristle in my breakfast steak.

"Beats me, sweetie-kins. Boom Boom was a gorgeous girl with a lot on the ball. She had a lot of well-healed boyfriends and she was always dressed to kill, no pun intended. I never could understand why she settled to work at that crummy Glad Gland joint."

"Who could give me . . . a postmortem rundown . . . on her?"

"She shared a place with a girl she worked with by the name of Wanda Latouche. If their address isn't in the phone book, I can probably get it from the masseuse at the health club."

"Great." I pushed my clean plate back toward the middle of the counter and wiped egg yolk off my chin. "And, what can you tell me about the Glad Gland's owner, Sal Valentinuzzi?"

"Sal? Let me tell you about that creep," Girtha spat. "Nothing means anything to him except money; not even his own family. He sold his own eighteen-year-old sister into white slavery—that's right; she's in the harem of some wealthy Arab potentate in the Middle East. Sal got a rush order one night for a virgin, and a big bonus was promised if he could deliver in a hurry. Know what he did? He raced over to the drive-in and pulled his sister, kicking and screaming, from the backseat of some kid's hot rod.

"I guess timing is everything," she philosophized. "In another five minutes, she'd have been another deflowered UCLA co-ed and disqualified herself from the sheik's special order."

"Girtha, you're a jewel. I'll take a rain check on your invitation and ingest megadoses of vitamin E in the interim." While kissing her hand, I slid the check into her apron pocket, and then ducked out the door.

Chapter 6

My next stop was the local precinct of the Los Angeles Police Department. The Hudson and I prowled around a few side streets when we got to the area until I found a meter that still had some time on it. After easing my rust bucket into the spot, and adding a few coins for good measure, I headed toward the station.

Near the end of the block, the precinct steps came into view, and my attention was distracted by a half dozen ladies of the evening. They were marching in an ellipse, with handmade signs that they waved in spirited fashion, demonstrating against police injustice. Although some signs contained scatological diatribes against the police, most of the commentary was an impassioned defense of the free enterprise system and the rights of citizens to pursue a livelihood without constabulary harassment. I was intrigued by their protest and sympathetic to their lack of professional status.

One of the demonstrators was a black Hispanic woman by the name of Lizelle; she was known professionally as "*Reina de la Cama*," which translates as "queen of the bed." Lizelle and I had occupied adjacent hospital rooms several years ago when I was recovering from a bout of gout, and she was convalescing from a mild concussion inflicted by an impatient nightstick. We kept bumping into each other in the hall while taking our morning and afternoon exercise walks and developed an immediate if not unlikely camaraderie.

Her recognition was simultaneous and prompted a warm greeting. "Chauncey, my main man. How's it hanging, honey?"

"Madam Lizelle, my warmest salutations. I'm fascinated by your little gathering. For what purpose do you and your cohorts congregate in recalcitrance?"

"Say what?"

"What are you and your friends up to?" I rephrased.

“That’s right. I remember now—you always did talk strange where a body could hardly understand you. Was yo’ momma scared by a dictionary?”

“I was an English teacher at an urban high school for a few years. Fearful of the violent crimes that were being committed on a daily basis, I opted for a safer occupation.” I had a feeling that my truthful response, told in a tongue-in-cheek manner, had sailed over Lizelle’s head.

"To answer yo’ question, we be on strike, honey, to protest police brutality."

Regardless of a word’s length, Lizelle always accentuated the first syllable, an act that invariably caused her red-Afro wig and pukka-shell jewelry to shake in emphatic concert.

"The man is always bustin' us and on our case. We stand on the corner minding our own business and we still get rounded up, herded into the wagon, and taken downtown to lock-up—for no reason at all. It costs a hundred bucks to get sprung and we have to cough it up out of our own pockets. We tired of this shit and ain't taking no mo’."

"You certainly seem to have a reasonable basis for your grievances. I see that labor is well represented in your dispute, but I don't see your management anywhere."

"Our management!" Lizelle echoed with a shrill laugh. "Let me tell you something, honey. Our ‘management’ don't come nowhere near a police station. Our management don't get up 'til four in the afternoon. Our management don't come around 'til two in the mornin’ when a limousine pulls up by the curb with a palm stickin' out the window for a piece of the take."

I shook my head sympathetically.

"And that ain't the half of it, honey. Times is tough all over. What with all them airline stewardesses, real estate broads, and wannabe actresses runnin' around and *givin'* it away, it's hard to find a paying customer. We getting killed by unfair competition. How come the president don't protect us like he do the railroads, steel mills, auto industry, and savings and loans?

“And another thing. The governor done vetoed a bill that would have increased the expense allowance of the legislature. This hurts 'cause some of our best customers is congressmen. We got no guaranteed minimum wage like plumbers and electricians. We got no health care, no dental plans, no pensions, no deferred compensation, no stock option purchase agreements, no credit union, no nothin'. We got no tax shelters, no Keogh plans, no 401(k) plans, and no group life insurance. We *do* got shitty workin' conditions, though, *and* job security if yo' able to crawl in the sack."

"I'm impressed by your knowledge of employee benefit packages, Lizelle. How did you acquire it, if I may ask?"

"From one of my Thursday tricks—a law school student over at the Public Law Center."

Sympathetic with Lizelle's lack of benefits participation, I promised to contact my state senator on her behalf.

"What about you, honey? You doin' good?" she asked.

"Without resorting to braggadocio, my professional services are highly sought these days."

"Say what?"

"The investigation business is going good right now."

"That's right," Lizelle recalled, "you a private dick. The invitation is still open, sugar man. Drop by on Tuesday afternoons when business is slow, and I'll give you a mercy hump and knock them cobwebs out yo' drawers."

"Thanks, Lizelle. I'll keep your offer in mind."

I entered the precinct and encountered the usual assemblage of colorful characters parading in and out and around, all preoccupied in some transaction involving human misery. At one grill-covered window, citizens who were being released reclaimed personal items they had surrendered at booking; at the next window, those being detained emptied their pockets, took off their belts, and unstrung their shoelaces. Seated along the opposite wall, children arrested while shoplifting tearfully feared the arrival of their parents, while mothers of missing children fearfully awaited positive news with hope. In the corridor, apprehensive first-timers ducked away from blasé recidivists while the dishonest types—pickpockets, thieves, embezzlers—gave wide berth to the mean offenders—murderers, batterers, and other purveyors of violence.

Attempting to blend into corners and shadows, families of the powerless tensely awaited the release of loved ones, and witnesses summoned for suspect identification exited quickly. The fear of victims and the scorn of predators intermingled incompatibly to sustain a milieu of tension.

Swarming throughout these groups were attorneys hugging their inseparable briefcases, and bail bondsmen chomping cheap cigars, their beady eyes in constant vigil for fresh catch.

In the midst of these factions is the policeman, the everyman who aspires for nobility but settles for less. Harassed and beleaguered, he dutifully records a plethora of real and imaginary transgressions, knowing full well that only a fraction of the legitimate ones will ever be solved. Caught between the presumption that our laws are just and the practical reality that their application may not always be, he steers a course between indifference and hostility. He is the living breath in a ponderous system that is neither good nor bad, but just is.

The desk sergeant yelled at an intercom to inform Lieutenant Del Dotto of my presence and pointed down the hall to the bowels of justice. Del Dotto was waiting for me, feet on his desk, actively engaged in the consumption of a bag of pistachios. As I passed through the door, shell halves flew across the room to a wastebasket, which accepted some and deflected others. He continued to munch while I squirmed into a chair.

Adding to my discomfort, as always, was Luther Del Dotto himself. Tall and thin, his long face was divided by a narrow nose and dark eyes that peeked from beneath heavy lids. His slick black hair was combed straight back and parted in the middle.

I had met Del Dotto a couple of years earlier while working on a missing person case. Although he disdained private investigators in general, he would grant me an audience from time to time for two reasons: I usually handled trivial cases that the police didn't want to be bothered with anyway, and he had in me an easy target for his jaundiced humor.

"Well, well, McFadden, what drags your tubby little ass away from the smorgasbord?" He was wasting no time today. "You finally drive the country buffet into chapter eleven? Or did they catch you licking roadkill off a tractor bumper?"

"Au contraire, lieutenant. I'm working on two cases of extreme promise."

"Extreme promise, huh? What are you looking for this time? The Loch Ness monster? Abominable snowman? Fountain of youth? Seven cities of Cibola? Atlantis? Judge Crater? More likely, some fourth-grade bully who's been stiffing smaller kids out of their lunch money during recess. Or, maybe you're looking for an easier way to tie your shoes? I can solve that one for you: buy loafers." He laughed derisively as he brushed some pistachio husks from his lapels.

"Actually, lieutenant, I'm interested in getting some information on the Cleotha Saperstein and Justine Rutledge murders."

"Why?" Del Dotto's face remained unchanged but one foot dropped to the floor.

"I've been retained to learn the identities of the responsible parties," I replied.

"Saperstein, I have no problem with; but who put you on the Rutledge case?"

"Judge Barrington."

"Now, wait just a minute, McFadden," Del Dotto snarled. He straightened and leaned across his desk. "Why would someone like the judge give a two-bit peeper like you the time of day? You're as useless as tits on a canary and as worthless as a Prussian food stamp."

For once, I could bait him. "Call the judge to verify my employment if you wish."

"I'll do that, porky, but if you're shining me, you're in for a world of hurt." He rose and left his office, slamming the door behind him.

Through the thin walls, I could hear him dialing a telephone on a nearby desk. I noticed his voice was initially agitated, but it soon abated into acquiescence. After he hung up, a period of silence followed for several minutes. Finally, the door opened and Del Dotto reappeared with two files, which he tossed into my lap.

"All right, McFadden, take a look and make it snappy. I ain't got all day to play librarian."

I first perused the Saperstein file and then the Rutledge folder. All police reports have the same format, diagrams, syntax, terminology, and typographical errors, so I flipped right to the parts I needed to see. A number of similarities did seem to exist between the two crimes, similarities that suggested a common perpetrator might have been involved. First of all, neither the Saperstein nor the Rutledge homes evidenced any signs of struggle or forced entry. The killer had either entered through an unlocked door or window or been admitted by an occupant. Second, both victims had traces of chloroform in their lungs, which explained how they had been subdued and rendered immobile.

The most obvious link, of course, was the unique method of murder. In Boom Boom's case, the deed had been performed by "Mr. Destroyer." Mrs. Rutledge had been impaled with an "Amazon's Delight." I also found one final parallel to be interesting. Some articles of clothing, presumably those worn by the victims right before their demise, had been neatly folded and placed on chests-of-drawers. Mrs. Rutledge's bra, panties, blouse, and slacks were her last earthly attire, and might have been folded when undressing. But, Boom Boom had apparently been surprised in a nightie and bathrobe. Folding a bathrobe is unusual, I thought—it would normally be hung in a closet or on a hook behind a door.

"Lieutenant, I notice in the Saperstein file that the death was ruled to be homicide by person or persons unknown, while the Rutledge death was deemed to be a probable accident. How did you reach the latter conclusion?"

"The way we read the evidence, Mrs. Rutledge tripped and fell on an upright vibrator which was plugged into the electrical outlet of her bathroom. In trying to dislodge it, she slipped on the wet floor and fell into her tub."

Del Dotto's smirk was even more annoying than the incredulity of his statement.

"Or, maybe she was playing submarine in the tub and got carried away," I offered just as facetiously. "Seriously, something is not clear here. I don't see in either file any speculation about the oddity of the vibrator's power source—vibrators are usually battery-powered."

"Usually, yeah. You get 'em to hum along on a couple of double-A's. But in both homicides, the batteries had been removed and replaced by an electrical cord, like you might find on a lamp, so that the power was supplied by a 110-volt socket in the wall," Del Dotto replied.

"Why would someone go to all that trouble to carry out a couple of executions?" I asked. "It would seem the killer selected and modified this specific device to make a statement. Otherwise, he could have grabbed any electrical appliance, like a toaster, plugged it in the wall, and tossed it into the occupied tub. The killer clearly had a purpose in killing them through vaginal means. Maybe he was trying to obliterate their sexuality or punish them for the way they had lived."

"You may have a point, my fat swami. I'll have my forensic vibrator specialist check this out as soon as the county hires one. Or maybe the feds can help. They may be able to free someone up from the Bureau of Alcohol, Tobacco, Firearms, and Dildos."

Del Dotto loved to laugh at his own humor. Perhaps one day he'll find another depraved soul on the planet who will appreciate it.

"Or," he continued, "maybe we should seek the services of a porno psychic. There's gotta be at least one working the fair circuit in the San Francisco Bay area. How about hiring a profiler who could create a psychological portrait of the killer? My money says it's an unemployed electrician who can't get it up, who was abused by his mother as a kid and forced to watch her have sex with the meter reader." His obligatory chuckles followed.

"I also don't see anything about physical evidence—you weren't able to find *any* physical evidence at *either* crime scene?"

"Nope, the bathrooms were as clean as whistles. No fingerprints were found. Not even a grain of sand to allow us to do a soil determination, nor a stray hair, nor any trace element. The killer either cleaned up real good or wore gloves and elastic shoe covers. This is all a moot point, anyway. The boys above said to treat the Barrington death as an accident until they hear otherwise from the judge and let us know different. He calls the shots on this one."

"It appears that you've ruled out robbery . . . Nothing was taken?"

"Nope. At both scenes, jewelry and money were lying around in open view."

"If this is the work of a serial killer, they usually leave a message or a signature memento. Sometimes they simply want to bait the police; other times they leave cryptic clues because they secretly want to get caught. Was anything like this found at either scene?"

"Come to think of it, we did find a 'Have Vibrator-Will Travel' business card taped to the bathroom mirror. It said to 'Wire Paladin-Hotel San Francisco'."

Del Dotto was continuing to have a field day at my expense.

"Did you check the national crime database to see if anyone else has ever died in a fashion similar to these two?"

"Of course," Del Dotto replied. "The closest we came was a Maine farm woman who died of a vaginal hemorrhage and infection caused by a pitchfork handle. Since this happened in 1832, and electricity hadn't been invented, we didn't connect it to these cases. Also, since it happened 150 years ago, we felt we could safely rule out a serial killer."

Del Dotto was on a roll, but I'd had enough.

"You're a great help, Del Dotto," I said. "If I run across a guy driving a van full of pitchforks, I'll alert you to the possibility of a copycat killer."

"You do that, blimpo. If you're through, take a hike. I got work to do."

"A final question, lieutenant—switching the focus to the Saperstein murder, are you pursuing any leads? I trust you'll refrain from your usual practice of arresting the first available derelict or homeless wino who has the misfortune of being without alibi."

"There is one clue you can check out if you want." Del Dotto had ignored my jibe to reply in surprising seriousness. "The coroner found traces of theatrical greasepaint on Boom Boom's face but not on her fingers or in her cosmetics tray. It's not the type of makeup you buy from the Avon lady or at the corner five-and-dime. Could be it was left over from her strut at the Glad Gland or that she was starring in some silver screen production of *King Dong*—one of the detectives thought he might have seen her before."

"That *is* interesting," I said. "Was greasepaint found on the Barrington body?"

"None indicated in the report," Del Dotto replied, scanning the folder.

"Why aren't your detectives pursuing this avenue of inquiry?" I asked.

"Plain and simple: I don't have the resources. If I had to round up all the skin-flick actors, directors, and producers in southern California, they'd stretch from here to Tijuana. It'd take me a year just to record fingerprints and mug shots. Besides," he smirked, "I have to tread carefully around members of the porn-film industry. If I put 'em out of business, the economy in L.A. County would collapse like a house of cards."

He picked up the police photos of the nude victims and looked them over—probably for the fortieth time. "I'll say one thing for vibrators," he noted sadistically, "stick 'em under water, and they'll fry nooky faster than a microwave." More wistfully, he added, "And look at the knockers on this Saperstein broad. Six midgets could sleep in the shade made by those tits. If I was driving down the highway and saw her over on the side of the road with a flat, I'd get out and change her tire with my dick."

Another thing about Del Dotto: he always managed to be more grotesque than the crimes he investigated. I tried to focus his warped mind back on the case. "A couple of possibilities present themselves," I observed. "She may have been dispatched by a third party after returning home from moonlighting in an off-site film session. Or, she could have been the involuntary headliner in a quickie snuff film at her home."

"Checking this out should be right up your alley, McFadden. You've spent so many Saturday afternoons at triple-X matinees doing the knuckle shuffle that *Hustler* magazine ought to appoint you film critic."

On that cue, I was ready to move on. "Thank you so much for your time, cooperation, and insight, lieutenant. Can you arrange for me to talk to the medical examiner now? I'd like to speak to a professional and get a forensics viewpoint of these murders."

Del Dotto picked up the phone. "At least, it'll get you outta my hair."

I started to stand up and the chair came with me. It was suspended at a forty-five degree angle from my butt, its arms clasping me in a firm embrace.

"Leave the chair, McFadden, it's city property." Del Dotto snickered, and another handful of pistachio shells went airborne.

I extricated myself from the pine lobster and walked to an adjacent building, where one of L.A. County's most interesting institutions was housed: the morgue.

Chapter 7

Dr. Ludwig Sartoris, the chief medical examiner, was a luminary in his field. He was a major contributor to the elevation of forensics—the interpretation of the shadowy region between circumstantial evidence and unassailable fact—to a science in and of itself. As an authority, he had written many texts on the subject of cadavers and how their mute remains could be coaxed to talk during autopsies. He was also frequently called upon to provide expert testimony in famous criminal trials; in fact, his medical evaluations and forensic opinions could make or break a case. It was easy to see why Sartoris had achieved cult status in the pale of law enforcement.

But the ME had also gained a popular acceptance that had spread beyond medical academia and into the living rooms of Middle America. His forensic opinions were as much at home on the front pages of checkout-line gossip rags as they were in prestigious medical journals. His eloquence and ability to easily transfer his knowledge to a lay audience earned him frequent invitations to appear on talk shows, and a dramatic flair for wit and wisdom garnered him guest spots on the leading game shows, further evidence that he had successfully drifted into the mainstream and pop culture. His affinity for giving interviews and showcasing the depth of his specialized expertise probably explained his positive reception.

"Your timing is good, Mr. McFadden. We are in the process of completing the toxicology report on Miss Saperstein; she's being examined as I speak. I have no problem sharing our findings with you since Del Dotto doesn't appear eager to act upon any evidence we may uncover," he said with undisguised disdain.

"You'll find me an extremely appreciative acolyte, Dr. Sartoris. I'm looking for anything you've found that may provide insight into the identity of her killer. What can you tell me about her death?"

"Not as much as you might expect. The vast majority of deaths by electrocution are accidental—being hit by lightning on a golf course, hitting a transformer or power line with a tree trimmer, stepping on a downed power line after a storm, that sort of thing. Homicides by electrocution are rare, which makes the Rutledge and Saperstein cases fascinating."

"What was the actual cause of death?" I asked.

"For both Justine Rutledge and Cleotha Saperstein, it was cardiac arrhythmia, or a change in the rhythm of the heart. When a shock from a low voltage electrical source, such as a wall outlet, is received by the heart, interference is created in the natural rhythm of coronary pulsations. Death can be instantaneous when this occurs, or it may take a minute or so; it depends on the amount of current and how long that current is received by the body.

"Here's the amazing part," Sartoris said as he pulled the covering sheet down to the corpse's knees. "Note that there is very little corporeal damage. At the vagina—the point of electrical contact—there's some very slight discoloration: the skin is red and slightly blistered. However, there are no obvious burn marks or signs of charring. If vibrators had not been left in the victims, the cause of death would have been more difficult to determine."

"How were you able to tell the time of death when the forensic evidence is so sketchy?"

"Rigor mortis," Sartoris replied. "In deaths by electrocution, rigor mortis occurs quickly and is localized in the affected area."

"Were there any signs of forced sexual activity?" I asked.

"That can't be determined. The amperage would have killed all sperm traces and neutralized the vaginal channel."

"There don't appear to be any other marks on the body that might raise a red flag," I observed.

"Correct. Both subjects were in excellent health. There were no signs on either body of a struggle or defensive resistance. We found traces of chloroform in the lungs of both women, which probably facilitated the assaults."

"Del Dotto said that no physical or biological evidence was found at either crime scene to assist in perpetrator identification. Is that your understanding as well?" I asked.

"You would have to speak to the crime scene investigators for information like that. However, I believe they've drawn a blank for the time being."

"Did you manage to learn anything from the vibrators?" I asked.

"Only that it's the first time I've ever seen them used for homicidal purposes. I'm expecting a request for them any day from Ripley's Believe It Or Not! or Madame Tussauds wax museum.

"Neither of them is anything special: just two run-of-the-mill vibrators that can be bought in any adult novelty shop or ordered through the mail. In each instance, the batteries had been removed and a hole drilled at the base of the shaft. An electrical cord was then inserted through the hole and its stripped wires connected to the battery clips.

"After the vibrator was inserted in the submerged victim, it was plugged into the wall outlet until its mission was complete. The same result could have more easily been obtained by just dropping the live end of the cord into the tub of water."

"I don't believe the killer minded the additional work," I responded. "This confirms my initial suspicion that by using a vibrator, the killer is either sending a specific message or a message to someone specific. Thanks, doc." I shook his hand and sighed. "Since science is not cooperating, I'll have to resort to shoe leather."

I left the morgue and walked to the Hudson. My departure, I noted, created two parking places: mine and that of a black limousine that merged into traffic behind me.

Chapter 8

I decided to follow up on Del Dotto's earlier tip regarding Boom Boom's possible involvement in the cinema. I didn't have much knowledge of porn-flick production, but a former client did—a big North Hollywood porn-film producer named Benny Pobloski. Benny fancied himself to be a producer of cinematic note, but his version of *Snow Whyte and the Seven Dorks* featured a septet with un-dwarf-like appendages who crawled naked over a raunchy Snow Whyte, looking for any available orifice they could plug.

Pobloski had hired me a couple of years back to find his runaway teenage daughter. I finally located her in Utah, at a maverick religious commune, the Church of the Parallel Divinity—a congregation whose members claimed to be direct descendents of Jesus' brother, Mycroft. I thought Mycroft was Sherlock Holmes' brother, but then theology was never my strong suit. Regardless, they appeared to be a pretty decent group, at least as much as I could tell.

They lived in a self-contained community in which each member had an assigned task relating to food production, shelter construction, or clothing fabrication. They seemed to pray a lot and extol the virtues of universal peace and the love of all mankind, values that even I could warm to. I actually felt guilty about abducting her in the middle of the night and returning her to her father, who wasn't exactly a shining parental role model. In any event, Benny had been grateful for my services and I figured he owed me a favor.

I found his office off Sunset Boulevard in a mid-rise building that appeared to be relatively new. The directory in the lobby indicated that French Kiss Productions was on the second floor, so I took the escalator up to the suite. The receptionist was paging through a tinsel town magazine when she glanced up. Add a few years and a few pounds, and she had a strong resemblance to the aforementioned Snow Whyte.

"Can I help you?" she asked dryly.

"I'm Chauncey McFadden, and I'm here to see Mr. Pobloski."

"Do you have an appointment?"

"No, but he'll see me."

"I'm afraid you'll have to wait. He's conducting a new talent audition and will be tied up for a while."

Knowing Benny as I did, I asked, "As soon as she gets dressed, will you tell him I'm here?" Then I thought maybe I'd score some points: "By the way, your face looks familiar. Did you star in *The Bondage of Snow Whyte?"*

"Why, yes," she brightened, looking up. "That was a few years ago. How kind of you to remember." She fluttered her false eyelashes, which were long enough to string a bow.

"Not at all. I'm disappointed to see that you've retired from acting. Were you abandoned by your thespian muse?" I asked.

She looked puzzled, but then responded. "No, I was abandoned by my tits, which started sagging to my knees. Rather than take on cameo bit roles, I decided to leave the silver screen altogether. I work out here when we're not shooting, but I assist Mr. Pobloski on the set when we're in production."

We were interrupted by the opening of the door to Benny's office. A nymphet came out holding some papers in one hand and stuffing her panties inside her purse with the other.

"Thank you, Mr. Pobloski. You won't be sorry," she cooed. "I can't wait to get started." She was positively bubbling as she sashayed to the elevator.

"Benny," I called out before he had a chance to duck back inside his office. "Remember me?"

Benny turned around, stared, and snapped his fingers. "McFadden, isn't it? You rescued my daughter from that cult. I owe you, man. What can I do for you?"

"I need a few minutes of your time."

"I was sneaking out to lunch, but come in. A few minutes are the least I can do considering what you did for me."

Benny scurried around, picking up items off the carpet and restoring them to their normal locations on the top of his desk. "Have a seat," he invited, indicating a chair that was lying on the floor.

Benny was constantly squinting, probably a combination of beady eyes and ill-fitting contact lenses. He compensated for his short weasel-like appearance with sartorial splendor: a natty tapioca-colored, double-breasted blazer and a garish silk handkerchief that spilled out of his blazer pocket that matched a wildly patterned necktie.

"Where's your casting couch, Benny?" I asked while setting the chair upright and looking around the room. "I don't see it anywhere."

"We don't use those things anymore," the articulate director replied, waving his hand in disdain. "You just stain the cushion fabric, get wrinkles in your trousers, and throw your back out. It's a lot easier to bend 'em over the desk and poke 'em from behind."

"The young lady who just left appeared to have passed her audition." I commented innocently. "Can she act?"

Benny looked at me incredulously. "That bimbo couldn't read a fortune cookie, but maybe she'll photograph well enough in the dying cockroach position. If not, I can always start her at the bottom of the career ladder—as a fluffer."

Stumped, I had to ask, "Benny, I must confess, you've piqued my curiosity. Assuming that performing vaginal, anal, and oral sex in front of a camera is the top of the career ladder, pray tell—*what* is a fluffer?"

Benny looked at me like the neophyte I, of course, was. "A fluffer is an extra who gives blow jobs to the guys between scenes to keep them hard for their next take."

"I see," I said. "I don't believe I've ever seen that job listed in the screen credits at the end of a film. Do they give Oscars out for that sort of thing? Do you have stunt fluffers? I mean, if the guy is unusually well endowed and the usual fluffer can't accommodate him . . ."

Benny's face lit up. "'Stunt' fluffers—what a concept! I gotta mention that to my casting director.

"What can I do for you, old friend? Did you drop by to pick up some free passes for the opening night of *Lickety Split,* my latest lesbian western? It's already won honorable mention at the Tijuana Film Festival—"

"I'll pass, Benny, but thanks. Actually, I need some information. Have you ever seen this girl working in the industry?" I handed him the picture of Boom Boom that Mrs. Saperstein had given me.

"No, but I'd hire her in a New York minute. With a looker like this, I could easily win an adult video award." Benny was practically salivating over the glossy.

"You'd be a little late," I advised. "She's dead."

"No problem. I could lower the lighting, use a fuzzy lens, and focus the camera from the neck to the knees."

Benny could be scary. "She's buried already, Benny, and I'm not going to tell you where. I like you and don't want to see you and your shovel get arrested." I was only half kidding; I could see him doing something like that. "How about snuff films? Could she have been used in one of those?"

Benny straightened his Windsor knot and then shook his head. "Snuff films are one of the great hoaxes of our times. Ever since the Charlie Manson incident . . . over ten years ago, in '69 . . . there's been a widespread belief that a network exists to kidnap kids and young adults and kill them while the cameras are rolling, then distribute the films underground to a perverted group of connoisseurs of the genre. They're just myths. The subject heated up again in '76 when the movie *Snuff* was smuggled into the states from Latin America. It was supposed to have depicted an actual on-screen murder of an actress, but it was also proven to be bogus."

"Then snuff films don't exist?" I asked.

"No more than the tooth fairy or the Easter bunny. I'll grant you there's been some clever fakes, but not one snuff film has ever been confirmed. Most of them have involved special effects. Others arise from rumors about serial killers who are supposed to have videotaped the last earthly moments of their victims before they were murdered. But think about it: who'd make a visual record of a murder that a jury could use to send them to the electric Lazy Boy?"

"Interesting point," I said. "I was just chasing down a lead but it looks like it ends up nowhere. Changing the subject, how's business these days?"

"Making money by the truck load," Benny beamed. "Ever since porn began being accepted by mainstream distribution channels, our production has been in high gear. *Deep Throat, The Devil in Miss Jones, Behind the Green Door,* and a few others paved the way and gave porn a wider audience and more respectability. All we need to do is keep pushing the envelope until American censors are forced to accept European standards of obscenity."

"Sounds like you've discovered unlimited potential in this niche market."

"The possibilities are endless. We started with man-on-woman, man-on-man, and woman-on-woman. Then we progressed to man-on-animal, animal-on-woman, robot-on-woman, ghost-on-woman, extraterrestrial-on-woman—we're only limited by our imaginations. I'm even looking at a script for plant-on-woman. A wacko botanist pollinates some huge Venus flytraps with a super aphrodisiac like Spanish fly. They turn on their master and hump him to death, then, after pulling their roots from the soil, escape the greenhouse to start a reign of terror on a nearby convent."

"I'll wait for the sanitized TV version," I responded. "I don't believe I could handle that in full-screen cinemascope with Dolby sound!"

Benny chuckled. "The only problem," he continued, "is that we're getting so popular we're starting to attract the attention of politicians. There's already rumors that somebody's thinking about proposing a bill to force porn actors to wear condoms to prevent the spread of syphilis and venereal disease. We already got mandatory physical exams."

"That's why you executives get paid the big bucks—to overcome those little operational obstacles." I stood up and returned Boom Boom's picture to my jacket pocket.

"Thanks, anyway, Benny. This visit was admittedly a long shot. By the way, how's your daughter doing?"

"Hey, she's doing great. She's starring in my latest sci-fi pic, *Star Whores.* Want some comp tickets?"

"Thanks, but I'll stick with the George Lucas version." I got to my feet and shook his hand. "Don't bother; I know the way."

On the way out, I spotted another nubile lovely sitting in the reception area, staring into a compact. She jumped up. "Are *you* Mr. Pobloski?" She tugged down on a tight leather micro-skirt.

"No," I replied. "I just got the lead role for his next picture, *Humpty Dumpty Shags Little Bo Peep.* Are you auditioning to be my co-star?"

She looked me over, turned up her nose, did an about-face, and left in a huff.

I felt a little better. I may have failed Benny's daughter, but I might have diverted this young girl from a career in porn—that would be some consolation.

Chapter 9

I drove to Dr. Rutledge's lab to learn what I could from his associate, Dr. Clovis Tubinski. Located in the west end of a Santa Monica neighborhood of small businesses and professional offices, the lab was a two-story cinderblock structure whose stucco had been haphazardly slapped on the walls like icing on the cake of a last-minute birthday party. Some dry, brown Bermuda grass lingered in front, in slightly worse shape than a struggling hedge; both fighting valiantly to survive the summer.

The building looked secure, with closed shutters covering the windows, but the heavy glass door was unlocked, so I let myself in. In the rear of the building, I could hear the sounds of laughter, a commanding but feminine voice, and boxes scraping across a floor. I walked down the hall toward the sounds.

I approached a rear door slowly, until I could see that it opened onto a loading dock. Another step and I observed two Chicano youths standing on the bed of a pickup truck, laughing as they engaged in a mock karate fight. Fuming at their horseplay was an attractive woman, in her early thirties or so, who was wearing a white smock over a tight lime-green jumpsuit. Her flaming red hair had been casually gathered into a bun, but now, loose strands of hair fell down from her temples to create a frame for her handsome face that featured a delicate but firm chin.

"Pongan sus culos en el camello, pronto!" she yelled. Her left hand was propped on her hip and her right hand brandished a roll of masking tape. She was obviously annoyed by the antics of the two boys who mimicked her instructions and gestures.

"May I be of assistance, madam? You appear to be experiencing some linguistic difficulty."

"I hired these two clowns to pack this computer equipment and drive it to a storage warehouse in Chatsworth, but I can't seem to get them to do anything."

"I believe I know the source of your problem," I offered modestly.

She turned and looked at me quizzically. "Then, care to share this deep, dark secret?"

"Pleased to oblige," I nodded. "Your instructions are the root of your difficulty. You're telling your minions to 'put their asses in a camel.' I suspect that you mean to say *'pongan las cajas en el camión,'* which means 'put the boxes in the truck.'"

"Why, thank you." She brightened, slapped the roll of tape against the palm of her hand, and yelled: *"Pongan las cajas en el camión."*

Accurate communication established her authority, and the youths began to load the truck without further ado. Her immediate problem solved, gratitude was replaced by suspicion. "Are you looking for someone?" she asked.

I introduced myself and my occupation and asked if she was Clovis Tubinski.

"Yes, I'm Dr. Tubinski. Do you have any ID?"

I showed her my PI license. "I'm also in the telephone directory if you care to check it out."

"It has already been packed. What do you want?"

"To ask a few questions, if I may."

"Ask away, but I'm not obligated to answer them," she countered.

I disclosed my retention by the Barrington family and stated the nature of my mission before asking my first question: "When was the last time you saw Dr. Rutledge?"

"About a week ago."

"Was that before or after his wife was murdered."

"His wife was murdered in the evening. I last saw him the afternoon of that same day."

"Have you heard from him since?"

"The next morning, I found a hastily scrawled note pushed under the door of the lab."

"Do you still have it?"

"No, he asked that it be destroyed after I read it."

"What did it say?"

"Nothing, really," she replied.

"Funny thing about 'nothing,'" I replied. "It happens most of the time, and in most places, but I don't believe it happened here."

She hesitated. I prepared myself to be told either an insignificant truth or a significant lie.

"He apologized for having to leave so suddenly and without explanation. He told me to close the lab and put the equipment in storage."

"That sounds like an extended sabbatical."

"Make of it what you will," she replied. "It was a surprise, of course, but closing the lab is understandable under the circumstances."

"It also sounds like you may be out of a job."

"Computer scientists are always in demand. I'm pursuing several attractive opportunities already."

"Such as?"

"I'm not at liberty to disclose the names of any suitors," she replied stiffly.

I thought her choice of words was interesting. "I'll bet. What else did Dr. Rutledge have to say?"

"He said to use the money left in the lab's bank account to pay off the staff."

"Anything else?"

"That's all I can recall."

"Did he say anything about sending for you at a later date once he got squared away?"

"That question is impertinent," she snapped, "but since you asked, no such invitation was issued."

"He didn't mention anything concerning his wife's death?"

"No. The subject of that . . . Mrs. Rutledge never came up."

"I gather you feel that Dr. Rutledge is not implicated in his wife's death in any way."

"That's right. Dr. Rutledge is incapable of such an act."

"Then why isn't he here assisting the police in their inquiries?"

"I have no idea."

"I understand that Dr. Rutledge was working on a government-related project at the time of his disappearance."

"Dr. Rutledge was involved in a number of projects. I'm afraid you'll have to be more specific," she said coolly.

"This particular project, as I understand it, was the design of a powerful computer that could process information faster than anything currently available."

"The research assistants and I performed a variety of tests and studies that involved harnessing the power and speed of laser beams to transmit large volumes of data. I'm not at liberty to disclose more information about the project than that."

"Judge Barrington indicated that Dr. Rutledge was apparently experiencing some stress over the past few weeks. In your opinion, were these conditions precipitated by his work?"

"It's possible. He did appear to be edgy and irritable from time to time."

"Were there problems with the project?"

"There were some minor delays, results that could not be readily validated or replicated. I can't say more than that."

"Can you identify some of his business associates and visitors?"

"Dr. Rutledge was a rare individual. He was an astute businessman as well as a brilliant scientist. He not only knew how to create breakthroughs in computational speed and transference of data but how to get his research supported by financial backers, as well. Perhaps that's what you're referring to."

"Or perhaps seeking a more lucrative market for a product already funded by others. Perhaps he was an auctioneer in addition to his other interests."

Her smile flickered but she was otherwise unruffled. "You'll pardon me if I don't participate in your unsavory speculations involving Dr. Rutledge's character."

"Did the good doctor ever do anything to indicate that he planned to suddenly leave on his own accord?"

"No," she replied, "his disappearance took us all by surprise."

"Did Dr. Rutledge ever discuss his wife with you?"

"Only in general or incidental terms."

"Did he ever mention his suspicions of her infidelity?"

"That wouldn't be general or incidental."

"How did he meet his wife?"

"He copied her name and phone number off the town water tower."

"It doesn't sound like you and the late Mrs. Rutledge were on good terms?"

"If you're looking for something positive about her, you can read the glowing testimonials on any men's restroom wall."

"You sound like you don't feel Mrs. Rutledge was good enough for her husband?"

"Let's just say, if he was expecting to deflower a virgin on his wedding night, he was about ten years too late. He was head-over-heels in love; but to her, he was just another conquest."

"If he didn't flee on his own accord, do you know who would have reason to abduct Dr. Rutledge or do him harm?"

"I've no idea. He wasn't the type of man who made enemies or lost friends. Look," she sputtered impatiently, "I hate to be rude, but I've got a lot of work to do and I'm paying these kids by the hour. If you'll excuse me . . ." Without waiting for a reply, she turned and walked away.

As I retreated to my car, I couldn't help but regret the closing of the lab. The secrets within its walls would have been illuminating. As to Dr. Tubinski's converse reactions to the Rutledges, her role in this affair, though not yet determined, was not to be casually dismissed.

I saw the black limousine parked about thirty yards behind my car, and I gave in to curiosity. I waved, and then approached the darkly tinted windows on the driver's side. When I got within a few feet of the car, its powerful V-8 roared to life and charged, barely allowing me time to sprint to the safety of the sidewalk. I didn't even have time to admire the grill as it flashed by.

Chapter 10

Having worked up an appetite, I retired to a little Mexican place at Balboa and Roscoe where I polished off a few tamales, a couple of tacos, and a stack of taquitos—oh, and a churro or two or four for dessert. Reasonably full and comfortably sluggish, I returned to my office to take a brief nap and determine my next course of action. I had acquired a lot of information that morning and needed a respite to ponder its significance.

I sensed something was wrong as soon as I opened the door to my office. The room was darker than it should have been for that time of day. I looked up and, to my shock, confronted the source of obstructed illumination. Standing on the other side of the room, in front of the window, was one of the largest men I had ever seen: he was easily seven feet in height, but I was equally shocked by his massive head, broad shoulders, and enormous hands. When my eyes finally focused on his face, I was confronted with even more disconcerting features—crater-deep acne scars and the fact that only one eye moved.

Hoping to appear unnerved, I managed to stammer, "I'm sorry but I don't see clients without an appointment." This was derring-do on the part of a cacophonous, one-man band whose shaking legs were causing my cheap shoes to squeak, my loose coins to jingle together in my pockets, and my ballpoint pens to rattle against each other in my plastic pocket protector.

"The Thing" pointed a finger the size of a rolled diploma at me. "Boss want to see you," it said in a guttural monotone.

I attempted to back into the hallway so I could turn and make a hurried escape, but with unexpected agility, The Thing kicked my chair aside with his left foot and leaped across the room in two strides. His right hand reached toward my stomach and swallowed my buckle as he picked me up by my belt and lifted me until my head almost touched the ceiling.

"Boss say now."

I concluded that cooperation was the best response for the time being, especially since I had lost the element of surprise and I hadn't remitted my latest health insurance premium. Besides, he was giving me a painful wedgie. I wheezed, "Okay."

He dropped me abruptly and pushed me down the deserted hall to the rear stairway, which led to an alley in back. Another push deposited me in the backseat of a familiar black Cadillac limousine and was followed by a forced scoot as The Thing entered and sat beside me.

The interior of the limo was as plush as an expensive coffin and as quiet as a tomb, analogies that brought little comfort. I looked to the front seat for an ally and noted only a nondescript Hispanic-looking man in a black chauffeur's hat behind the wheel. The Thing and I sat in silence.

I attempted to bolster my sagging spirits by reasoning that this abduction was benign in purpose. If death was to be my destiny, The Thing would have squashed my corpus and left the grisly residue lying in a pathetic pile swathed in green-checked polyester.

No, this abrupt, peremptory summons indicated I was obviously of interest to someone of importance, although not of apparent importance to someone of interest. A thick plastic partition had risen between the front and back seats, which added to my feeling of isolation—and fueled my struggle against claustrophobia. It didn't appear to bother The Thing, however. He stared straight ahead in a stolid trance, apparently lost in thought, but that would have been gratuitous since I suspected that thinking would have been a bit too anthropomorphic for The Thing's particular rung on the evolutionary ladder. I decided to test my suspicion.

"The car smells new," I said to The Thing.

"Traded other car in," The Thing replied. "Blood stains on upholstery wouldn't come out."

My uneasiness returned but was interrupted by a loud thump from the rear of the car as we accelerated from a stoplight.

"Maybe you should stop the limo and secure your cargo," I suggested, planning a dash for freedom at the first opportunity.

"Not stop," said The Thing. "Just a body. Keeping there 'til The Cleaner from Chicago can acid-wash."

"The Cleaner better get a move on," I advised. "It's going to be hard getting the crew at the car wash to vacuum the trunk with a dead body sprawled in it." The Thing stared straight ahead without reacting. "As an option, you could prop him in line at the social security office: it'd be months before they discovered he was dead."

Still, The Thing stared straight ahead.

In thirty minutes, we arrived at a Century City office complex in West Los Angeles. The limousine pulled up behind a modern glass and steel high-rise and stopped at an alcove where a private elevator awaited.

Instead of a push, I was pulled from the limo and The Thing and I ascended to the uppermost level. A private security guard nodded to us as we exited and stared after us until we entered a small foyer. The Thing tapped three times, then twice on a large door that dominated the foyer. Momentarily, a buzzer sounded as the door unlocked, allowing us to enter.

The sole occupant of the room was sitting in a large leather chair with his back to us talking on the phone. His baritone voice was resinous, educated, and vaguely foreign. As we waited for his attention, I looked around the room in an effort to determine the identity of my host and his interest in me.

He qualified for tycoon status if the décor was any indication, as all the furniture—desks, chairs, credenzas, wet bar, and bookcases—were made of hand-carved, highly polished teak. The floor was covered by a rich burgundy carpet that was matched by heavy open drapes. The drapes framed two ceiling-to-floor glass walls that joined at a right angle to form the corner of the building; they afforded a panoramic view of the city skyline. The view was currently obscured by a hovering purplish-brown smog, probably the residue from the fires in Bakersfield.

His conversation concluded and the phone was dropped into its gold cradle, an act that preceded the mysterious voice rotating in its swivel chair until I was centered in its focus.

"Welcome, Mr. McFadden. How good of you to come. Allow me to introduce myself. I'm Armand Duvalier."

Duvalier's features were every bit as pleasant as his voice. The face was handsome and crowned by impeccably styled silver hair; his trim body, showcased by a gray silk jacket, probably Italian and custom-made. Although he projected an affable charm, Jake's warnings over his alleged brutality made me somehow feel safer with The Thing.

"Sit down and let's chat, Mr. McFadden." He didn't bother to rise or extend his hand. "I believe you've met Roger . . ." With a wave of his hand, he directed my attention to his myrmidon, who had plopped down in a chair opposite mine and begun nibbling on a fresh chrysanthemum from a Ming vase.

"Somehow, 'Roger' doesn't seem to fit," I opened. "A more truculent appellation like Igor would seem appropriate."

Duvalier smiled. "We don't know Roger's last name. He misplaced it some years ago. Oh, I suppose we could review the personnel records of the hospitals for the criminally insane and find the name he was admitted under but why bother? 'Roger' is enough of a handle and he's very good at what he does."

"Which would include ensuring that your invitations always get accepted."

Duvalier nodded. "But, let's drop Roger as a subject of conversation for the moment, if we may, Mr. McFadden, and talk about you."

"A very inconsequential topic, really—hardly worth your time," I informed him.

"Ordinarily, I would agree. You lead a very undistinguished existence, Mr. McFadden—flotsam in the backwater of life, in a manner of speaking."

"That's not entirely true," I rebutted. "The trash man once slapped a 'star recycler' decal on my garbage can."

Duvalier continued. "My interest in you is confined to your activities since yesterday—specifically, what business did you have with Judge Barrington, Lieutenant Del Dotto, and Dr. Tubinski?"

I had already used my amazing deductive powers to realize I'd been transported here by the same black limousine that had been following my every move. As a result, I recited the standard lines I used when someone was trying to breach the confidentiality of a client relationship.

"Your sources are well-informed regarding my recent whereabouts," I complimented. "You must realize, however, that the communication between a private investigator and his client is privileged information, which I'm not at liberty to disclose.

"You see, Mr. Duvalier, a detective is like a doctor, or a priest. We are bound by a code of conduct—a canon of ethics, if you will—to take no action that might be prejudicial to the best interests of those we represent. Once retained, an investigator has a supreme responsibility—in fact, a sacred trust—to be discreet and divulge nothing regarding the subject of his employment relationship.

"This obligation goes beyond good business; it emanates from fundamental moral precepts. To breach this confidentiality would be worse than death; it would be dishonor. Why, the very thought of it is abhorrent and repugnant to every fiber of my mortal being. A thousand horses couldn't drag this information out of me."

"I would hardly incur the expense of a thousand horses, Mr. McFadden," Duvalier said dryly. "But let me be clear. You'll either tell me what I want to know or I'll allow Roger to introduce you to some of the many thresholds of unbearable pain. This room is soundproof and I'll put a headset on to block out your screams of agony."

By this time, Roger had devoured the rest of the flowers and turned a glass ashtray into powder with his hand. Having heard Duvalier's warning, he had scooted forward to the edge of his chair in excited anticipation. The prospect of impending sadism was whipping him into a frenzy, and he began to drool and emit strange noises from the back of his throat.

It didn't take long for me to reconsider my position. "Well, I don't suppose professional standards were intended to be cast in concrete. I can be flexible to modification when extraordinary times and circumstances dictate," I conceded.

"You've made a wise decision, Mr. McFadden. You could hardly be of service to your clients if bits and pieces of your body were scattered throughout the South Bay area like fragments of a poorly constructed kite."

Roger's mind, dull as it might have been, had sensed that he was, at least on this occasion, to be denied the joy of dismemberment. He expressed his petulance by banging his fists on his knees.

"Now, now, Roger, don't pout. I know you're disappointed," Duvalier soothed, "but I'll make it up to you." He appeared to think a moment, and then offered some recompense. "How would you like to break into a mortuary tonight and select a playmate to take home with you?"

Roger seemed mollified by this counterproposal. He leaned back in his chair, no doubt with visions of necrophilia dancing in his head.

"You have, as they say, dodged a bullet, Mr. McFadden. Roger's only source of pleasure in life comes from committing atrocities upon his fellow men. He prefers his subjects to be alive, but he'll take a corpse in a pinch. Now, what was it you wanted to tell me?"

I started at the beginning, with Rubella Saperstein's visit, and continued through my encounter with Jill Barrington, the meeting with her father and the information provided by Del Dotto and Tubinski. "That's everything I know up to this point, Mr. Duvalier."

Duvalier leaned back in his chair, digesting the information I had disclosed. He then leaned forward. "I'm inclined to believe you. And, I have a proposition, which you'll, of course, accept.

"I have no personal interest in the murders, so you can pursue their resolution at your leisure. My sole objective is Rutledge. Locate him, and I'll instruct you how to deal with the judge and the police. Is that understood?"

I glanced at Roger out of the corner of my eye. The casket Casanova was preoccupied bending quarters into ninety-degree angles with his thumb and first two fingers of one hand. I nodded without hesitation.

"Mr. Duvalier, I know very little about Rutledge. If I'm to find him, I need more information than I now possess."

"Such as?"

"For example, is it Rutledge you want or the plans for the supercomputer?"

"If I have Rutledge, I'll have the plans," he replied evasively, "but there's other unfinished business to be settled as well. You don't want to know any more than that."

"Other than you, who else would have a reason for abducting Dr. Rutledge?" I asked.

"If I knew that—"

The main door to the office opened at that point and an attractive brunette stuck her head inside. "Hi, love. Your secretary's away from her desk and I thought . . ." As soon as she realized Duvalier was not alone, she stammered an apology and shut the door.

Duvalier glowered, knowing the damage had been done; that I had recognized Jill Barrington. "Our little chat is over, Mr. McFadden. Find Rutledge and it's worth ten thousand dollars to you. Fail, and you'll make Roger happy beyond words. Find your way to the first floor and Gasper will drive you back to your office."

"Can we make that ten thousand dollars . . . plus expenses?" I asked, pushing the envelope with uncharacteristic and momentary boldness.

"By the looks of you, McFadden, the expenses could very well exceed the fee." He tapped a platinum letter opener on the marble surface of his desk. "Very well, your expenses are covered—if you're successful. Good day."

I sighed in relief at being released from Duvalier's custody, but not before I was reinstated in the backseat of the limousine. After a few sighs, I finally did begin to relax and spread out to enjoy the comfort and to savor the prospect of yet another client on the same basic case. While running my hand across the luxurious leather, my fingers brushed against an object that had been wedged between the seat and the armrest. Curious, I pulled it free and surveyed my find.

It was a book of matches, and the outside of the cover contained a rough anatomical outline of a young woman from the waist down wearing a G-string and high heels. On the inside of the cover, the name of the advertiser rang a bell of familiarity: The Glad Gland.

Chapter 11

I left my apartment late the next morning and didn't get to Cosmo's for breakfast until half past ten. Girtha was her usual attentive and jovial self, spellbound as I related my progress on the case—with the exception of mentioning the kidnapping, which would have disturbed her. She slipped my check into her pocket with her usual good-natured grin as I left the diner.

The streets surrounding my next destination were empty, not surprising for this time of day, except for a group of Japanese tourists who, I guessed, had taken a wrong turn on the way to Disneyland. The steep fall of the dollar against the yen had them flocking to the U.S. in droves this year. Like penguins, they huddled together as they walked en masse. Each was attired in a somber-toned suit or dress and bent over at the neck from the weight of a dangling assortment of cameras and telephoto lenses. They chattered merrily and pointed excitedly at anything of remote interest.

Finding the Glad Gland was easy. The building appeared to have been a grocery market at one time—a long, single-story building with large glass windows in front. They had been painted over, of course, and the exterior façade was now plastered with glossy posters of performers in various stages of undress. A sign over the door advertised a five-dollar cover charge and two-drink minimum, standards for that type of business.

I could tell the club was not open, but standing outside the door, I heard the sound of chairs being dragged across the floor inside. Curious, I wandered to the rear of the building, where I discovered an unsecured employee's entrance that would allow me access; I walked inside. What I could see of the interior through a hazy film was North Hollywood Gothic. The stench of cigar smoke and spilled spirits was strong and resisted dissipation by any of the several portable fans that had been placed around the premises.

As my eyes began adjusting to the dim lighting, I saw an elderly black man placing the last few wooden chairs on the tops of small round tables. When he finished with the chairs, he picked up a worn mop and started swabbing back and forth across the dull tiles. He starting humming to himself, and was soon joined by the vocal offerings of a middle-aged Hispanic woman in a yellow peasant blouse who was behind the bar busily bagging empty cans and bottles, presumably destined for the dumpster out back.

Across the room, on the stage, a slatternly peroxided blonde was walking through a dance routine in a leotard that was stretched to the limit and too old to remember how it used to fit. Probably rehearsing for an upcoming alumni night, I hoped; her last dance was likely on the lap of Teddy Roosevelt. In my best accent, I asked her where Sal Valentinuzzi might be found. *"Discúlpeme, señora, donde está el jefe?"*

"Está en la oficina al final del corredor," she replied.

Guided by this information, I walked down a dark hallway past several unlocked storage closets before coming to a door with "Office," "Private," "Keep Out," and "This Means You" signs nailed to it. I raised my hand to knock, but froze as I heard a familiar name—

"Rutledge? Honest to god, boss, we ain't seen or heard nothin' about Rutledge . . ."

"Sure, I got the word out like you said—ten big ones to the guy what fingers him . . ."

"Yeah, we ripped up Boom Boom's place like you told us . . . No, nothing . . ."

"Naw, Wanda's ain't showed up yet. She's still on the lam . . ."

"As soon as we get her, I'll let you know first thing . . . I won't let you down, boss . . ."

"Yes, sir. I know what happens to people who let you down. . . ."

"Yes, sir . . . Yes, sir . . . Yes, sir . . . Good-bye."

So, Wanda Latouche, Boom Boom's roommate, was missing. That was unfortunate since she had become a pivotal figure in the case. I took a deep breath and knocked on the door.

"Who is it?" roared the voice from the other side of the door. “Whaddoya want?”

"Sal Valentinuzzi?" I queried as I stepped inside the small, cluttered room.

"Who wants to know?"

"My name is Herbert Rice. I'm an investigator with the Golden Indemnity Insurance Company. May I have a moment of your time? I'm looking for some information on two of your employees, Miss Cleotha Saperstein and Miss Wanda Latouche."

His surly expression indicated I was not going to have long to play out my little charade.

"What kinda information you lookin' for—and why's an insurance company interested in those two snatches?"

"This is an official investigation, Mr. Valentinuzzi, and I hope that I can secure information from you voluntarily without resorting to subpoena ad testificandum."

"Speak English, pal."

"Miss Saperstein took out a five-hundred-thousand dollar, ten-year, renewable-and-convertible term policy a year ago with us. Miss Latouche was the beneficiary designated to receive the proceeds. Each of our policies has a two-year suicide contestability period which relieves us of the liability to disburse benefits if the insured should take his or her own life."

"What's this gotta do with me?" Sal asked, while removing the band from a cigar.

"The police are not pursuing this case with vigor. They have not classified Miss Saperstein's demise as murder, accident, or suicide. They have left this determination open, pending the discovery of further information. Naturally, my company would prefer a ruling of self-inflicted death."

"So you cheap bums wouldn't have to pay off," Sal snorted. "Now I got your angle. You insurance chiselers are always lookin' for a loophole."

I pretended to be offended and retorted huffily. "That is not the case at all. We have every intention of honoring our contractual obligation. In the interest of fairness to all our policyholders, however, we must make every effort to determine if Miss Saperstein was contemplating suicide when she applied for this coverage. If so, adverse selection existed and we must resist payment or stand in violation of our most cherished actuarial principles."

"You bums might as well write the check now," Sal chortled. "Boom Boom wasn't the type to punch her own ticket. She was rolling in dead presidents and had plenty of rich dicks fightin' for her favors."

I was intrigued by this last point. "Rich boyfriends, you mean? Like who?"

"Who knows? You gotta understand, a joint like this, we get three kinds of customers: kids, bums, and big bucks. The kids come in with fake IDs to see a naked broad for the first time without any staples or airbrushing. They whoop and holler and try to out-macho each other. They memorize every physical detail so they can go to school the next day and bullshit about the great lay they got. The bums collect soda bottles for their deposit and sell blood to scrape up enough to pay their way in. They just want to see something to help them get it up so they can run in the head and bop their bologna."

"Big bucks come in to get a taste of the forbidden. They're makin' it big in the business world, but things ain't so interesting at home. They been married fifteen, twenty years and the old lady's already sleeping in a separate bed smothered in cold cream and hair curlers. A lot of the girls, like Boom Boom, date the big bucks but what they do on their own time is their business. As long as they bring 'em into the club and keep 'em buyin' champagne cocktails, I don't give a damn."

I was impressed by Sal's philosophical dissertation on his clientele and the basis of their patronage. While he spoke, I scrutinized him at great length. He was in his late forties with an accent straight from Jersey City. He was shorter than I was and had a dietary problem similar to my own. His hair, probably dark and wavy in his youth, had receded and thinned with age. Dark, heavy jowls wouldn't have objected to a thrice daily brush with a razor, as I suspected he had a five o'clock shadow that started forming right after breakfast.

As for his clothing, he was wearing a brightly-colored, hand-painted tie, a wide one that was probably straight from the 1940s. It stopped halfway to his belt and appeared to serve the dual role of napkin, evidenced by the number and variety of stains and some crumbs from a recent meal, and slalom for his Macanudo ashes. The lower part of his short-sleeved shirt was being strained by his expanding paunch, which allowed patches of his hairy, white flesh to show through the oval openings between the straining buttons.

"If Boom Boom never mentioned a boyfriend to you, would she have done so with someone else—perhaps her close friend, Miss Latouche?"

"Could be, but Wanda ain't showed up for work in several days and we don't know where she is. The loss of both Boom Boom and Wanda is killin' business, Wanda especially. She was a tall, good-lookin' kid . . . and built like a brick shithouse."

Based upon what I heard during my earlier eavesdropping session, I suspected Sal's ignorance of Wanda's whereabouts to be truthful.

"Did Boom Boom have any known associates other than Wanda?"

"Beats me. Like I say, I don't mix in the personal lives of these broads. Boom Boom and Wanda shared a house, and I don't imagine either one of 'em ever spent a lonesome night if she didn't want to. Wanda especially; her heels were behind her ears more often than they were in a pair of shoes."

Sal concluded his last statement with a loud belch which added the essence of garlic, onion, and green pepper to the disagreeable odors that already occupied the room.

"How long have the two ladies been in your employ?"

"Wanda . . . about a year. Boom Boom, a little longer."

"Do you have a picture of Wanda that I could borrow? If I run across her, I'll be sure to let you know."

Sal reached in his desk drawer and tossed me a publicity still of Wanda. "You can keep it. We got plenty."

“Thanks. Other than dancing here, did Boom Boom have any other jobs that you’re aware of?”

“Like what?” Sal asked suspiciously, leaning forward in his chair.

“Like modeling . . . or acting in low budget film productions . . .”

Sal seemed to breathe a sigh of relief for some reason. “Not that I know of. Why you asking?”

“Just part of our routine inquiry since the amount of insurance is so large,” I replied. "Since Wanda is unavailable, would it be possible for me to interview some of the other performers?"

"Suit yourself. Most of 'em show up around five or so even though they don't go on 'til later. They rehearse on Monday mornings, too, if you're around."

"Thanks. A couple of final questions. Did Justine Barrington ever come in to the Glad Gland?"

Sal paused before answering. "Who's she?"

I watched Sal's face closely for a reaction to my next question: "Was Kevin Rutledge an occasional visitor to the club, or did he come in often?"

Sal played it deadpan and scratched his crotch, which I presumed to be a gesture of thoughtful repose. "Rutledge did you say? Don't know nobody by that name."

Despite Sal's denial, his earlier conversation had established Rutledge as a possible link between his murdered wife and the murdered stripper.

"Look, pal, I ain't making no money shootin' the breeze here with you. Hit the road and forget how to find your way back."

I'd obviously hit a nerve.

Sal labored to his feet, lumbered around the desk, and pushed me out into the corridor, slamming the door behind me.

I’d barely taken a step before bumping into the Mexican woman who’d been cleaning up behind the bar. She had obviously been eavesdropping, and motioned for me to follow her outside the club.

"I overheard part of your conversation, señor. Is it true you look for señorita Wanda?"

I nodded, surprised at this turn of events.

"And you wish to give her a lot of money from insurance policy, no?"

"I wish to discuss this possibility with her, yes."

"Listen." She lowered her voice to a bare whisper and looked around the parking lot anxiously. "I can tell you are no friend of señor Sal. He is an evil man. Tell you lies. Wanda was afraid of him . . . afraid he would kill her."

"Why was she afraid of Sal? I want to help Wanda get out of whatever trouble she's in."

"Wanda never say. She run and hide, but I know where she is. The night Boom Boom was killed, Wanda calls me from hotel. Says she needs help, bad, but can't go home or to work. I pick up her clothes and other personal things at club when no one is looking and take them to her. I loan her the little money I have. If I tell you where to find her, you will give her insurance money, and tell her that Rosarita help her, yes? Then she can pay me back."

"Rest assured that I will do everything I can, Rosarita. What's the name of the hotel where she's staying?"

My informant leaned forward and whispered in my ear. "Wanda left hotel. She is in Long Beach now. Got new job at a Joy Stick Lounge. She is wearing a wig and using name of Wilma Lattimore. Hurry, por favor. She need money to leave California. Tell no one where Wanda is. Her life depend on it. You can trust no one in this city. Bad place."

"Rosarita!" Sal roared from the back door of the club. "Get your wetback ass back to work. I ain't payin' you to siesta."

I silently thanked her as she scurried back inside and turned toward the Hudson. A couple of tough-looking thugs, eyeing me threateningly from an adjacent alley, encouraged me to walk briskly; I was glad to leave the Glad Gland, posthaste.

Chapter 12

I had just left Jake's kiosk after borrowing a street map of Long Beach when I spotted a familiar figure across the street. The stooped carriage, short, shuffling steps, and twitching ears indicated the unmistakable presence of one person: Judge Barrington's butler. Despite my desire to get to Long Beach, this was an excellent opportunity to interview the butler away from the muting influence of the mansion. I didn't have to hurry to catch up with the decrepit majordomo on the corner.

I tapped the feeble soul on the shoulder. "Excuse me, aren't you Judge Barrington's man?"

The elderly head looked up and peered over the right shoulder. "Quite correct, sir. Have we met?"

"I'm Chauncey McFadden, the private investigator."

"Indeed. Thank you, but I have no need for a private investigator's services at the moment."

"I wasn't soliciting business, my good man. We met at Judge Barrington's home. I was merely making an introduction."

"Introduction, you say? Quite so. I'm Montrose Pecklingham. And who might you be?"

"Chauncey McFadden," I repeated. "Look," I sputtered, attempting to suppress my exasperation, "as I'm sure you know, Judge Barrington has retained my services on a family matter of utmost importance. I'd appreciate a few moments of your time to acquire some information, so that I might more properly discharge those responsibilities. May I accompany you?"

"Oh, that would be difficult, sir."

"Why is that, pray tell?"

"I'm not going any place."

I slumped. "In that case, how about some lunch?"

Montrose stopped and rubbed his head. "Terribly sorry, sir, but I wasn't asked to prepare anything. If you like, I'll check with the cook to see what can be done on such short notice."

I suggested weakly, "I have a better idea, Montrose. How about me taking you to lunch?"

"I don't lunch, but there's an adequate tea room around the corner. A cup of Lord Grey's and a scone wouldn't be objectionable, I suppose."

"Tea and scones, it is, then. Lead on, Montrose."

The Bombay Tea Room was, in actuality, a Southern California yuppie diner. Overhead, a plethora of hanging baskets was suspended from the ceiling filled with Boston ferns, prayer plants, scheffleras, English ivy, caladiums, and some omnipresent philodendrons. Every nook and cranny was similarly filled with a planter containing a *Ficus benjamina,* a palm tree, a fiddle leaf fig, or a rubber tree. Scattered flower pots, interior window boxes, and vases on each table all effused with foliage, giving the room a verdancy that a South American rain forest would have envied.

All the fashionable causes du jour were championed in framed posters on the walls. One poster featured an environmentalist hugging a giant sequoia to protect it from a chainsaw-wielding lumberjack. Another poster showed a seafarer dangling over the bow of a charter boat tossing mullet to a lip-smacking whale, while a fishing vessel sank in distant waters. A third poster depicted two penitentiary guards strapping a struggling inmate into an electric chair. The prisoner had a cherubic face highlighted by a glowing halo. His two tormentors, on the other hand, looked like bad clones of Vlad the Impaler. Strangely, I didn't see a poster featuring a coat hanger and an unborn fetus, but I assumed this to be a philosophical oversight. It seems like protection was being advocated for everything except unborn human life. But, then, I guess with so many causes and so little wall space, priorities have to be set.

We were seated at a table in the rear that was sprinkled with a dozen small leaves of various shapes. Montrose sniffed in disdain, took out his whisk broom, brushed the leaves into his palm and deftly deposited them inside his jacket pocket. This housekeeping duty accomplished, he prepared for tea by removing his false teeth and dropping them into the glass of water brought by the waitress. I was prepared for anything and determined not to react. The waitress took our order with some apprehension, however.

"So, Montrose," I began after she had left, "what can you tell me about the Barrington sisters?"

A lengthy pause followed and Montrose took on the look of a man who knew a lot and didn't know where to begin. Some editing and summarization was going to be necessary—no small feat when the subject was two siblings with such colorful and eventful lives.

"Judge Barrington did instruct me to cooperate with your investigation, sir. Therefore, I am obliged to do so. Miss Barrington—Jill—can perhaps best be described as a collector."

Without his teeth, Montrose sounded like a bad re-broadcast of a nineteen thirties radio show. "You mean like a numismatist or philatelist?" I asked.

"Not exactly, sir. You see, Miss Barrington is a collector of orgasms."

His response caused my head to jerk back, flinging my clip-on bow tie into adjacent shrubbery.

"She is reputed to have one of the largest collections in the occidental world. After Mrs. Barrington, the mother, went away, I assumed many maternal duties. Nature abhors a vacuum, you know. I'm everlastingly chagrined that I didn't do a better job. Jill developed rampant promiscuity early on, long before graduation."

"College?" I asked while retrieving my bow tie.

"Junior high," he replied. "By the time she entered senior high school, she had become an accomplished fornicator. I spent the better part of her formative years breaking up illicit trysts between her and a succession of juvenile paramours. On more afternoons than I care to remember, I was forced to break up her couplings in the pool cabana with a fire hose. On other occasions, a bucket of cold water was sufficient to chase her and a nude lover from the garage or the guest house. The various bathrooms on the estate were the most troublesome love nests, but I interrupted these rendezvous of the flesh by pouring ammonia under the locked doors." With his teeth in aquatic storage, each deep inbound breath that passed between his bare gums produced a low whistle. “I must say, Jill had a fertile imagination—the young men locked in her embrace were always different, and I don't believe I ever saw her in the same position twice."

Montrose said all this very innocently. He could have been discussing macramé or origami.

The waitress brought our order and made a fast retreat. Before I attacked my cucumber sandwiches and sherry, I asked, "How about Justine? I understand that she was also an indulger in the sybaritic pursuits."

I munched on my cucumbers while Montrose dunked his scone in his tea and nibbled on the softened dough. The agitated movement of his little cheeks caused his wispy sideburns to jump up and down like cotton balls on a trampoline.

"To use an analogy, I’d say that both sisters enjoyed food, but Jill is a gourmand while Justine was a gourmet. No, the difference was more distinct than that. . . . I'd say that Jill is a glutton while Justine was an epicure . . . yes, that’s a better comparison.

“In addition, Justine went through the normal states of pubescent experimentation, but she wouldn't be caught dead in a laundry room with a clumsy, inexperienced varsity football player. Her relationships were with more influential, more experienced men, men of substance; and her sexual adventures took place in affluent penthouses, luxurious hotel suites, and oceanfront condominiums.”

"How did all this affect the judge's wife?" I asked, dabbing my lips with a napkin.

"Not very well, I'm afraid. When the girls were younger, Bernice—Mrs. Barrington—experienced a series of severe emotional breakdowns and was eventually confined to institutional care. Mrs. Barrington never got along well with either of her daughters. She couldn't deal with their behavior and it finally nudged her over the edge.” Montrose dunked another section of scone and nibbled off another bite.

“Judge Barrington, on the other hand, had a strange love-hate relationship with his daughters. Their activities were an embarrassment but he coped by ignoring what they did, by looking the other way.

Parenting was the only endeavor in life in which my master had ever failed. He never forgave his wife for leaving him and forcing him to face the child-rearing burden alone."

"How is Mrs. Barrington these days?"

"Occasionally, she appears to be lucid, but most of the time she just babbles."

"Is it conceivable that Jill could be involved in Justine's death?"

The off-duty butler tucked the last bit of scone in his mouth and washed it down with a final sip of tea. "Jill *has* been subject to cruel impulses from time to time. As a small child, she would tease her playmates by inciting them to want something very badly, like a toy or candy, and then withholding it from them. And, as she grew older, these behaviors did worsen. Fortunately, she outgrew the practice of tossing an occasional hamster into the compost shredder. Jill was jealous of Justine but murder is not an arrow in her quiver—she enjoyed the competition too much."

Montrose had been unexpectedly wordy, and I gratefully noted his observations while brushing away an infestation of thrips that had abandoned the plant above us for my coat sleeve.

"One final question, Montrose. Did any of the Barringtons have an acquaintance with a dancer at the Glad Gland nightclub named Boom Boom Saperstein?"

Montrose extracted his teeth from his water glass with a fork and took a moment to reset them in their place.

"Boom Boom Saperstein? Not to my knowledge, sir. I should perhaps mention that a former romantic interest in my life had the name Saperstein, though: Rubella Saperstein. I haven't seen her for many years, but I believe she's a housekeeper for a Mr. Armand Duvalier."

I nearly choked on the last sip of my sherry.

Chapter 13

After Montrose and I parted, I sat in my car, summarizing the growing web of connections between the Supersteins and the Barringtons. First, were the similar and bizarre murders of Justine Barrington Rutledge and Boom Boom Saperstein. Second, it appeared that Jill Barrington and Armand Duvalier, Rubella Saperstein's employer, were enjoying a physical relationship. Third, Sal Valentinuzzi, employer of Boom Boom Saperstein, had launched a manhunt at the direction of his boss to find Kevin Rutledge, husband of Justine Barrington. Fourth, Kevin Rutledge apparently frequented the Glad Gland, where Boom Boom Saperstein plied her trade. Fifth, Montrose, the Barrington butler, and Rubella Saperstein, Duvalier's housekeeper and Boom Boom's aunt, had shared a romantic past.

A short while later, I pushed these reflections aside and headed for the San Diego Freeway and Long Beach. Rosarita felt that Wanda was in danger, and I resolved to reach her before she was found by others of more sinister intent.

I arrived in Long Beach around two in the afternoon. The sky was overcast, which gave the downtown area an even more dismal appearance than usual. I found the Joy Stick Lounge on a little street off Long Beach Boulevard and eased into a space against the curb.

Inside, I gave my eyes a moment to transition from sun-drenched sidewalk to dark, chilled bar. My adjusting vision disclosed the Joy Stick to be a typical neighborhood watering hole, complete with the obligatory jars of pickled hard-boiled eggs and a rack of Slim Jims at the end of the counter. Behind the bar, a few neon signs flickered intermittently, like pinioned fireflies. Beside me, at the door, I looked down upon a vacant pool table whose slate guts were peeking through a tear in the jaded green felt.

At the bar, a couple of alley queens with faces as weather-beaten as old concert posters on a barrio fence were singing along to an

Englebert Humperdinck ballad that oozed forth from a scratched recording in the juke box. Neither the queens nor Englebert were appreciated, however, by one thin desperado with a ponytail whose face was sprawled on the bar between empty glasses and an overflowing ashtray.

There's a bar like this in every navy town. At night, the cash registers are kept ringing by sailors on liberty, women who materialize from nowhere to help said sailors enjoy their liberty, and night workers getting fortified for the third shift. In addition to those seeking a good time and laughs, others come and drink to remember or to forget. I've never been able to distinguish one group from the other; I'm not sure they can either.

The day is a different story. The stools are filled halfway to capacity by mid-morning with all the gallimaufry in the area. Hugging the bar are welfare recipients trying to accelerate the tortuous, slow passage of time and retirees who spend their days in meaningless chatter and sauterne—people who, for the price of a drink, get a bit of conversation and attention that is otherwise difficult for them to secure. Their dialogue is always about the future or the past—current circumstances are conspicuously avoided. The regulars entertain each other with apocryphal tales that recall successes in days gone by or anticipate the big score that lies ahead, as soon as they get that one long-awaited, long-overdue break.

A few patrons stare blankly into eternity, their visual rigidity interrupted by occasional sips of gin. I always suspected that the stares were deceptive; that behind the placid masks raged a turmoil created by the conflict of memories rehashed into oblivion, dreams deferred, and ambitions thwarted—blank faces that served little purpose but to give identity to the manifestation of death. Their shoulders sagged, as if already slumping under the burden of the grim reaper's cloak.

Looking around, I didn't see anyone who'd have been carded in at least four decades. The only things needed to complete the transformation of this place into a senior citizens center was for the government to deliver free surplus cheese or a Baptist Sunday school class to pass out peanut butter-and-jelly sandwiches on paper plates or a country-western social club to conduct line-dancing classes. I felt the eerie chill of death's waiting room: lonely souls trying to fan the embers of their youth but the ashes would have none of it. I suspected that when a regular died, they either propped him up against the juke box or pickled him for posterity, like the hard-boiled eggs on the counter.

The bartender acknowledged my presence and walked nonchalantly to my end of the bar. "What'll it be, bub?"

"I'll have what the locals have," I replied.

He returned a moment later with a double shot of rotgut and a beer chaser. "That'll be two singles."

"Got a moment, friend?" I asked.

He leaned on the bar with a scowl, which suggested that hospitality was not to be taken for granted. His gray, steel-wire flattop crowned a square face, a jutting jaw, and two cauliflower ears. His short-sleeved shirt was open to the waist so that it displayed parts of a tattoo mural that began at his knuckles, advanced to his clavicles, and descended to at least his navel. The design was difficult to follow, but it must have been etched while he was in a drunken stupor in the studio of Diego Rivera during the latter's most fervent anti-gringo period.

Resisting intimidation, I said, "I'm looking for a woman—"

"Ain't we all—" he interrupted. "Take your dance card someplace else, bub. The women here will either puke in your shirt pocket or die on you halfway through the two-step."

"I'm looking for a specific woman," I continued, "my cousin, Wilma Lattimore. She dropped me a card recently saying that she had procured employment at your establishment. However, I don't see her at the moment. Is she here today?"

He flexed a few times and grunted.

"Yeah, Wilma just started here but she don't come in 'til five or so. What do you want her for?"

"Simply to repay a small sum she was kind enough to advance me several months ago. Her unavailability does present a small problem. You see, I'm passing through town on my way to San Francisco and I need to see her as soon as possible. My bus leaves in an hour. Would you happen to have her address?"

Concluding that I looked harmless enough, he responded after a pause,"Yeah, she lives at the corner of Broadmoor and Clancy, number four."

"You have been most helpful." I left a five dollar tip on the bar and left.

Back in the Hudson, I pulled Jake's street map from the glove compartment and found Broadmoor and Clancy without much difficulty. Only a few miles from the Joy Stick Lounge, the streets intersected inside a rundown neighborhood several blocks from the beach. The houses had forgotten their last coat of fresh paint, and the dead, drooping fronds of neglected palm trees gave them a lugubrious appearance.

I found the building quickly, partly because my attention was drawn by the carcass of a rusted and battered Ford Pinto that slumped in the yard. Its axles were parked atop cement blocks, and a wadded rag substituted for its gas cap, while faded tourist attraction stickers had been plastered willy-nilly on the bumpers.

Like the surrounding houses, the curb appeal of this quadruplex had faded sometime around the Korean War. To complement the look, a string of broken Christmas lights sagged between nail supports on the fascia board, and four plastic chickens in knee-high grass appeared to have gotten lost while attempting to navigate their way between two rubber tire planters that encircled flowers long dead.

I knocked for several minutes at number four, the bottom left unit, but no response was forthcoming. Wanda was apparently not at home, which was disappointing—I couldn't bear the thought of having come all this distance just to go away empty-handed. I gave the neighborhood a quick scan and confirmed that I had not attracted any attention. Buoyed by this thought, and not wanting to accept the prospect of failure, I reasoned that boldness was my best recourse. The door wouldn't budge, but the window next to it was open and the screen had a small hole in it. I enlarged the hole, reached through with my right arm, and leaned far enough around to unlock the door from the inside. This full forelimb extension and the uncomfortable position of balancing my body upon my right foot left me winded.

After regaining my breath and rubbing my leg, I entered the apartment cautiously and found the living room in shambles: two chairs from a dinette set lay on the floor along with a broken lamp, and a coffee table had been knocked upside down and partially covered by a scattering of magazines and newspapers. The kitchen, on the other hand, appeared to be fairly tidy, which indicated that the fracas had been relatively restricted.

I headed toward the bathroom and stuck my head around the corner to peek inside—instead, I froze in the doorway.

My body trembling, I leaned against the door for support. Nervous perspiration oozed from every pore . . . and my glasses clouded over with an opaque, foggy film . . . my collar and belt felt like they were shrinking, causing me to breathe with difficulty.

I wobbled back into the living room and sat down on the sofa for a few minutes to dispel the dizziness and regain some strength in my legs. Several minutes later—though it was the last thing I wanted to do—I knew I had to return to the bathroom. At least the shock was behind me.

She was still there, still lying nude in the bathtub, completely submerged in water. Her eyes and mouth were wide open; a frozen testimonial to the pain that had racked her body as electricity stilled her heart. Running from between her legs to the lavatory was a black electrical cord. It had been plugged into a socket below the medicine chest and then extracted when its task had been completed.

Like Boom Boom Saperstein, the vaginal area displayed skin discolorations and nascent blisters. Her brown hair floated languidly in the water like a South Seas mermaid in aquatic repose. I also noticed her fingers and toes were curled back, an interesting effect which made the corpse appear to be more in a state of suspended animation than the finality of death.

I glanced at the picture I'd obtained from Sal and confirmed that the airbrushed girl in his photo and the body in the tub were one and the same: Wanda Latouche, alias Wilma Lattimore. Now that I'd seen her in reality, I had the nagging feeling that I had seen her before but I couldn't remember where until I walked into the bedroom and saw her long blonde wig lying on the dresser. Then it struck me. *The corpus delicti was the same blonde who had visited my office three days ago and vanished without explanation.*

Why had she come to see me? Had she wanted me to find the killer of her best friend, Boom Boom Saperstein? Or had she sought personal protection? Why had she left so suddenly? Had she changed her mind, or been scared away? Had she been frightened by the approach of Rubella Saperstein? Was Rubella something more than she claimed to be? Was she *really* Boom Boom's aunt? Was hiring me her idea or was she following the directives of another? What did Wanda, Justine Barrington, and Boom Boom have in common that had incited their murders?

I pushed these and other questions to the back of my mind, reasoning that looking for clues had a higher priority. I conducted a methodical, room-to-room search, taking pains to leave the contents as undisturbed as possible. I ran across nothing of relevance, except to note that Wanda's housecoat and lounging pajamas had been carefully folded and stacked upon her dressing table. This was significant. A copycat murderer could be ruled out since this facet of the case had never been publicized in the press.

I took a deep breath for fortification and ventured back into the bathroom to search it one last time. While I was down on my hands and knees, looking into the cabinet beneath the lavatory, something shiny winked at me from behind the toilet. How could I have missed *that* the first time? But then I glanced up and over to the bathtub, again, and forgave myself for my initial oversight.

At least I had noticed it now . . . lying atop the damp dust behind the commode—an expensive-looking lady's cigarette lighter. The surprise came when I turned it over.

There, in Old English script, were the initials "JB" . . .

Jill Barrington?

I dropped the lighter into my pocket and turned my attention back to the corpse in the bathtub. My first impulse was to locate a nearby telephone booth and report the murder as an anonymous tipster. However, the bartender at the Joy Stick Lounge could identify me as a person who'd been asking "Wilma's" whereabouts, so non-involvement was impractical. I decided, instead, to drive to the Long Beach police station, where I reported the crime as a good citizen.

There, I was introduced to Captain Barnwell, who proceeded to interrogate me for the better part of an hour. He asked questions from all different angles and reviewed my story a number of times to check for inconsistencies. Eventually, I satisfied his suspicions regarding my innocence and intentions of good will. I had even told him the truth, except for any mention of a cigarette lighter that I'd stored in my locked glove compartment.

As soon as a sergeant finished copying information from my PI license, I was released with the usual instructions to not leave the Long Beach area without checking with the captain first. "We may be wanting to talk to you again."

Not under similar circumstances, I hoped.

At least Long Beach was out of Del Dotto's jurisdiction.

Chapter 14

The lighter was excellent circumstantial evidence; however, it was not conclusive proof of any involvement on the part of Jill Barrington. Sal Valentinuzzi, on the other hand, had emerged as a suspect who was worth further scrutiny. I was fairly confident that he was more involved than he was telling, and I was convinced that if I could get a few moments alone in his office, I might discover information that could move the investigation along.

Gaining access to Sal's office during normal hours wasn't feasible, which suggested the necessity of a nocturnal investigation. But a break-in was out of the question—not because I was particularly averse to criminal trespass, but because I didn't know how to disable the burglar alarm system. No, to successfully search Sal's office, I was in need of two things: a strategy and the nerve to carry it out.

It was slightly after midnight when I arrived at the Glad Gland. The strategy I had devised was to be viewed as a gentleman who was out for the evening to enjoy a walk on the wild side. My clever disguise? Well, I gave my gray toupee and its matching handlebar mustache one last straightening and my derby one final twirl before reaching the door.

Inside, I took a seat at the bar, at the rear of the room, and sipped a tepid beer. Only a few of us sat there, since most of the patrons chose to crowd around ringside tables at the stage to be near the strippers. A perfunctory quartet provided the musical accompaniment, but they were almost drowned out by the shouts, jeers, and whistles of the crowd.

At the moment, we were privileged to be entertained by one Jambalaya Bordileaux, who went by the sobriquet, "Queen of the Creole Strippers." She was a pulchritudinous redhead, blessed with disproportionate mammary development, who pranced and danced quite spiritedly about the stage in a voodoo mask and a brief loincloth made of Spanish moss. In addition to her statuesque comeliness, her theatrical appeal was enhanced by her considerable athletic prowess. Judging from crowd reaction, her pièce de résistance was probably the simultaneous clockwise and counterclockwise rotations of her bosomy protrusions.

After this theatrical tour de force, the rest of the show was downhill. I was particularly unimpressed with the simulated soixante-neuf act that ended the show and Chiquita and Her Horny Burro.

The club started to clear out around one-thirty, and I slipped unobtrusively from my bar stool to move toward the dimly lit hallway. I crept along until I came to an unlocked door next to Sal's office. I opened it slowly and ducked inside.

A cleaning closet! Of all the luck; but at least I knew it would not be used this time of night. The glow of my pen flashlight confirmed that the small room contained cleaning materials and restroom supplies, an incredibly filthy sink, a noisome collection of mops, brooms, and rags, and several cartons of toilet tissue and paper towels. On the bright side, while squeezing around, trying to get comfortable, I dislodged some boxes of little goldfish crackers, which the club used for hors d'oeuvres. Fortuitously, I discovered that the more boxes I ate, the more space I created for myself—space I badly needed so I could wiggle my toes and stretch my legs from time to time to deter the onset of numbness and cramps. I squirmed in the closet for about twenty minutes before I heard footsteps and the door to Sal's office being unlocked, then opened and closed. A couple of long belches identified Sal as the probable occupant and reassured me that the thin wall separating us would easily accommodate the eavesdropping part of my plan.

For ten minutes or so, it sounded as if Sal was merely rummaging through some papers. Then, despite the late hour, he stopped to make a couple of telephone calls. Nothing was particularly interesting until I heard that magic word.

"Boss? Boss, this is Sal."

My attention became quite focused.

"Naw, we still got nothin' on Rutledge. We know he's outta the state, though. Nobody on the coast has seen him . . ."

“I touched base with all the usuals . . .”

“He was snatched or took off in his car . . .”

“No, he didn’t leave by commercial train, boat, or plane. We’re checking on rental cars and chartered boats and planes, but that’ll take some time . . .”

“He ain’t used his credit card so there’s no transaction trail so far. Listen, I don't know if you heard the news—it ain't in the papers yet—but Wanda was found snuffed this afternoon down in Long Beach—done in with an electric pickle, like the others . . ."

"I don't know. No, some private dick tripped over her. According to my inside fuzz, nothing of interest was found . . ."

"But, we still can't connect Rutledge and his computer project with whoever's been cooking the coochie . . ."

"Dunno. All I can tell ya is what we pieced together so far. It looks like Boom Boom was runnin’ a little blackmail racket and got a little careless; then she got herself croaked. Wanda may have been in on it, or she might’a been runnin’ her own gig . . ."

"I know our partners are gettin' impatient, but we're doing everything we can . . ."

"Sure thing, boss. Look, it’s closing time; place should be cleared out by now. I gotta lock up and call it a day."

Sal dropped the receiver, flipped off the light switch, closed the door, and walked back down the hall. In another twenty minutes, the building seemed deathly quiet. I brushed the goldfish crumbs from my jacket, peeked warily outside the closet door, and walked softly from room to room, prowling with confidence. Even the big performance room was dark, with the exception of a couple of night-lights behind the bar.

Satisfied the club was empty, I returned to Sal's office. I pried the door open with a chisel from my pocket and entered the dark room, then wasted no time. I lodged my flashlight in my mouth and began to rifle through drawers in the desk and filing cabinet, looking for anything that could even remotely be of relevance.

Sal was sloppy and had shoved notes, papers, invoices, and other documents into vacant receptacles and spaces without any sense of organization. Other than a torn bra and a half-eaten package of cotto salami, though, I found nothing out of the ordinary.

I had just gotten to the last drawer when the light was switched on. I froze where I was, bent over, my back to the door. I swallowed as a cloud of malodorous smoke drifted into the room and settled above my head like a sinister cloud.

"Well, well . . . whatta we got here?" Sal chortled. "Turn around, pal, before I put coupl'a red holes on either side of your brown round one."

I turned timidly and raised my arms slowly. A large .45-caliber automatic was the reason for Sal's confidence and at least part of his high spirits. He waved the barrel carelessly, slavering on a stubby Cohiba.

"You wanna tell me what you're doing here, or you wanna tap dance to a bullet serenade like in the old westerns?" he asked.

A number of possible retorts rattled through my mind. If I was Philip Marlowe, I would have said something like, "If you're looking for trouble, I come from where they make it," or perhaps, "All you cheap crooks are alike. You think a gat in the hand means the world by the tail."

However, I was Chauncey McFadden, and I only managed to stammer.

"Please be careful with that pistola, Mr. Valentinuzzi. While I'm *sure* it's the farthest inclination in your mind, the hammer could accidentally be released to discharge the resident projectile with fatal consequences; and though I fully recognize that my presence in your sanctorum at this inauspicious hour raises questions regarding my purpose and intent, I, nonetheless, assure you that a reasonable explanation does exist."

"I *never* heard such a mouthful of shit before—at least not all in one breath." Sal concluded his coarse evaluation with a loud burp and accompanying flatulence. "Hey, wait a minute . . ."

Sal reached out and used his pistol barrel to flip the derby and toupee off my head. "You're that insurance snoop who was here this morning! What're you doing in my office this time of night? Insurance people don't break and enter; they just keep losing the paperwork until you die of old age waiting for the claim to be settled." He took the effort to stretch and peek around me, then settled back onto both feet. "You weren't tryin' to rip me off 'cause the door to the safe is still open, and it don't look like nothin' is missin' . . . That's why I came back—to close it," he explained. "*Give,* pal, and make it good before I create some overtime for the morgue."

Sal, in his own forthright fashion, had convinced me that full disclosure was the best course of action.

"I'll be candid with you, Mr. Valentinuzzi. My name's Chauncey McFadden and I'm a private investigator. I've been retained by certain parties to discover the perpetrator of the so-called vibrator murders. I was looking for Wanda Latouche this morning, as I told you. My purpose, however, was not to confer insurance proceeds but to acquire any knowledge in her possession that might have had a bearing on the Rutledge and Saperstein murders. I did manage to locate Wanda this afternoon; but, unfortunately, I arrived too late. My objective in searching your office was to obtain information that you might not have voluntarily shared."

"So, you're McFadden," Sal snorted.

He surprised me by lowering his pistol and tucking it inside the waistband of his trousers. "Why didn't you say so this morning and avoid nearly gettin' your asshole used for target practice?"

I was flabbergasted by Sal's sudden acceptance. He observed my bewilderment and explained.

"Mr. Duvalier told me he hired you yesterday to find Rutledge. He knew you might be pokin' around and asked me not to kill you if I could help it. You see, I work for Mr. Duvalier, too. He owns this club."

Chapter 15

Sounds began drifting into my subconscious around eight the following morning. First, I tried to block out the noise of metal trash cans being emptied, then slammed down on the sidewalk, loose to roll to a final resting place. Between can serenades, I tried to ignore the grinding gears of the garbage truck as it inched down the street, thudding heavily over each pothole and drain grate. Next, I tried to mask the beagle in the apartment below that was howling mournfully to the tunes of the trash men's transistor radio and the screaming of a teething baby who was stubbornly defying pacification. For another few minutes, I even tried to bury the mélange of a retired coal miner coughing to soothe his blackened lungs, an argumentative wife demanding to know why she couldn't get more grocery money just because her combative husband didn't get enough sex, and a deaf violinist who was still attempting to locate a harmonious note.

Is it any wonder why I seldom sleep late?

I gave up.

My morning shower took the better part of an hour—thirty minutes to get wet and another thirty to rinse—thanks to water conservation devices that our parsimonious landlord had installed in all the shower heads in the building. The continuing drought had prompted this reduction in the water pressure to little more than the drip irrigation systems used by the larger farms and groves. Not even the toilet was spared—added to my monthly rent was a one-time surcharge for the cost of two bricks in the tank.

While drying the little hair I had left, I sniffed around the kitchen for something to eat and found some leftover pizza, which I carefully warmed up over a gas burner. It was going to be a good day: I only singed two of my fingers this time.

A half hour later, I was on my way to the state mental hospital, Camino Real Sanitarium, some sixty miles away. Besides the elusive Mr.

Rutledge, Bernice Barrington was the last major figure in the case to be interviewed. I hoped she could provide some insight into Jill that could be added to my growing list of incriminating, albeit still circumstantial, evidence.

Heading northwest on the Ventura Freeway through the San Fernando Valley, I passed through the communities of Calabasas, Agoura, and Westlake Village. At one time, they were small, quaint residential outposts; but then came the advent of mandatory busing for schoolchildren in Los Angeles, which caused the communities to swell and overflow with an influx of evacuating families seeking to remove themselves from the jurisdiction of the court decree. This mass relocation of the populace was the fourth largest in California history, ranking behind the Gold Rush that was triggered by the discovery at Sutter's Mill, passage of the Homestead Act that offered free land for the first to claim it, and migration to Canada that helped many avoid service in Vietnam.

Because no rain had fallen for more than six months, the rolling, gently sloping hills through which the ribbon of highway dipped and curved had become dry and brown. The tall grass that covered the land had been parched and turned to a golden hue by the summer drought, stirring only faintly when a breeze from Malibu passed over the Santa Monica Mountains. Some of the hills appeared to have a smooth texture, like beige silk or the sands of the Sahara. Others were rougher in texture, more like the skin of an old camel.

Grazing wherever vegetation was to be found, flocks of sheep took occasional respite from the heat in the shade offered by gnarled oaks that dotted the hillsides and in the shadows created by passing clouds, which were small and fleeting like smoke from a musket barrel. An early morning fog had not quite burned away and resembled diaphanous cotton candy as it nestled in the gullies and arroyos between the soft ridges.

Come winter, the skies would crackle with thunder and lightning and open up to release torrential downpours. The hills would drink their fill of the drenching storms and when they could hold no more, the runoff would trickle down the slopes in search of lower plateaus. Everywhere, the dormant vegetation in the dry adobe soil would explode in colorful growth, and these same hills would be magically transformed into large scoops of green chiffon in celebration of the arrival of spring. I was again reminded that nature was often poetry unspoken.

I left the city of Thousand Oaks behind me, to struggle with growth control ordinances and rising property taxes, and crawled up a long grade until the road dropped into the Camarillo Valley, the center of agriculture in Ventura County. On both sides of the highway, the rich black soil stretched as far as the naked eye could see and was well-organized into sections and straight rows of corn, tomatoes, okra, cabbage, squash, and string beans. On makeshift dirt roads among the rows, flatbed trucks patrolled to collect filled baskets of produce. From the cab of the closest truck, a burly arm dangled out of the window, slapping the metal door in time with an upbeat country tune. A cloud of dust trailed the crawling truck, suspended in midair, like breath on a still, frosty morn, waiting to cling to anything passing by.

The fields were sprinkled with Mexican aliens in bright bandannas and light cotton clothing who engaged in the laborious task of harvesting by hand. Their dark and deeply etched faces reflected their fatigue and their status as a people with no future and no past, just a dismal present offering opportunities to nowhere. If cotton was substituted for today's crops, this picture wouldn't appear much different than the old daguerreotypes and engraved illustrations of plantation life in the antebellum South. Just another reminder that this land of plenty was being at least partially sustained by underpaid labor.

I pressed on and shortly passed through a grove of eucalyptus trees whose branches formed a canopy over the highway for a couple of miles. Their distinctive smell was an aromatic treat for my nostrils. It wasn't long before I reached the turnoff to the hospital and I left the main highway behind to meander through orange groves. No fences or walls were to be seen; in fact, the only indication that I was entering the grounds of a state mental facility was a large roadside sign with three caveats:

> "The state reserves the right to inspect vehicles entering or leaving"

> "Severe penalties apply to anyone who assists a patient-resident under legal hold to leave a mental hospital without permission"
> "No photographs are allowed without the permission of the executive director"

I encountered no gates or guards, so I continued down a two-lane asphalt road that bisected lettuce fields until the hospital complex came into view.

From this distance, the hospital looked more like a junior college campus than a mental institution, but as I neared, directional signs pointed toward the Psychotherapy Clinic instead of a science building and the Center for Schizophrenic Studies instead of business administration classrooms. The buildings reflected a Spanish architectural motif with white stucco walls, red tile roofs, and rounded arches framed by decorative ceramic squares. The grounds were attractively landscaped and the shrubbery almost succeeded in hiding the iron bars that girded some of the windows. An atmosphere of serenity and tranquility prevailed and succeeded in contradicting any institutional stereotypes.

I found the building labeled Admissions and Visitors and walked in the main door. Behind a wooden counter in the lobby, a receptionist was rolling her lips together, cementing a fresh application of high-gloss lipstick. She tilted her head forward as I approached to peer at me over the top of glasses that were perched on the end of her nose. The oversized tinted lenses were set in large pink frames, studded with rhinestones. She looked at me in haughty examination, apparently trying to decide whether I was a patient or a visitor. Her prolonged hesitation was somewhat disconcerting, and I was relieved when she finally asked, "May I help you?"

"Yes. I'm here to see Bernice Barrington."

"Do you have a completed visitor's card on file?" she asked.

I fought to tear my eyes away from her orange bouffant, which swept upward and to the rear, suggestive of a pumpkin in flight, and nearly swallowed her nurse's cap. "No, this is my first visit. I do have

Judge Barrington's permission, however. You can contact him to authenticate my request if you wish."

She paused, relented, and reached under the counter. "Very well." She handed me a card to fill out. "Write your name, address, and who you're here to see—and remember to sign out in this register before you leave."

After completing the registration procedure, I walked down a short, white corridor to a large room. Mrs. Barrington was in a separate cottage, I was informed, a short distance away from the visitor center and would be transported here, to the waiting room, by her personal attendant. I'd been warned that it might be fifteen minutes before she arrived, so I made myself as comfortable as possible in a squeaky metal folding chair designed for someone half my girth. Situated in the chair, I looked around the sparsely furnished room.

About a dozen people were milling about; they all appeared to be patients except a young black man who was sporting a medium Afro and wearing a white short-sleeved shirt, white pants, and white shoes. He, apparently an attendant of some kind, also sat in a metal chair, reading a large textbook and rubbing what appeared to be a *gris-gris*—an African fetish charm that hung from his neck. He didn't pay much attention to his charges; that is, unless they became unduly noisy. When that occurred, he would get up and, with infinite patience, propitiate them in a rich bass voice and involve them in some less agitating activity.

About half of the patients were swathed in bathrobes despite the summer heat. They varied by age, sex, and race and were involved in a myriad of unusual activities, some of them discomforting to an unprepared observer. One elderly patient, in particular, was fidgeting in anguish and biting her lip as if trying to recall some previous but elusive happiness. She looked as lonely as an abandoned child's bicycle leaning against a decaying fence in a forgotten wood. Conversely, other patients scurried around in surprising animation, bumping into each other like ant scouts walking point before an advancing column.

The attendant must have noticed the look of concern of my face. "Don't get uptight, man. They're not as bad as they look. They're harmless enough when you get to know them. The only difference between them and us is that they faced bad problems and responded to them in ways unacceptable to our culture. Their only offense was in not conforming to the social norm in their reaction to whatever set them off."

"I'm sure you're right," I agreed. "I believe it was George Santayana who said that even the most intelligent man holds a lunatic on a leash."

The attendant smiled broadly and countered with, "Or, only a fool would wish to be normal after he discovered what it would be like."

I smiled equally as broadly and a tacit bond of understanding was formed. These were his people and I was giving them the respect they were due, and he liked that. He crossed the room and I shook the extended hand of Rudy Williams. We were proceeding to exchange pleasantries, and some psychopathological observations, when he noted I was continuing to watch an unkempt lady in her early forties who was sitting on the floor engaged in an interesting pantomime. She appeared to be scrubbing her hands and even periodically dipping them in an imaginary pan of water.

"She's a victim of an obsessive-compulsive reaction," Rudy volunteered. "Constantly washing her hands is an acquired defense mechanism that she engages in to eliminate feelings of guilt, which she would have if her original impulses were satisfied. No one's sure what causes her to do this. Maybe these washings are compulsions to protect herself from guilt feelings somehow related to infant sexuality. Maybe she's obsessed with the idea that she will reach out and touch someone on the genitals. Who knows? Anyway, she's a kind soul who does no harm."

Only once in a while would errant breezes waft through open windows and disturb the room's thin curtains from their lethargy; but the breezes always withdrew as quickly as they had arrived, sucking the curtains back against the mesh screens and then releasing them back to their former position. Overcome by the power of visual suggestion, the perspiration on my face, neck, and arms quickly became rivulets. I shed my bow tie and opened my shirt at the collar to get some air.

"How about the young man squatting on the floor with his hands clenched tightly behind his neck? He's been that way since I came in. That's got to be terribly uncomfortable."

"He probably doesn't notice it," Rudy said sadly. "He's a catatonic schizophrenic. He'll stay in that fetal-like position for hours at a time, refusing to talk to anyone and ignoring what goes on around him. He's probably aware of environmental stimuli; he just chooses to deal with them in a non-responsive manner."

Having established a rapport with a sympathetic ear, I asked, "How about Bernice Barrington?"

"She's not in the general ward so I don't see her very often. She's got bread so she gets special treatment. She has her own cottage and attendant—fellow by the name of Calvin Nately. I haven't seen her medical diagnoses, but I believe she's a simple schizophrenic, possibly with recurring bouts of paranoia or dementia. Half the resident population here is schizoid because it's a condition that has resisted all treatments to date. Are you a relative?"

"No, I'm a friend of her husband's. I'm seeing her on his behalf."

Rudy nodded. "Sometimes she seems clear as a bell, but most times she comes across as apathetic, withdrawn, or indifferent. Good luck."

"Thanks. I'm impressed with your clinical knowledge of the troubled mind, Rudy. How did you acquire it?"

"I'm going to California Lutheran College under the GI Bill and working here part-time. I'm planning on majoring in psychology," Rudy replied.

"I admire your ambition . . ." I stopped mid-sentence because an attractive lady, probably in her late fifties, was being pushed into the room. She sat in a wheelchair that was being pushed by a gangly youth in a uniform identical to Rudy's—white shirt and pants, spotless and wrinkle-free. The young man, in contrast, had a bushy mustache that was overgrown and in need of pruning and dark hair that was cut in a Prince Valiant style that had looked better on the prince. I presumed this to be Calvin Nately.

Mrs. Barrington appeared as out of place as a Quaker at an S-and-M party. Her luxuriant gray hair was coiffed in a becoming fashion. She was elegantly slim and had the formal, reserved bearing of a dowager at ease with wealth and its privileges. She had undeniably been a looker in her day. Oddly, her blue eyes, though sparkling and clear, were impossible to read.

I nodded politely and pulled my metal chair closer to her. Rudy pulled out a couple of cigarettes and invited Calvin outside for a smoke, which gave me some appreciated privacy.

"Mrs. Barrington, thank you for seeing me. I'm Dr. McFadden, Jill's psychiatrist." I wasn't sure how much she remembered, so I avoided any mention of Justine.

"Jill's doctor. How nice," she said with a faint smile.

"Mrs. Barrington, Jill is currently under my care. To render the best treatment possible, I need to know her better than she knows herself. Please tell me about her."

"Jill," she repeated slowly, wrinkling her brow and biting her lip. "Yes . . . yes . . . there was a Jill in satanic mythology. She was the high priestess of zoophilia. She habituated with the Republican elephants and Democratic donkeys. She ran naked through galleries and museums wearing nothing but a rebozo, desecrating great works of art and plastering 'Out of Order' signs on all the elevators. She nurtures wild beasts by letting them suckle at her breasts, feeding them venom disguised as milk before she slits their throats with a poniard, allowing the poisoned blood to flow over the earth, like Sherwin-Williams paint."

No one had said this was going to be easy.

"Fascinating, Mrs. Barrington. By any chance, do you happen to know any other Jills?"

"Oh, yes, *lots* of them!"

I brightened. "Could you tell me about them?"

"Let's see, there was a Jill who went up the hill with Jack to fetch a pail of water. Jill fell down and broke her crown and all the king's horses and all the king's men couldn't put her back—"

"Do any other Jills come to mind?" I interrupted.

"I suppose so," she said darkly after a lengthy pause, "but I don't want to talk about her."

"Why not?"

"She's bad . . . very, very bad. When I think of her, I get a terrible headache." Bernice closed her eyes and slowly massaged her temples.

"Perhaps you and I could talk about her. Most people find that when they discuss something that's upsetting them, they feel better afterward because the troublesome thought isn't bottled up inside them any more—they have released it, and by doing so, they have become free." I could see I wasn't getting through. She just stared at me hypnotically.

The prolonged pause that followed was awkward and challenging. I was reluctant to press harder for two reasons: I didn't want to provoke a scene since her hold on emotional stability was so fragile and I didn't want her to retreat into silence.

In the meantime, it was nearing midday and the temperature was approaching ninety degrees by this time. Without air conditioning in this wing of the hospital, I dabbed my damp face with my handkerchief and wrung the collected perspiration into a potted plant before tucking it back inside my pocket.

As I deliberated my next move, my thoughts were interrupted by the shuffling of feet. I looked up and noticed that almost everyone had stopped what they were doing and were migrating to the open windows. Out of curiosity, I stood and went to join them.

Initially, I saw patients in wheelchairs and rockers on the front porch of an adjacent residential building. But, then I focused on the object of their attention: an ambulance had quietly glided up the driveway and was slowly circling the building. Still under full gaze, it backed up to a door in the rear. A few minutes later, a gurney and its sheet-draped cargo was wheeled out by two briskly moving attendants.

I would not easily forget the looks on the patients' faces. They knew the bell had tolled, and while it had not tolled for any of them on this occasion, its clarion call would not indefinitely be denied. They turned away and shuffled back to their previous pursuits, comforted by relief that it was not them on the gurney, but saddened by the inevitability that death was one day closer.

Time is a bitch, I thought. Lips that used to laugh, now mumbled; hair that used to glisten and cascade, now was as sparse and dull as colonial pewter; fingers that used to excite and create, were now brittle and frail; and eyes that used to sparkle and attract, were now listless and pale. My thoughts were startled by a voice.

"Jill was an evil child," she said softly.

Her face and voice had changed and now reflected a matter-of-factness that raised my hopes that the forthcoming dialogue would be more . . . reality-centered.

"The seed was sown in the devil's garden, so it had to be. Jill resisted earthly guidance and received her directions from the world below. When she was growing up, she tried to kill her sister—twice. Once, she pushed her into Sunset Boulevard in the middle of heavy traffic. Another time, she tried to back over her with a car."

I had my notepad out and was writing hurriedly. Bernice had closed her eyes and was speaking as if in a trance.

"I see Jill laughing at me. She's mocking me, taunting me. She's dressed in a long, black soutane with a hood, standing behind an altar in a large, dark cave which has torches flickering along the walls. There are bodies on the altar covered with blood. There are other people in the cave also dressed in robes. They're chanting in a medieval tongue and approaching the altar one by one, dipping their fingers into the blood and smearing it on their faces. Enough. I'll talk no more of Jill."

She was breathing heavily now and I allowed her a few minutes to regain her composure before asking about the last family member. "This Jill, did she have a father?"

"Ah yes, Jill's father. He was once a minor deity who resided in the dark forest and enjoyed the favor and esteem of the major gods. In a moment of drunkenness during a bacchanalian orgy, he insulted Zeus and was forever banished to endure the trials and tribulations of mortal man. He mated with a scorpion to produce two vile harpies who constantly pluck at his eyes and ears to torment him. So sad . . . so sad." She closed her eyes, dropped her chin, and in a few seconds began to softly snore. I put my barely scratched notepad away, sighed, and left her reluctantly.

I ran into Calvin in the corridor and asked him a few questions in the hope that he would be more intelligible. He amiably relayed that he had been employed by a state mental hospital in Oregon before moving south a year ago and becoming Mrs. Barrington's private attendant. He told me he did his best to make her residency more enjoyable, and he detailed some of the special things he did for her like giving her rides in his van around the spacious hospital grounds and getting her food from nearby restaurants when the institutional fare was too bland and repetitive. It was obvious from his voice, eyes, and mannerisms that he found his employment relationship to be anything but onerous.

I thanked Calvin and stopped by the visitors counter to sign out. Since the receptionist was nowhere to be seen, I took advantage of her absence by thumbing through the register to see if Mrs. Barrington ever had any company. I had only flipped through a week of register sheets when a familiar name appeared on the third line down from the top of the page. The handwriting was small, but I couldn't mistake the name: *Cleotha Saperstein!*

Chapter 16

I rolled the windows down on the way back to Los Angeles hoping that the incoming air would usher in some clarity. What business did Boom Boom have with Bernice Barrington? What could *possibly* serve as a link between those two? Was Boom Boom's visit somehow connected with her subsequent murder? Was Mrs. Barrington in any danger?

I also needed to consider the fact that connections to Jill Barrington kept turning up. She was attracting more and more suspicion and had to be regarded as a prominent suspect in the case. If the latest information was correct, if her mother's memory was to be believed, Jill had exhibited homicidal behavior toward Justine long ago—had she finally been able to make good on her juvenile attempts? Jake had mentioned rumors of jealousy between the sisters—that *could* suggest an undivided inheritance as a motive. Even Montrose had detailed Jill's predilection for cruelty.

Perhaps Boom Boom and Wanda had discovered Jill's fratricide and decided to make their silence available—for a price. If that was the case, they evidently underestimated Jill's passion for this sort of activity and paid for their shortsighted greed with their lives—that was the impression I'd gotten from listening in on Sal's phone conversation. Admittedly, all this was circumstantial . . . except for the lighter that had turned up in Wanda's apartment. For lack of a better plan, I decided to confront Jill with the hard evidence and soft hearsay and see what she had to say in response—or in defense.

Further development of any plan of action was interrupted by my stomach's expression of impatience at my neglect. Normally, I would have been ravenous by this time of day and made my presence known to any one of the many junk food palaces in the region, where my dining exploits were legend. However, I felt I was really on to something today and resisted seduction by the beckoning pangs of appetite.

I turned into Halcyon Hills and repeated my earlier pilgrimage along Regal Place. The security patrol picked me up immediately and followed at a respectable distance until I turned into the palatial driveway of the Barrington estate. Montrose responded to my intercom announcement, then answered the doorbell and admitted me. I was prepared for my nemesis this time and was determined not to be upstaged.

"Good afternoon, Montrose. I'll keep my coat on if you don't mind."

"But you aren't wearing a coat, sir."

I made a mental note to strangle the little troll as soon as this case was over. "Is Judge Barrington in?" I queried.

"In where, sir?"

"Is he at home, Montrose?"

"Home, sir? So soon? But you just arrived."

I draped my arms around a banister for support.

"Would you care for a cocktail, sir?"

Ah-ha! He wasn't going to get me this time. "No, thanks," I declined, even though my mouth was dry and would have liked nothing better.

"That's too bad, sir. I just made a nice pitcher of martinis for myself," he said, picking up a frosty glass from behind a vase of flowers on a foyer table. "Mmm," he sipped, closing his eyes and smacking his lips in appreciation. "Absolutely perfect, if I say so myself."

"Actually, it was Miss Barrington I really came to see," I continued weakly. "Will you tell her I'm here?"

"I'm afraid not, sir."

"What? Why not, pray tell?"

"She's not at home, either, sir. My word, but you look a bit pale. Is anything the matter?"

I groaned. "My head is swimming."

"Swimming? Oh, no, sir. Miss Barrington is taking tennis lessons at the Halcyon Country Club. I don't expect her for another hour or so. I have some pressing duties in the other wing of the manor and will not be able to attend you, but you are welcome to wait in the study."

"I accept your invitation but before you depart, I have a question to ask relating to my investigation: were the bedrooms of Jill and Justine near each other?"

"Oh, no, sir," Montrose exclaimed. "They would never have consented to that arrangement. Jill's bedroom was up the stairs and to the left—the last room at the end of the hall. Justine's bedroom was up the stairs, to the right and all the way down the opposite end of the hall. Will that be all, sir?"

"Yes, indeed. Go right ahead, Montrose. Don't let me detain you."

"Very good, sir." Montrose turned and shuffled off in usual fashion, as if his ankles were tethered together by a six-inch rope.

When he finally disappeared from view, I puffed up the spiral staircase, hung a left, and wobbled my way down to the end of the hall. The length of my trek made me wonder if the two bedrooms actually resided in the same ZIP code. But, finally, I turned the knob on the last door.

Even without directions, I would likely have identified this as Jill's bedroom. Catherine the Great's boudoir would have paled in comparison. From the lush pile carpet to the murals on the cathedral ceilings, it was a decorator's dream. Everything was done in vivid pink, from the furniture to the drapes. The majestic king-sized canopy bed was covered by a mink duvet and enough pillows to muffle a dynamite explosion. And four players around a small card table could have fit inside the fireplace.

I ignored the cavernous walk-in closet for the time being because it resembled a swanky women's wear section in a small department store and would have required more time to search than I had. Instead, I began with a custom armoire and was rewarded by the discovery of something interesting in the twentieth drawer. Crumpled up and stashed beneath a black leather body stocking was a receipt for six vibrators from Ortenzio's Sex Shoppe in Laguna Beach. I slid the sales slip into my jacket pocket and descended the stairs.

Montrose was in the large entry hall when I got there, twirling an olive that had been impaled by a toothpick.

"*So, there* you are, Montrose," I said, to get the butler's attention and make him think I had been looking for him—in case an alibi for my absence had been necessary. But I needn't have worried. He turned around slowly with a look of mild surprise.

"Oh, it's you, sir. Back again already?"

"Quite so, Montrose. My need to talk with Miss Barrington has just assumed some urgency. Would you be good enough to give me directions to the country club?"

"Of course, sir. Take Regal Place to Winding Lake Circle. Don't be misled by the name. We're entirely landlocked here. Take a right, and go one and one-quarter miles to Delacroix Lane. Take a left and proceed to Ramon's Escort Service—unless, of course, it's been put out of business by the local citizens committee again; in that event, you'll see a 'Commercial Building Ready for Occupancy—Lessor Anxious' sign instead. There, you'll find an intersection where four roads converge, but not at right angles.

"Take the road at fourteen hundred hours—you can tell you've taken the correct street if you pass a large bed of orange and yellow marigolds three miles down, on the left. This lovely flower bed can be identified by the bronze statue of Northcote Smedley-Winston standing in the middle of it, though he may be difficult to recognize because of the many layers of pigeon guano disrespectfully deposited about his head and shoulders. Go about another quarter of a mile to where Dinky Vandermint crashed his Alfa Romeo last year. Poor Dinky, he never could learn to stay away from the steering wheel of a motorcar when he had a snoot full of gin. At this point, you'll be on Danziger Drive. If no one is looking, take a left turn and drive as fast as you can for three blocks."

"Why is that?" I foolishly interrupted.

"Because you'll be driving up a one-way street in the wrong direction," Montrose explained as if I should have known.

"At that point, you'll be on Sasquetooney Avenue. The Sasquetooney Indians were the original inhabitants of this area, you know. They were cheated out of its possession by Commander Smedley-Winston, who pioneered the exploration of this territory right after the

Revolutionary War. In exchange for ten thousand acres, he gave them diseased cattle, typhus-infected blankets, and infertile seeds.

"The Sasquetooney tribe eventually disappeared into extinction because of starvation and illness, but before the last shaman died, he placed a curse on Smedley-Winston's memory. With his dying breath, he used his big medicine to call upon the spirit of all flying creatures to denigrate the commander's remembrance. To this very day, whenever any pigeon has gorged himself, especially on purple berries, he will fly over the commander's statue and defecate on his fedora. The pigeons are simply reacting to some primeval, inexplicable instinct, sort of like the swallows who return to Capistrano each year."

This time, I decided not to interrupt.

"Now, remember, you're still on Sasquetooney Avenue, heading north. When you get to the Schwartz house, take a hard right. Poor Mrs. Schwartz, God rest her soul. She was out in the gazebo one night in 1936, shucking corn, when a sudden electrical storm came up. A bolt of lightning hit the gazebo and incinerated it. When Mr. Schwartz returned from a business trip the next day, all he found was a pile of ashes, the remains of his dear departed wife, and a swimming pool full of popcorn.

"That right will be Swanson Drive. Take Swanson past the Montessori School and the Clenet showroom and you're there." He turned away from me at that point without explanation and began rummaging through a drawer in a foyer table.

I had honestly attempted to jot down directions when Montrose first started his monologue. But, I lost a sense of direction somewhere between the pigeon guano and the one-way street. If Montrose had given directions to Columbus, we'd be eating out of rice bowls. "Thanks," I said dryly. "I don't think I could miss it if I tried."

Montrose turned back around and handed me a piece of cardboard. "Take this, sir, and stick it under your windshield wiper. It will gain you admittance to the club. Have a pleasant afternoon." With that, Montrose twitched his ears and shuffled off.

I hadn't been on Regal Place for more than a few minutes when I looked in the rearview mirror and noticed that I was being tailed by the Halcyon Hills security patrol again. This time, I was glad to see them. I flagged them over to the curb and asked for lucid directions to the country club. Surprisingly, they provided them with no offer of an escort.

The elderly guard at the gate of the club looked at my car suspiciously. The last time he had seen a 1952 Hudson was no doubt in 1952. I explained that I made my fortune restoring antique automobiles, and he nodded as if he believed me. I smiled, waved my pass, and scooted on past. After maneuvering into the available parking space between a Ferrari and a Bentley, I began a stroll around the facilities to see how the other half lived.

The Halcyon Country Club was some layout. It appeared to have every pampering and leisure device known to man. Featured were two eighteen-hole golf courses outside and a score of racquetball and squash courts inside. But, in this heat, it was the free-form pool, which could have easily qualified as the seventh largest freshwater lake in the state, that served as the social center of the club.

Almost all of the pool crowd was bronzed and fit and only occasionally tested the water since swimming was just an incidental ruse for the mating games and seduction tactics that were in progress. Lucky suitors could expect, through amorous attention, to capture either the virginity of a teenage nymph, or a few lusty moments of afternoon delight with a bored housewife, whose not-so-subtle flirtations were competing for the same young studs. The swimming pool was a stock exchange for the brokerage of sex, and floor trading looked pretty active. My guess was that more scotch was being used than chlorine and sun screen.

Moving on from hard-body haven, I finally found the tennis courts. Only three were in use, but it wouldn't have been difficult to identify Jill Barrington in any event. She was wearing a bright yellow outfit with matching sweatbands on her head and wrists. The sensuous canary was apparently in the middle of her lesson, which was being given by a young man, who was standing directly behind her. His lean and tanned body was pressed tightly against her back, his arms encircling her torso. He appeared to be giving her instruction on her grip, but had found the going difficult when her left hand inched its way down the front of his shorts, found the object of its search, and exhibited a grip of its own.

I sat down at a courtside table and ordered a lemonade from a waiter who appeared out of nowhere. He reappeared momentarily with a large glass and an even larger check. I peeked at it and caught my breath: I've had cars repaired for less. I passed myself off as Jill Barrington's guest and conned him into charging it to her tab. As I took a sip, I noticed that Jill had grown tired of digitally volleying inside her instructor's shorts. After she spotted me at the table, she dismissed him with a well-placed pat. He grinned and walked toward the pro shop while she approached me like a model on a catwalk. As she neared, I saw that no perspiration was in evidence, but she dabbed her face and arms with a plush towel as if she had just completed ten sets at Wimbledon.

"McFadden, isn't it? What on Earth brings you here? Did you find the whip-dick who put a dent in my new car?"

"Fellow by the name of Joaquin Fandango," I answered. I had obtained his name from an MVR that I had a friend at an auto insurance agency run.

"Good. I'll have the son-of-a-bitch arrested. Did you get his address?

"Yes, but it won't do you much good."

"Why not?"

"Mr. Fandango reported his car stolen the day before the accident."

"Thanks a lot," she said disgustedly. She threw her towel over a bougainvillea-covered pergola and sat down across from me. "It wasn't the damage so much—I just wanted to make the bastard pay. Serves me right for driving in the spic part of town, I suppose."

She snapped her fingers, and in a moment's time a vodka and tonic arrived. She played with the straw while looking at me in an odd sort of way. "What brings you to the club?" she asked. "It couldn't be tennis. I would venture that you and exercise don't even have a nodding acquaintance." She put down the straw and pulled a tennis ball from her bag. "Have you found my sister's killer, yet?"

"I have some clues. That's what I came to see you about."

She looked at me with amusement while squeezing the tennis ball in her right hand.

"Why would you want to see me?"

I decided to try a direct frontal assault. "Primarily because everything I've come up with so far points to you as the killer. Interested in confessing?"

She had a nice laugh. It carried across the courts and prompted a couple of heads to turn.

"I might. What do you have in the way of evidence?" She extracted a filtered menthol cigarette from a gold case and waited. I pulled the cigarette lighter with the initials "JB" from my coat pocket and lit it.

"I believe you lost this at Wanda Latouche's apartment. Considering the circumstances, though, I wouldn't feel right accepting a reward for its return."

She tilted her head back and laughed again, then took a lengthy swallow from her drink. After returning the tennis ball to her bag, she took the lighter from me and turned it over in her hand a few times. "It's a nice lighter," she commented as she handed it back to me. "The only problem with your theory is that it doesn't belong to me. Anything else?"

"I would like to see *your* lighter if you don't mind. You don't impress me as the matchbook type. That is, if you have it on you." I gave her my patented smirk, which, granted, could have been improved by a little orthodontia.

Jill had draped a long, lithe leg over the arm of her patio chair and was polishing the lenses of her sunglasses with a cocktail napkin. "Why, I don't own a lighter, Mr. McFadden. I can *always* count on a man to light my smokes—as you just did."

Ouch! There's nothing more humiliating than being used as a witness against yourself. "I find it hard to believe that you never smoke alone," I said.

"I'm an improvising kind of gal. If I can't find a fire, I start one. What else have you got?"

Yes, it was time to move on to exhibit B: the vibrator receipt that was in my pocket. "I happened to be in Ortenzio's Sex Shoppe this morning. Ortenzio tells me you're a regular customer. In fact, he says he could pay his overhead just off your vibrator purchases. Large markup on those things, you know."

"Big deal," she scoffed. "A gal can get lonely. I go through vibrators the way the Dodgers go through baseball bats."

She was very good. I don't believe I had ever met anyone who could talk so casually about such an intimate subject.

"That may be," I countered, "but the baseball commissioner takes a dim view of the Dodgers using their bats to maim opposing team members." I waited for a reaction that did not come.

"Moving on to another topic, I was at the Camino Real Sanitarium this morning and spoke with your mother. Interesting lady. She told me your relations with your sister were strained, to put it mildly. In fact, she recounted how you tried to harm Justine once or twice in your impetuous youth. I got the distinct impression from her that you finally succeeded."

Jill got the waiter's attention and asked for another vodka and tonic. She looked at me and I added a wine spritzer to the order.

"My mother doesn't have both oars in the water, isn't playing with a full deck, is a few bricks short of a full load; her elevator doesn't go all the way to the top, or any of a number of phrases commonly used to describe the crazy among us. I'm afraid she wouldn't make a very good witness in court. Any first-year law student could rip her testimony to shreds.

"But, out of curiosity, what did dear old mom have to say about me, anyway?" She leaned back and blew almost perfect smoke rings that floated lazily upward until they dissipated on the underside of the courtside umbrella.

"Let's talk instead about your several attempts on Justine's life. They strike me as more than a little naughty."

"Those were merely childish pranks, the type of things sisters do to each other without ever really thinking about the consequences. I eventually did hit her with a motorcycle and broke her hip. It turned out to be a favor, actually—it kept her from losing her virginity until she was fourteen. I beat her by two months, and she never got over it . . . I outmaneuvered Montrose one afternoon, and gave a shot of leg to the pool maintenance guy in the cabana."

"Is that the last time you tried to harm your sister?"

"My memory gets a little hazy after that point. Sorry." She put another cigarette between her lips and waited for the obligatory light.

Her body language suggested I take a different approach, so I did: "What's your relationship with Armand Duvalier?"

"He's a fascinating guy who knows how to show a girl a good time. He has power and knows how to get what he wants. I like that. Most men today are boring, boring, boring."

"Did you ever meet Boom Boom Saperstein or Wanda Latouche?"

"I saw them doing their acts, if that's what you want to call it, at the Glad Gland. I'm surprised both of them haven't died from bad silicon transplants or terminal herpes," she said cattily. "Armand and I used to drop by once in a while for laughs. He owns the place, you know."

"Yes, I do." I decided to try and bait her. "And when did you find out that Armand was having relations with some of the dancers at the club?"

"I'd call that an employer's prerogative. But I really can't see Armand stooping to dip his quill in the village inkwells," she replied with eyes flashing.

My earlier shots may have missed their targets, but this one had enjoyed a closer proximity to center.

"If I was a man, I wouldn't hump any of that Glad Gland riffraff unless I was double-rubbered *and* wearing a raincoat." She sat up in her chair and pushed away from the table. "If you'll excuse me, McFadden, I really must shower now. It's been an interesting afternoon."

She rose to her feet, tugged her tennis skirt down, and headed undulatingly across the courts to the locker room. The fact that two doubles matches had to halt their play to permit her passage didn't faze her in the least.

Chapter 17

It was still afternoon when I pulled up in front of my office building and parked behind a large, new Chevrolet. After noting that it somehow looked out of place for our neighborhood, I entered the building and climbed the stairs, stopping for my customary rest at the top to catch my breath. When I puffed into my office, I was surprised to find two men waiting for me.

At first glance, I thought they were twins. They were Caucasian, clean-cut, average build, mid- to late-twenties, and wearing three-piece gray suits with white shirts and narrow black ties. In each left breast pocket, a piece of white cloth peeked out, no doubt one of those fake handkerchiefs—a piece of cotton scrap stapled to a cardboard square—furnished for free by the dry cleaners. They appeared to be perfect reincarnations from the 1960s. They stood up at the same time and simultaneously reached inside their coats to produce shiny badges. Fortunately, only one of them spoke.

"Good afternoon, Mr. McFadden. I'm Operative Moore and this is Operative Nelson. We're from the National Investigation Agency. Your note on the door said you'd be back by noon; it's almost 2:30."

"My humble apologies, gentlemen—field work. Now, answer in the following order succinctly and without digression: who are you, what do you want, what does it have to do with me, and what is the National Investigation Agency?"

"All of this will be explained in due time by our field director, whom you'll be meeting shortly. If you'll be good enough to accompany us, we have a car waiting downstairs."

"Not so fast, gentlemen. It's been a rather trying morning and I'm fatigued. I hadn't planned to go out the remainder of the day. Please convey my regrets to your director. Some other time, perhaps."

The non-speaking twin opened his coat and tapped the handle of a .38 Smith & Wesson; standard government issue.

“Oh, come now. The government doesn’t go around shooting civilians,” I pointed out.

“The government denies we exist,” replied Operative Moore, “and they don’t much care how much collateral damage we create as long as we clean it up. We would prefer that you come without resistance. You can walk down the stairs under your own power, or we can expedite things by tossing you through the window.”

Without further ado, I preceded my escorts down the stairs and we climbed into the new Chevy I had noticed earlier and left the city. When we reached Woodland Hills, we exited south on Topanga Canyon Road and drove a couple of miles uphill on the narrow, winding two-laner until we reached an overlook where another car was parked. The view offered a scenic panorama of the San Fernando Valley. The more distant portions of the valley were obscured by a hazy, miasmatic smog—the fires were still burning—but it was an impressive view, nonetheless.

The parked car was a long white limousine with tinted windows. Another young man, in a similar gray, three-piece issue, leaned against the front fender, smoking a cigarette, which he extinguished after a final long drag. Nelson and Moore instructed me to join the director in the tonneau of the limousine. It was with curiosity, but some trepidation, that I did so while they remained in the Chevy.

I crossed over to the limo’s door, which was opened by the driver, and ducked down to slide inside. Turning to greet my fellow passenger, I almost did a double-take. I don't know what I expected, but the director was different than any preconceptions I may have entertained. He was a morbidly obese man, attired in a white suit with a pink carnation in his lapel, and though he reclined against the back of the seat, his bulk made him appear to be leaning forward, supporting himself with two ring-laden, pudgy hands that clasped the ivory handle of a walking cane.

"Mr. McFadden, I see you made it after all. I trust your ride was comfortable?"

His unique appearance was further accentuated by his habit of keeping his eyes closed as he spoke in a rasping, wheezing voice. I expected him to have an attack of angina pectoris at any moment. Training on his face, I could see that he was bald, had a thin, black mustache, and a large nose that formed a porte cochere over his small, rosebud lips. A monocle covered his right eye.

"Comfortable enough, although I'm getting a little annoyed at all the command appearances I've been 'requested' to make lately."

"You do deserve an explanation, of course. I'm the director of the National Investigation Agency. You can address me by my code name, 'Apollo.'"

Far be it from me to comment, but he was as close to Apollo as I was to Don Juan. "I've never heard of the National Investigation Agency. Is it a bureau of *our* government?"

Apollo smiled condescendingly. "Yes, we're a covert arm of the CIA. Our existence is not generally known, and I ask your cooperation in keeping it that way. I rarely even leave Washington. It's only matters of extreme national importance that cause me to venture into the public arena and risk identification. I beg your indulgence, but this type of meeting protects my anonymity and assures the privacy of our discussion."

"I see. I'm surprised your henchmen didn't search me. How can they be sure that I'm unarmed and unwired? That I'm not a threat to your person or organization?"

The thick, protuberant lips formed a small smile. "You were never important enough to warrant the creation of a dossier in our files, so we've had to scramble the past few days to learn something about you. And, although you do own a pistol, you wouldn't be considered dangerous even if armed. To be candid, Mr. McFadden, you're a penny-ante player swept by circumstances you don't understand into a high-stakes game."

"What did you want to see me about, Apollo?" I asked brusquely, treating myself to the luxury of sounding impatient. My mortal insignificance was becoming too widely known for my liking.

"We're seeking the location of Dr. Kevin Rutledge and are interested in any information you may have stumbled across during your investigation."

Since I had learned nothing about Rutledge, I faithfully related—for the umpteenth time—the events of the past four days to Apollo. During my exposition, he kept his eyes closed, but he nodded periodically to indicate his comprehension. Several minutes later, I concluded with my own brief foray to find out what the National Investigation Agency knew.

"I could be mistaken, but I don't believe Rutledge is connected with the murders. In fact, I have another suspect in mind and evidence to support my hypothesis. That information aside, I would guess you are more interested in Rutledge because of his computer invention than because of his possible malpractice with a vibrator."

I could tell I had piqued his interest because of the respiratory agitation that emanated from his chest and a twitch that started in his right eye, which caused his monocle to jump. Apollo hesitated, appearing to choose his words carefully. "Our government is involved in an international race for computer supremacy that will determine which nation will come to dominate the world in the economic, scientific, and, most importantly, military arenas.

"In the military arena, every advanced country's national defense and offensive weapons systems are dependent upon the support of computers. Weapons laboratories have long used computers to design nuclear warheads. And intelligence agencies have employed computers to crack enemy codes and to process intelligence data.

"In the future, computers will become the very heart of battle management systems. Computers are being developed to assist military commanders in configuring defense strategies and attack patterns; to help fighter pilots make split-second decisions in dogfights; and, more momentously, to update the detection and destruction of intercontinental missiles, long-range bombs, and stealth torpedoes.

"Even conventional forces will be replaced by computer-directed soldier-robots and driverless vehicles that can invade our adversaries using sensors and machine intelligence to achieve their objectives."

"Okay, so, GI Joe will be replaced by R2-D2," I quipped. "Where does Rutledge fit into this?"

"The genius of computers is, of course, their ability to process and manipulate large amounts of data extremely quickly. And current computer technology, which is based upon electronic circuitry, like circuit boards and semiconductor chips, has served us well.

"But, Dr. Rutledge's mission has been to design a totally new supercomputer technology that will handle massive amounts of data—XV-1000 is the project's working name. Its intent is to increase computational speed by astronomic orders of magnitude. Rutledge determined this goal wasn't achievable using electronic circuitry, so he looked elsewhere for a solution—brilliantly concluding that laser technology was the way to go. At the time of his disappearance, he was well along in designing a supercomputer that focused on a black box technology—beams of treated, infused light that capture, store, calculate, and transmit data faster than anything imaginable.

"I don't think it's being overly melodramatic to say that those who possess the fastest computers will be the inheritors of the Earth, Mr. McFadden. Dr. Rutledge *must* be located immediately, and by representatives of *our* government. If he slips through our fingers with this secret . . . well, I believe you can now understand our urgency."

"Indeed. But, if Dr. Rutledge successfully developed the XV-1000 himself, why can't he sell it to whomever he pleases? Can our government rightfully seize his work in the name of national security?"

"Confiscation is not necessary in this case. Mr. Rutledge's research was subsidized by a federal grant, so anything he develops is the property of the U.S. government. We're merely trying to recover what we've paid for."

"How do you know the XV-1000 works? Couldn't Dr. Rutledge have been pulling off a colossal scam, parking your funding in some secret offshore bank account in the Grand Caymans?"

"We suspect that the XV-1000 has not been completed, but we're convinced he was making exceptional progress. Grantees are required to submit periodic status reports in order for us to verify that substantive effort is taking place and that demonstrable results warrant continuation of funding. Our scientists were optimistic about Rutledge's notes and were able to duplicate his work, up to a point. When his reports became increasingly dilatory, we assigned operatives to keep him under surveillance. Due to an unfortunate contretemps, he eluded our vigilance and disappeared."

"I understand that he may have acquired some limited partners other than Uncle Sam. Couldn't other countries be involved in his disappearance?" I asked.

Apollo rotated his head in my direction to study my face, and I could see traces of talcum powder that had mixed with perspiration and sebum to cake between the folds of skin in his neck.

"It is *not* probable that he's been abducted by a foreign government. You see, each predator country has an espionage network that operates in other target nations. If these target nations become aware that foreign agents are operating within their boundaries, they can feed those agents false information to tie up the predator's lines of communication in nonproductive transmissions.

"Target nations can also proselytize the agents of the predator nations and convert them into counterspies. The predator countries, if they discover counterspies at work, can then either neutralize the counterspies by feeding them inconsequential information or outright fabrications, or they can re-proselytize the counterspies and turn them into a counter-counterspies, which has the effect of restoring them to original spy status."

"Target nations can also have their agents proselytized by predator countries and turned into counterspies. Target nations also have the same option of either making their disloyal agents useless counterspies by making them transmitters of valueless information, or they can make them counter-counterspies by re-enlisting their ideological repatriation. This whole scenario is what we call the *covert* network."

"Is there a Cliff's Notes version of this?" I asked facetiously.

Apollo's rosebud lips widened perceptibly, which I assumed to be a smile. "If there was, we'd have to sanction Cliff with extreme prejudice." I think he made a funny but government-speak is not my forte.

Back to business, he continued without pause. "We also have an *overt* network, which operates somewhat differently."

I could hardly wait.

"In the overt network, the agent of the predator country makes his identity very apparent while operating in the target nation. The predator country therefore knows that any information received through this overt agent will be false since he is *known* by the target nation to be a spy. In the espionage business, it's as important to know what is false as it is to know what is true. However, if the overt agent did not make his true identity conspicuous enough to the target nation, then the information he obtains could be true since he was, in effect, unintentionally acting in a covert capacity. In this event, the information is neutrally regarded, and corroboration by a trusted covert spy is usually required.

"So you see, Mr. McFadden, with so much deceit, duplicity, treachery, and betrayal in abundance, it would be impossible for a foreign power to come into the possession of something as significant as the XV-1000 without us knowing about it."

I could see why this man was a director. I wouldn't have been able to wade through that reticulation with a cue card.

Apollo continued. "Observe the gentleman pacing back and forth outside this car, for instance. He's one of our west coast operatives who was selected to drive me here today." Apollo went on as I glanced out the window. "He is, in reality, a double agent employed by the *Komitet Gosudarstvennoy Bezopasnosti.*

"Say what?" I asked in my best Lizelle impression.

"The KGB. He doesn't know that we're aware of his perfidy; therefore we can use him to send the wrong signals to his bosses as long as they aren't aware that we know his true identity. Since he serves a purpose for the time being, we allow him to live and serve his purpose.

"If we did decide to terminate him, we would then have to be prepared to accept retaliation by having made advance arrangements to place one of our less-effective operatives in harm's way, where he could be executed by our enemies.

"If we get one of theirs, they must get one of ours. It's an unwritten law in the code of reciprocity. It's a callous but effective way of pruning our less fruitful organizational branches. Since we perform this same service for them, everyone benefits in a way; this is one of the reasons that espionage stays at such a high, state of the art, level."

Apollo then asked me a few other questions about Rutledge and, satisfied that my ignorance was genuine, dismissed me with a wheeze.

Back in town, the car slowed and had almost come to a complete stop when I was pushed out of the rear door near my building. Equally surprised was Chen Lee, owner of the Chinese laundry by my office, who bolted from his store gesticulating wildly and jabbering in rapid-paced Cantonese. He had witnessed my fall, which ended up being cushioned by the rack of unclaimed shirts he had set out on the sidewalk to sell. I got to my feet and unwrapped myself from the surrealistic, variegated montage of sleeves and collars, restored the rack to its upright position, and replaced the now-soiled shirts. Serendipitously, I discovered two of my own shirts that I had forgotten to pick up at some point in time.

I finally made it upstairs to check the mail and feed the mice—and relax.

I could only groan as I was welcomed back by some stimulatory grunts coming from behind the bathroom door—Melkoff was using my toilet again. As soon as I can financially forego the twenty dollars a month he pays me for restroom privileges, I'm going to start locking my office door when I leave and banish him to the Texaco station down the street.

Chapter 18

The next morning, I stopped by Jake's to return his map and bring him up to date on the case.

"Chauncey, you sophist shamus; you distended detective; you prince of peepers," Jake greeted. "How goes it?"

"Things are looking promising; almost as good as your alliteration," I confided. "I have a suspect in mind and after breakfast, I'm going to present my evidence to Del Dotto."

"I got news for you, too," Jake said during a mouthful of *souvlaki.* "But you go first."

"Jill Barrington is the culprit, to my way of thinking," I told him. "She had motive, opportunity, and—" I stopped because of the disquieting look that had swept across Jake's face. "What is it, Jake?"

"That's the news I was going to tell you, Chauncey," Jake said quietly. He looked at the ground and scraped some imaginary mud off the bottom of his shoes. "I was listening to the police band on my shortwave radio a few minutes ago . . . They found Jill Barrington's body in a motel room about an hour ago."

I was dumbfounded by Jake's revelation and almost collapsed on his counter.

"A place called the Magic Fingers, on Reseda, in the valley. The cops and the meat wagon boys are over there now." He concluded with a soft apology: "Sorry I had to be the wet blanket."

This case was getting to be nothing but one setback after another.

The Magic Fingers Motel was about what I expected, but I was at a loss to understand what someone like Jill Barrington would be doing there. It was a one-story, fifteen-unit affair, squatting like some evil toad under a half dozen large oak trees in the northern part of the San Fernando Valley. It had probably been attractive at one time, but age and neglect had taken their toll. The color on the exterior walls was now an indecipherable pastel, and the paint on the wooden doors and trim had faded and cracked in surrender to a merciless sun. Like many other once-proud lodgings bypassed by the freeway system, it had been allowed to deteriorate by uncaring owners, and made its living these days catering to the needs of a low social and moral stratum. Its specialties were hourly rates and around-the-clock pornographic movies on cable TV.

It wasn't difficult to identify the room involved. Policemen, reporters, and representatives of the coroner's office were milling around number fifteen, at the end. Two men were wheeling a body out on a collapsible gurney to a waiting ambulance when I walked up.

I took a deep breath and ducked under the yellow crime scene tape, then unzipped the body bag before anyone could object. It was Jill Barrington all right. Her eyes and mouth were wide open, contorted in a chilling death mask. A feeling of déjà vu flashed in my mind, but I wasn't prepared for the startling effect of her lifeless form. I zipped the bag back up and shivered.

"What's the matter, McFadden? You never seen a stiff? You're playing with the big boys now, so you're gonna have to take the training wheels off your bike. What are you doing here anyway? Did the motel call you to report a stolen cherry?"

It was Del Dotto and I wasn't about to tell him I'd been on my way to his office to report my suspicions about Jill Barrington.

"Who found her?" I asked.

"The maid. No one answered her knock, so she let herself in with a passkey to clean up. These rooms are usually rented out five or six times a day, unless some outfit is shooting a skin flick."

"Was she . . . the same as the other three?"

"Yep, sucking current at low tide." He raised a clear plastic evidence bag to eye level. "This one's a King Dong Tunnel Teaser." He smirked as he tried to hand it to me, but I slipped my hands into my pockets and ignored his offer.

"This is getting out of hand," Del Dotto remarked, referring, I assumed, to the use of vibrators as murder weapons. "The next thing you know, the killer will be selling advertising space on them—hey, that's not a bad idea. The Del Dotto model could have 'Billy Bob's Country

Barbecue Restaurant, Chattanooga, Tennessee' written up the shaft. On the McFadden model, they could *maybe* squeeze in 'IHOP.'"

I was so glad Del Dotto could entertain himself.

Then, out of the blue, he whistled. "What a body on that broad," he said wistfully. "I'd give a week's wages to be the coroner's assistant who preps her for autopsy. I've never been inside one that's been cooked. I usually prefer mine rare, if you know what I mean."

"Has Judge Barrington been informed?" I asked.

"Not yet. Hey, I've got a great idea!" Del Dotto snapped his fingers. "Why don't *you* tell him, McFadden? I'll bet the judge is just crazy about the terrific job you're doing for him. If you stay on the case much longer, his whole family will be wiped out."

I didn't need Del Dotto to point out my lack of success. Now that Jill Barrington was dead, I was out of suspects.

"Mind if I go in and look around the room?"

"Stay out of there," Del Dotto growled. "The medical examiner's staff and crime scene investigators are still going through the motions and bagging anything that looks like evidence. I hope they brought enough bags by the looks of the place."

"Did you find anything you could directly relate to this murder?"

Del Dotto's mouth widened into an evil grin, revealing two rows of teeth the color of saffron. I could tell he was torn between the alternatives of keeping me in suspense by withholding information of interest or delivering another put-down by bragging about what he had accomplished to reinforce what I had not. He chose the latter.

"You could say that . . ." Del Dotto's tone was that of a braggart and he went through the motions of performing an impromptu inspection of his fingernails, "we caught the killer." He dropped this disclosure like a bomb and luxuriated in my astonishment.

"They're bringing him out now," he added, motioning with his head toward the open door to the crime scene.

I was speechless when four patrolmen led Roger out of the room in manacles. Because of his size, two of them had a firm grasp on each arm, while fingering their truncheons nervously. But they got Roger into the backseat of the squad car without difficulty. He seemed uncharacteristically calm, which was puzzling. If Roger had been antipathetic to incarceration, it would have taken most of the precinct to wedge him into a black-and-white.

"You look like you know him, McFadden. Where from?"

"He's the human compactor who does odd jobs for Armand Duvalier. But something doesn't make sense here. Jill Barrington and Duvalier were going at it like the expiration date for lust was quickly approaching. Duvalier wouldn't risk having her killed—that would put him in the crosshairs of the judge's political machine.

"Besides, if he and Jill had become estranged, he would simply have told her to park her shoes under someone else's bed. Perhaps Roger was acting on his own. I admit that the murders are sordid enough to bear his signature. May I ask him a few questions before you take him downtown?"

"Nope, we wanna hurry up and get him booked before the sedation wear off. He's only half human and one quarter sane by the looks of him. If he gets frisky, we got nothing else with us to stop him. You'd need at least a .357 Magnum and a perfectly placed shot between the eyes to drop him at a full gallop."

"Did he confess?"

"He ain't said nothing. When the maid discovered the body in the tub, she screamed and started to run out of the room. On the way, she tripped at the door and saw Roger sitting in a dark corner with a confused look on his face—she was scared, double-shitless.

"We picked her up about four miles down the road. She was picking 'em up and laying 'em down and not looking back. We had to wait until the soles burned off her tennie pumps before we could bring her into custody."

"Were there any other witnesses?"

"Not that we've found. After the maid started screaming, people in the other rooms got dressed in a hurry and split. The place emptied faster than a bottle of cheap wine at a hobo convention."

"I suppose the motel register was its usual exercise in fiction."

"You got it. There were seven George Washingtons and six John Smiths. The towns listed by these sex-heads ain't even been discovered by Rand-McNally yet."

At a loss and a dead-end, I sat in my Hudson and watched as the lab men finished their work and packed their equipment. Soon after, the door to number fifteen was padlocked and posted with a police quarantine sign. After that, the small crowd began to evaporate. Almost everyone there had been acting in an official capacity, and surprisingly few spectators had drifted in from the neighborhood. I suspect in that locale, the sight of police cars and ambulances is rather mundane stuff.

Before leaving, I went into the office to ask the front desk clerk a few questions. I knew she had already been interrogated by Del Dotto's men, but I felt a follow-up visit conducted in an unofficial capacity could prove of value.

A bell jingled when I entered the office door, and a pretty blonde head in pigtails popped up from behind the counter. In her late teens, she had large, brown eyes and deep dimples that parenthesized a glossy white smile.

"Hi! Can I help you?" Her voice was as sparkling and refreshing as her pert, fresh-scrubbed appearance. "You can have any room you want except number fifteen. Everyone's checked out and everything else is available, even the Congo Room."

"Oh? Why is the Congo Room so popular?"

"It has a waterfall shower, a vibrating rope hammock, a zebra skin carpet, *and* a vine hanging down from the ceiling. Somehow, though, you don't look like the Congo Room type."

Her pixie voice and the cute way she had of tapping her forefinger against her lower lip made it impossible to take umbrage.

"You look more like the Roman Room type. It has a lot of pillows thrown around on the floor and an in-ground Jacuzzi you can roll into."

"It sounds delightful, but I left my toga at the dry cleaners. What can you tell me about the occupant of room fifteen who was found murdered this morning?"

"Are you another cop?"

"Private," I replied. "How did room fifteen register?"

"Let's see," she said while flipping the page to the previous day. "She checked in last night under the name Martha Washington."

"What was your impression of her? Was she upset? Did she say anything you can recall?"

"I wasn't here last night when she came in. I only work the morning shift, from six 'til noon. I go to Cal State at Northridge and have afternoon classes this semester."

"Who would have been on duty last night?"

"That would have been old Mr. Jurgens. He comes on at six and works until midnight. I don't think he'll be able to help you much, though."

"Why not?"

"He doesn't hear or see very well. And, even if he had his five good senses, the owners want us to be as unobservant as possible. Take the money, get some kind of name and address to satisfy a state law, and give out the key. That's all we're supposed to do."

"Did you see the man who was led away in handcuffs?"

She suddenly shifted into Valley Girl speak: "Yuck! Gag me with a spoon! That thing was groady to the max—I didn't check him in. He'd give me piss fits for months!"

"Can you see if he checked in at all? His name is Roger, and I don't think he's smart enough to invent an alias."

She ran her finger down the previous day's registration sheet again and returned to her co-ed persona. "No 'Roger' here. He *must* have been in the room when I punched in this morning, though."

"Why do you say that?"

"Well, first, I'd have noticed him if he'd arrived while I was here. And second, there were two cars in front of number fifteen when I came in. One was a Rolls Royce; hard to miss that. The other was a beat-up 1966 Ford Mustang; my boyfriend has a car like that. The police wrecker towed both cars away, so I figured one of them was the dead lady's and the other one belonged to the hulk who was arrested. They're the only people who wouldn't have been able to drive away themselves after the police came."

"I commend you on your deductive powers. I'm surprised to find someone like you working at a place like this."

"This isn't bad. The work's not hard and it gives me a lot of time to study. It's only twenty minutes to school so it's ideal. Better than some part-time jobs I've had."

"Such as?"

"My first job was two years ago. I typed labels for a sperm bank over on Melrose. I met some really neat donors and dated a few of them. Then last summer I was a toe-tagger at the county morgue. I really was a records clerk but attaching identification tags to the corpses was one of the swell things you had to do. This job is neat because it's giving me some practical experience. I'm majoring in hotel management."

I didn't have the heart to tell her that working at the Magic Fingers Motel to learn about hotel management was like analyzing camel manure to gain insight into the engineering of the pyramids.

"By the way, do you know who owns this place?"

"Yes, he signs our payroll checks. Man by the name of Valentinuzzi."

Sal again. Did he own the Magic Fingers in his own name, I wondered; or was he fronting for Armand Duvalier?

"You want to know something funny?" she asked as I was getting ready to leave.

"What's that?"

"That police lieutenant who was here this morning—"

"Lieutenant Del Dotto?"

"Yeah, that's the one. He's been here before—as a customer, I mean. And, you know what? He likes 'em young—younger than me. About fifteen or sixteen. A real baby-groper for sure."

Outside the office, I spotted a familiar figure getting out of a late-model Oldsmobile: Lizelle, Reina de la Cama. She was accompanied by a nervous-looking accountant type who was pulling his collar up and looking around anxiously. Lizelle patted his arm and told him there was nothing to worry about.

"Hi, Lizelle," I greeted. "Everything's vacant except number fifteen—even the Congo Room."

Chapter 19

The next day was Friday, the fifth day of the case, and I wasn't much further along than I had been on Monday. I had dropped by my office to check the mail and pick up any phone messages from the answering machine, but as I passed the open door to Melkoff's office, I could tell from the conversation flowing into the hall that he was again involved in his dedicated pursuit of the perversion of justice. I knew I shouldn't indulge in this guilty pleasure, but I stopped to listen anyway.

"I know what I'm talking about, Mr. Strickland. I've handled hundreds of these cases before. If your wife is seriously contemplating divorce, you've got to act quickly and strip the marital assets clean before she can lay claim to the share that would fall to her under our community property laws.

"First, take out the biggest second mortgage you can get on your house. I know a bank in Switzerland that will hold your funds with the utmost discretion. Trick your wife into signing the loan papers; if you can't get her to sign, I know someone who can forge her signature if necessary. Remember, any joint equity you have now should look like Moscow on the eve of Napoleon's arrival—the old scorched earth approach.

"In a similar vein, convert your savings bonds and money market certificates into cold cash. You can deposit those funds with me; I'll then use that deposit to cover my legal fees and other expenses. Of course, I won't be able to give you a receipt . . ."

"Why not?" Melkoff's baffled client asked.

"Because, we can't very well give the courts an audit trail with which they can trace the money, can we?"

"No, no, I suppose not," the poor man responded. "It's just that I won't have any proof that I gave you those funds."

"Tut-tut" clucked Melkoff. "As your attorney, your well-being is my foremost concern."

"Okay . . . and how about the children? Can you guarantee me custody of them? Won't the courts hold my homosexuality and alcoholism against me?"

"Not to worry. The courts are becoming much more lenient where gay parenthood is concerned, and your drinking hasn't materially affected your employment record. Besides, if things begin to look doubtful, I know a couple of `professional' witnesses who'll testify that they've had unorthodox sex with your wife and have done so for a number of years. They can also claim she snorts cocaine while in their company. Courts always give boozers preference over dopers. If all else fails, I have a couple of other contacts who can abduct your two children and take them across the state line to you in Arizona. Believe me, Mr. Strickland, my record in these cases . . ."

The bones were almost bare, so I abandoned my eavesdropping addiction and walked cautiously into my office—after the past few days, I no longer knew what to expect behind door number two. Someone was inside, sitting in the overstuffed armchair, but to my relief, it was Rubella Saperstein. Her eyes blinked rapidly as she knotted and twisted a small white handkerchief in her lap. She was upset and had obviously cried a great deal recently. Her small chest shuddered and she dabbed her eyes quickly to prevent the welling of tears. She looked pitiable, and I felt worse than ever that I had not been able to find her niece's killer.

"Mrs. Saperstein—I wasn't expecting you. Have you been waiting long?"

"Just a few minutes, Mr. McFadden."

"I'm afraid I don't have anything to report to you. I've uncovered a lot of clues, and I thought I had determined the identity of the killer, but she came up with an ironclad alibi herself this morning."

"What was that?" Though she tried to give the impression of being interested, it was apparent that her heart and mind were absorbed by something else.

"My suspect was found murdered this morning in a valley motel. She was killed by the same procedure as your niece."

"That's what I came to see you about . . ."

With that declaration, she had my undivided attention, and I leaned forward to avoid missing even one soft-spoken word. "They arrested Roger for the murder of Jill Barrington."

"That's correct, but how did you know?" I asked.

"Mr. Duvalier told me. He received a call from the police this morning."

I had forgotten that she was Duvalier's housekeeper. "All right, but why did Duvalier tell you? Why would he think you'd be interested?"

"Because," she sighed, "I'm Roger's mother."

I was glad that Rubella continued without prompting, because I was speechless.

"I might as well let the other shoe drop, I suppose. Montrose Pecklingham, whom I suspect you've met by now, is Roger's father."

I removed my glasses and pretended to clean them with my handkerchief. I had a thousand questions to ask, but they had all rushed to exit at the same time and become jammed in the doorway.

"Montrose and I were married in England after the Korean War. We moved to the United States for opportunity, and I became pregnant with Roger shortly after our arrival. He was five weeks premature and was born after a good deal of labor. Roger developed behavioral problems early on and they worsened with age. When we couldn't do anything else for him, we had no choice but to have him admitted to a children's hospital.

“His problems had created a terrible strain on our marriage, and Montrose and I were divorced a year later. Roger became worse under institutional care, and since Montrose and I no longer maintained a family unit, he was sent to an orphanage.

“One of Roger’s problems was that he was very large for his age; another was that he enjoyed assaulting other children. After being examined by government psychiatrists, he was consequently committed to an institution in the Pacific Northwest where he stayed until several years ago. He escaped during a fire that destroyed the asylum and its records and, when Roger came home to me, Mr. Duvalier took him on at my request. Mr. Duvalier is such a kind man. I don't know what I'd have done if he hadn't taken an interest in Roger."

"Mrs. Saperstein, I'm truly sorry. What can I do?"

"I want you to see Roger and get his side of the story. I know he's innocent. He couldn't have done such a terrible thing. Will you try?"

"All right," I agreed, "but I'll need to ask you a few questions. Are you up to it?"

She nodded her head and stifled a sob.

"When was the last time you saw Roger yesterday?" I asked. "Remember, I can only help your son if I know the truth."

"Yesterday morning, when he left with Mr. Duvalier. He was running errands all day, and was put on a special assignment last night," she replied.

"Can you explain how he happened to be found in a motel room with a warm corpse? Without some logical explanation, it's going to be difficult for Roger to beat the charge."

"No, but I'm certain that Roger had a good reason for being there," she responded dejectedly.

"What makes you so certain that Roger is innocent of the murder of Jill Barrington, and possibly others?"

"Roger knew that Mr. Duvalier and Miss Barrington were keeping company and that Mr. Duvalier thought a great deal of her. Roger wouldn't do anything to hurt Mr. Duvalier," she said.

"Allow me to pose a question, albeit a hypothetical one. *If* Roger had discovered that Miss Barrington was somehow deceiving his boss or causing him some harm or embarrassment, could he then have reacted violently?"

"He might have, but that wouldn't explain the other murders."

"No, it doesn't. But, the police are looking for a fall guy and if they secure Roger's conviction, look for them to add the other three homicides to charges brought against your son. Did Roger know Justine Barrington, Boom Boom . . . uh, Cleotha, or Wanda Latouche?"

"Possibly. He may have known that Justine and Jill were sisters by overhearing conversations at Mr. Duvalier's home or office. He didn't know that Cleotha was his cousin, but he could have seen her and Wanda performing at the Glad Gland. I know he used to drop in there from time to time to catch the show and deliver things from Mr. Duvalier to the manager."

"Thank you, Mrs. Saperstein. I'll keep in touch," I said as I escorted her to the door.

After she left, I drove to the precinct to see Del Dotto and request permission to talk to Roger. Del Dotto was in his customary position, leaning back in his chair with his eyes closed, making no attempt to suppress a yawn. I tapped politely on the door to gain his attention, and then entered when no objection was forthcoming. His feet were propped up in the center of his desk, separating a thick police file on one side and a half-eaten cheeseburger and cup of coffee on the other. The burger reminded me that I was missing lunch, again, a fact verified by my ability to slide into the visitors' chair without the wooden sides groaning from the pressure of my pandurate profile.

"I'm underwhelmed by your visit, McFadden. What do you want?" He appeared to be a little sleepy, which no doubt accounted for the absence of his usual invective.

"You seem a bit lethargic, lieutenant, no doubt the result of your demanding responsibilities and the exhaustive, conscientious manner in which you carry them out." Given his sluggish condition, I was optimistic that I might have the upper hand for once.

"Listen, peeper, I got called outta bed at six this morning," he lamented. "I was supposed to have the day off, but an early morning backpacker found a body dumped in one of the gullies at the bottom of Topanga Canyon Road. Looks like he'd been dead about twelve hours."

"Was the victim, by any chance, a Caucasian male, in his late twenties, and dressed in a gray three-piece suit?" I asked.

Del Dotto's eyes widened. He even took one foot off his desk and looked at me with a sudden interest. "Yeah, how'd you know that?"

“There was no identification, I presume," I added.

"Nope, his head and both hands were missing, severed with almost surgical precision. No dental evidence or fingerprints. This ain't your everyday mugging.”

“If disposition of the body is a problem, you can always call The Cleaner from Chicago,” I wisecracked.

“Who?” Del Dotto asked.

“Never mind. I would sit this hand out if I were you. Your corpse was a foreign double-agent planted in a covert operation in one of our national intelligence agencies. His usefulness apparently expired late yesterday afternoon. Your chief will probably be getting a call from Washington, if he hasn't already, and the instructions will be to make this an unsolved John Doe who died as a result of misadventure at the hands of a person or persons unknown.”

I then described my encounter with Apollo—without details or names, of course—while Del Dotto listened with unprecedented respect. He didn't look very happy, probably because he recognized a situation where his authority and influence were nil.

"This valuable information, which I share with you on a professional basis, certainly merits some reciprocation on your part, don't you agree, lieutenant?"

"If the price is right. What do you want, porky?”

"Thirty minutes with Roger to see if I can get anything out of him. Have your storm troopers had any success with their rubber hoses and cattle prods?"

"Nope, he hasn't said a word since he was arrested. You can talk to him. I don't see any harm in that. Here, you can even take a look at his file." Del Dotto nudged the thick brown folder across the desk with the heel of his shoe.

"Thank you, Luther. That's decent of you. Your magnanimity suggests to me that you think your case against Roger is unassailable, and that his conviction is assured."

"Open and shut. That's the craziest rap sheet I've ever seen. I don't know if he's guilty or not, and I don't give a shit. With those priors, he'll go over for it just the same. The captain talked to Duvalier this morning and he's willing to let Roger swing for it. He just wants his name and relationship with Roger and Jill Barrington kept out of the papers."

I opened the folder and read the contents. Roger did indeed have a colorful history. Bizarre crimes seemed to break out wherever he hung his hat. At first, he managed, aided by the patron saint of the kinky, to elude arrest. However, his patron's aegis had failed, at least on one occasion, to shield Roger from indictment. His preoccupation with corpses to fulfill his sexual needs had been proven and earned him time at a state mental hospital outside of Portland. Since his arrival in Los Angeles, if there had been an occasional foray into an undertaker's parlor to snatch the guest of honor, it had gone unreported. But that's L.A. for you.

"I see what you mean. Roger certainly manages to squeeze twenty-four hours out of every day being a bad boy, doesn't he?"

"I'll level with you, McFadden. We've got about twenty other old, weird, unsolved crimes still hanging around that we'll close the books on once Roger gets gassed. The relatives of the victims will be happy, the taxpayers will be happy, the newspapers will be happy, and we'll be happy. Convicting a freak like Roger can tie up a lot of loose ends.

"I'll tell you one thing, though," Del Dotto said between bites of burger. "If humping stiffs was a crime, I'd be serving time. You ever meet my first wife?" Del Dotto chuckled at his own humor, then wiped his chin with the sports section and leaned across the desk with as serious a look as I've ever seen him muster. "Which brings me to this point. You start screwing things up, and we'll bust your balls. If Roger goes free, I'll nail you in his place."

"Lieutenant, please . . . have some professional respect. I wouldn't *dream* of exonerating Roger unless I could come up with an equally acceptable substitute."

"Good. Now, take a hike. I'll call lock-up and tell them you've got fifteen minutes, no more."

I hadn't been waiting in the visitors' room long before an apprehensive guard brought Roger in. His blue denim shirt and pants, issued courtesy of the county, were too small, which made him appear even more awesome. He sat in the chair opposite me on the other side of the Plexiglas divider and stared straight ahead. I picked up the phone on my side of the partition and motioned for him to do the same with his.

"Roger. Remember me? I'm Chauncey McFadden. You brought me to Mr. Duvalier's office."

Roger continued to stare ahead without reaction. With his shoulders slumped and his face blank, he seemed less ominous. The partition provided welcomed separation as well.

"Mr. Duvalier is very concerned that you've been arrested," I lied. "He feels you're innocent and has asked me to help prove it. To do this, I must ask you some questions. If you don't confide in me, there's a strong possibility that you will go to trial and be found guilty. If that happens, you'll be locked up for the rest of your life at best or go to the gas chamber at worst. Will you talk to me?"

Roger adjusted the phone in his hand until the mouthpiece was under his chin. "What you want to know?" came out haltingly.

I nodded in appreciation. "First of all, did you kill Jill Barrington?"

He shook his massive head from side to side.

"How did you happen to be found in her room by the police?"

Roger's face looked pained. Recollection was probably not his strong suit.

"Miss Barrington . . . she was at Mr. Duvalier's apartment last night. She leaves. Says she has an important appointment. Boss tells me to tail her. She drives to motel . . . goes to room at end. I park on street and wait."

"What time was this?"

"Don't know. Before midnight."

"Then what happened?"

"Someone came out of room."

"Did you recognize that person?"

Roger paused. "Dark. Can't see."

I had a feeling this last statement wasn't true—he turned his head and his voice had a different emotional inflection, but I continued.

"What did you do then?"

"I wait. Miss Barrington, she doesn't come out. I park in front of room and go in. I see her in bathtub . . . naked . . . dead. I know I'm in big trouble. Boss going to be mad at me for letting this happen. I was told to follow her and look out for her. Boss worried about her since her sister killed."

"What happened then?"

Roger put his gargantuan hands over his gargoyle face. “I sit in room to think. The police come . . . stick needle in arm . . . bring me here. That's all I know."

"Other than the maid and the person you saw come out of the room, did you see anyone else enter or leave room fifteen?"

"No."

"Roger, I think you recognized that person. They have vital information to give us about the murder and I need to talk to them."

"No!" Roger was clearly animated now, and other communicating couples, startled by the outburst, turned their heads in our direction. I lowered my voice, hoping Roger would imitate my example.

"Is this person a friend of yours? Is that why you are concealing their name?"

"Yes."

After Roger’s outburst, the guard had uncrossed his arms and walked over to his window. Roger rose from his chair without prompting and left through the same door he'd entered. As big and brutish as he was, there was something almost forlorn about his departure.

Chapter 20

On the way home, I started to feel tired and nauseated . . . My vision began to blur . . . my legs grew weak . . . my face felt hot to the touch. By the time I got home, the symptoms were acute, and I crawled immediately into bed. I awoke only briefly, I believe it was the following morning, just long enough to remove my shoes and coat; then dropped off again.

After hours of abyssal repose, I came to realize I was tossing and turning without control. Suddenly, I awoke to the sound of my own coughing and the fact that I was gasping for breath. I clawed at the sheet that had somehow wrapped itself around my windpipe and waited for consciousness to come to me. Before long, I heard a melodious but concerned voice calling my name over and over, at first gently then with more insistence. The voice was real—I had a visitor. I wrapped myself in a tattered bathrobe and put my ear against the apartment door.

"Chauncey, please open up. It's Girtha. Hurry! This pot's getting heavy."

I released the four dead-bolt locks, opened the door, and let her in. Girtha, bless her heart, staggered in struggling with a large kettle. It was still hot, and the aroma of chicken, noodles, and broth quickly filled the room. She hoisted the large pot to a front burner before collapsing wearily into a chair.

"God, I didn't think I'd make it. Four cats followed me down the hall rubbing their butts all over my ankles. It's the closest thing to an erotic experience I've had this week."

I barely heard her, since I was furiously ladling chicken and dumplings into a plastic Dodger batting helmet. I had broken my last bowl several weeks earlier and was forced to improvise. The steam from the kettle fogged my glasses but I deemed it a minor annoyance, considering the promise of its source.

After she caught her breath, Girtha remembered the primary purpose of her visit. "Chauncey, sweetie-kins, where have you been? You had us worried to death. No one has seen you since Friday morning. You didn't return my calls Friday night or yesterday. What with the cases you've been working on, we were afraid something had happened. I called your landlord and she said your car was here, so I figured you were probably sick and laid up in that nasty bed. You look terrible. What's the matter, honey?"

I was touched by Girtha's concern and would have properly expressed my appreciation except for the fact that doing so would have interfered with the frantic introduction of nourishment into my famished body . . . golden, thick, soft dumplings and succulent, tender morsels of chicken swimming together in a rich, savory broth . . . it was sustenance fit for a king.

"Well, it looks like you're starting to recover," she remarked in response to my harried spoon action.

Too preoccupied with slurping and chewing, I momentarily parked my spoon in the helmet and reached over and patted Girtha's knee.

She smiled. "I'll tell Jake you're all right, then." She took her eyes off me for the first time and looked around the apartment. "This place is a mess!"

I glanced up—but only for an instant—and saw her shaking her head.

"I don't know how you can live in such a dump. But, you men are all alike. You'd rather drop something on the floor than put it back where it belongs. What you need is a woman around this place. No, I take that back. What you need is to set fire to this dump and move into a woman's place." She paused for a moment while straightening her back and shifting to a more comfortable position in the chair. "I know a woman who *might* be interested, if she was asked nicely . . ."

She crossed her legs, as much as her ample thighs would permit, and smoothed the back of her head as if reinforcing the placement of her short, brown curls; all the while, she looked out the window, pretending indifference to whether or not a response from me was forthcoming.

My only acknowledgment was a final series of slurps as I upended the helmet, but that was enough to prompt Girtha into taking off her watch, slipping on a pair of latex gloves, and wading into the dirty dishes around the sink. Sometimes I felt guilty about taking advantage of her good-natured companionship, her love of sharing her cooking with an appreciative eater, and her preoccupation with cleanliness and organization—but the feelings were only brief. I only hoped that our relationship, as one-sided as it seemed, was giving her some satisfaction or fulfilling some need in return.

I finally put down my spoon. "Girtha, what day is today?" It dawned on me that I had lost track of the passage of time during my illness.

"Sunday. It's my only day off, remember?"

"I've been out since Friday? That's almost two days. What time is it?"

"It must be around eleven," Girtha said. Soap bubbles rose to the ceiling and popped as Girtha, the human cleaning tornado, used a steel wool pad with zeal to attack her avowed enemies, dirt and grime.

"Why don't you take a break and give the case a rest?" she asked over her shoulder.

I thought a minute before responding. "A murder investigation is like a balloon with a slow leak. To keep it airborne, you have to periodically blow fresh air into it in the form of new facts or new insights. Left unattended, it will gradually deflate and land in the dust bin of oblivion, attracting as much interest as a used condom."

Girtha seemed to ponder the allusion before speaking again. "I'll be through in a minute. Oh, before I forget, I brought the obits section of the Sunday paper. They're burying the youngest Barrington girl at Melody Meadows this afternoon at two. I thought you'd be interested. That's all they're talking about at the diner." She removed her gloves and wiped her hands on her apron, then handed me the newspaper.

I thumbed through the pages looking for the obituaries and funeral arrangements. Finally, I found the column and located the object of my search, fourth entry down.

"Listen to this, Girtha," I said, clearing my throat.

BARRINGTON, JILL MORGAN, beloved daughter of Judge Alfred Matthew Barrington and Bernice Lafollette Barrington, died on August 26, 1980. She is also survived by an uncle, Ralph Husted Barrington of London, and an aunt, Matilda Ramsay Crawford of New York City. Miss Barrington was a member of the Debutante Coterie of 1974 and graduated with a degree in Fine Arts from the University of California at Los Angeles in 1978. Memorial Services will be held Sunday, August 29, at 2:00 p.m., at the Olympian Timocratic Temple, 2100 Regal Place, Halcyon Hills. Interment in the Melody Meadows Thanatopsis Park immediately following.

I set the paper down, got up, and scoured the closet for a clean shirt. After a quick shower, Girtha adjusted my clip-on bow tie while I explained why I was going to the funeral—something about feeling at least partially responsible for Jill's death.

Chapter 21

Melody Meadows was down in Orange County, about a two-hour drive through Sunday afternoon traffic. I made the trip under a dark, cloudy sky, which was unusual for this time of year. By the time I arrived, mourners had left the memorial service at the temple and were already parking at the cemetery.

From the size of the crowd, I saw that Jill Barrington was getting the same degree of attention in death as she had in life. The black limousines, which transported family and close friends, were the head of an automotive serpent that must have stretched for a mile. A number of motorcycle patrolmen were on hand to direct traffic and give directions. They were rarely consulted, however, since for most attendees, this was the second farewell to a member of the Barrington family in several weeks.

It seemed every prominent family, business organization, and political group was well represented. Salutations were exchanged and business transacted as the crowd jostled its way up the flagstone footpath to the burial site at the crest of the hill.

Since I suspected Jill had few personal friends, I guessed that most attendees were there out of respect or hatred or fear. I overhead one expensively dressed matron mention to a companion that it was considerate of the two sisters to get murdered so closely together, since it had saved her a trip to her safety deposit box to fetch her special-occasion diamonds—she hadn't had time to return them after the first funeral.

The grave site was an elaborate pageant. Hundreds of floral arrangements nudged each other for visual prominence, and several large green-and-white striped tents had been erected over rows of wooden folding chairs to accommodate family members and a small number of associates.

The officiating minister, who was dressed in a golden robe, resplendent with shiny sequins, looked familiar; after some thought, I identified him as Ralph Waldo Fitzpatrick, the greatest of the Sunday morning showmen and master of televised, electronic ministry. He'd constructed a temple and Bible college in Orange County that took longer to build than Khufu's Pyramid. His gray pompadour was styled to perfection and cemented with enough hair spray to withstand gale force winds. Rings flashed from each finger, and several glittering medallions encrusted with what appeared to be precious stones hung from his neck.

The sky was worsening to inclemency as the show started and finally gave tangible proof of its sullen disposition in the form of a heavy drizzle, increasing darkness, and ground fog after the first few words. It was the first rain in more than six months, and the majority of the crowd had not brought umbrellas in spite of the morning's solemn skies. This provoked a stampede to the protection of the tents and led to the trampling of some of the floral arrangements and the less agile mourners. I assisted a number of elderly ladies to their feet afterward and brushed away muddy footprints from the backs of several Rodeo Drive jackets. One lady's fur stole fell into the open grave in the rush, and she surprised everyone by jumping in to retrieve it. She was lifted out of the hole by employees of the mortuary. The stole looked a little bedraggled by the experience—the fur was wet and slick, and mud had caked over the shiny glass eyes in the fox's little head. Once rescued from the abyss, the dowager removed her stockings which were riddled with runs and tossed them back into the hole. They drifted down and settled profanely at the bottom of the grave.

As the drizzle became more pronounced, the only people remaining outside the tents were the good minister, the choir members, and the slower afoot. Miffed that the weather was detracting attention from him, Reverend Fitzpatrick overcame an initial sulk and sought to prevail over the elements through exhortative oratory and flamboyant gestures. As thunder rolled in from the heavens and lightning flashed across the distant horizon, he decided to change his strategy by interpreting the sudden change in weather as divine sanction, becoming even more theurgical.

I didn't see Montrose until the doddering servant shuffled over to his dead mistress's grave and placed an object on the top of her wet casket. Curious, I waited for his departure and sauntered over to see what he had left. There, lying on top of the metal lid, was a vibrator with a black bow tied around it. I was sure this touching gesture, presumably to provide a source of pleasure to his mistress in the afterlife, would establish a funereal benchmark by which all others would be measured.

I walked back to the main tent and looked for the family section and located Judge Barrington. He appeared devastated and grief-stricken. Montrose was just returning from his casket farewell and was standing by the judge's side, rendering moral support. I could only guess what was going through his mind as he witnessed the final rites of the last Barrington mistress knowing that his secret son was in jail as her alleged murderer.

Bernice Barrington was several people removed from the judge. She was sitting in her wheelchair, with Nately standing behind her. She did not appear to be especially disconsolate—she was, rather, huddled in a silk shawl filing her nails.

I approached them and inched through the condolence line to pay my respects before walking back to my car. I sat for awhile, waiting for the storm to subside, but decided before long to proceed. Somewhere on the way home, the windshield wipers stopped working, and I was forced to drive slowly in the right lane, my chest pressed against the steering wheel as I squinted through the rain. Periodically, I stretched my left hand outside to scrape the rain aside with the lid from an empty take-out box of fried chicken. Fortunately, I got home just as the cardboard disintegrated, leaving the face of Colonel Sanders stuck to the glass.

Chapter 22

It was now Monday morning, which meant the case was entering its second week. I still had not located Dr. Rutledge, and I was back to square one as far as the deceased Barrington sisters were concerned. The strategy offering the most promise was to collect more information about Boom Boom Saperstein and Wanda Latouche: specifically, what did they have in common that necessitated their elimination? And, how were they connected to each other and the Barringtons?

The best leads for this information were likely the performers at the Glad Gland. Sparkling clean, thanks to Girtha's efforts, I left my apartment around ten o'clock to drive over to the flesh palace.

I parked in back of the club beside a couple of black limousines and entered through the rear door. I found no one in the bar area, so I proceeded to walk down the corridor to Sal's office. My knock interrupted muffled voices.

"Whaddoya want?" Sal's foghorn voice boomed out into the hallway.

I opened the door and walked in, surprised by the unusual assemblage of occupants in the room. In addition to Sal, who was selecting a cigar from an open Romeo y Julieta box, the faces of Armand Duvalier and three other men stared back at me.

One of the other men appeared to be Japanese, around my age, dressed in a double-breasted dark suit. He was small but compact, and flashed an insidious grin as he slowly rubbed the edge of a dagger with his thumb.

The other two men, some twenty years his senior, were darker complexioned and dressed in the flowing white desert garb of Arabs—they looked like a couple of used camel salesmen from a second-hand oasis lot. These two sat on the edges of low chairs at opposite ends of a coffee table; their intense facial expressions and body postures indicated they were engaged in some sort of contest. I looked down at the table and, to my horror, saw two giant scorpions circling each other. They were hideous creatures, brown in color and over six inches long.

Gathering that I was no threat, the two men prodded the scorpions with pencils to get them moving again. Over on the sofa, I saw two large black metal boxes with air holes, which I assumed to be their homes when they were not locked in gladiatorial struggle. I backed away from the table and sat in a chair by Sal's desk.

Duvalier smiled at my uneasiness. His sartorial splendor was a stark contrast to the slovenly, unkempt Sal, who looked like he had just rolled out of a waterfront gin mill. "Good morning, Mr. McFadden. I believe introductions are in order." Always the gentleman, Duvalier did his best to put me at ease with his affability and charm.

"I understand you've already met Sal. May I present Mr. Hyakawa to my right and Sheik Omar Al-Sahudi and his brother, Kasmir, who are amusing themselves in the Arabic equivalent of a cockfight. Would you care to play?"

"Thank you, no. The lottery is as adventuresome as I get." I watched the fight long enough to notice that whenever the scorpions appeared lethargic, their owners would prod them back to activity.

I looked over at Hyakawa and noticed that the tip of his left pinky finger was missing. From that, I assumed he was a *Yakuza* gang-banger who had offended his boss and been forced to commit *yubitsume* as an apology. "Better not screw up again, Tojo. The next time you have to offer penance, they may want you to lean over the knife. I believe you call it hara-kiri."

He didn't look amused. In fact, he snarled and tossed a piece of paper in the air and cut it into thirty-two pieces with four flicks of his wrist.

"Let me know when your shift starts at Benihana. I like my Kobe beef sliced thin," I said.

"You're fortunate that his English is limited, McFadden," Duvalier said. "Otherwise, he would have skinned you like a rabbit. Incidentally, the preferred, formal term for ritual suicide by disembowelment is *seppuku*, not hara-kiri."

"Getting my cultural horizons expanded at the Glad Gland—who would've thunk it? And all this time, the only thing I thought I would pick up here was clap from the hookers and crabs from the toilet. Live and learn," I said.

"Changing the subject, this is a colorful little group you have here. Are they foreign exchange students who've stayed twenty years past their visas or new cast members of a Glad Gland freak show you're producing?" I asked.

Duvalier smiled. "You're not even close. The sheik and his brother are militant Palestinians who want Rutledge's supercomputer because they think it will give them the military edge they need to wipe Israel off the face of the Earth and reclaim their homeland.

"Mr. Hayakawa wants to sell Rutledge's project to North Korea or Libya so they can stir up trouble in the world. His organization has a way of making money off of unstable international conditions.

"Enough of this talk, though. To what do we owe the pleasure of your visit?" Duvalier asked.

"I'd like to talk to a couple of your dancers if they're available."

"That shouldn't be a problem. You should find a few of them in the dressing room in back of the stage. You don't mind, do you, Sal?"

"No, boss. Whatever you say. I'll give 'em a ring and tell 'em to be nice." Sal dialed the backstage extension and barked a few words into the receiver.

"How is your search for Rutledge coming?" Duvalier asked. "Do you have anything to report?"

"Not yet, I've been focusing on the homicides. My feeling is that the identification of the killer will provide the clue to Rutledge's location," I said.

"I'm surprised to find you still investigating the murders," Duvalier said. "The police informed me that they had arrested a suspect for those crimes."

"Roger's in custody, as you know, but his guilt is doubtful, at least to me. It must be dubious to you as well, which makes me wonder why you're letting Roger take the rap."

Duvalier shrugged to minimize the impact of his response. "Because of his frequent skirmishes with the authorities, Roger has become a liability. While loyal and effective, he has been attracting a lot of attention, something I don't need. I'm afraid he'll have to work this one out on his own. His past record, plus the fact he was found with a smoking vibrator in his hand, so to speak, should seal his fate with any reasonable jury."

"How do you know this tawdry frame-up will stick?"

Duvalier smiled. "Appropriate arrangements have been made. Roger will have a lawyer whose only mandate is to stay awake during the trial and provide Roger with a defense that is anemic at best. A fellow named Melkoff, I believe."

I was startled but shouldn't have been. Melkoff was forever reaching up the skirt of Justice and would have her bare-assed as soon as he could snatch her panties and subvert them for his own enrichment. "I see," I replied. "And, if that fails, embracery—jury tampering—is your second line of defense, I suppose."

Duvalier's smile offset Sal's frown.

"I was surprised by your absence at Jill Barrington's funeral. I didn't expect you to be heartbroken, but I did think you might make a brief appearance to wish her a bumpless bon voyage to the great beyond."

The smile disappeared before Duvalier spoke about Jill. "Like Roger, Jill had ceased to be useful," he said. "My interest in her was primarily for surveillance purposes. Since she was Rutledge's affectionate sister-in-law, she kept an eye on him and apprised me of his activities without arousing suspicion. When Rutledge disappeared, and his wife was killed, Jill's value dropped sharply and she became expendable. I don't mind admitting that whoever killed her spared me the unpleasantness of ending our relationship." He had made a point of faking a sad facial expression. "Death is such a tidy way to end an affair."

"You're not exactly a poster child for Valentine's Day, are you? How about Boom Boom and Wanda? How did they fit into your blackmail operation?" I might as well get answers while he was in a talkative mood.

Sal lurched forward in his chair, presumably to throttle me, but Duvalier's manicured hand reached over and grasped his arm. "You interest me more and more, McFadden. I don't know how you found out about our little operation, but I may as well be candid since it's been disbanded . . . due to the death of the participants."

I doubted that, but I nodded my understanding and Duvalier continued while Sal fidgeted.

"Boom Boom and Wanda weren't only attractive, they were intelligent and ambitious—perhaps too much so for their own good. They weren't content with the money they were making at the Glad Gland, and they began looking at opportunities for additional income. They were big drawing cards at the club, and we weren't anxious to lose them, so I took their requests under consideration.

"In the beginning, I fixed them up as escorts for important business clients, positions in which they performed admirably. Their sexual skills gave me a much larger competitive edge over my rivals than even I had anticipated. Then, Sal suggested that we enhance their value by having them provide the same services for local politicians and bureaucrats. The girls performed ably in that arena, as well. With their special talents, I was able to be more 'influential' in such transactions as obtaining hard-to-get liquor licenses, getting properties rezoned, selling worthless parcels of land to the state at obscene profits, having city inspectors approve shoddy wiring and plumbing as up to code, and so forth. I'm sure you get the picture."

"Yes, I do—they were busier than maggots on a rotting rhino. Any number of people might have wanted them dead," I said.

"That was my thinking, as well. I suspect they tried to become freelance entrepreneurs in the subtle art of blackmail and, how do you say, bit off more than they could chew."

"Possibly, but that doesn't explain the murders of Jill and Justine Barrington. I'm sure you'll agree that the uniqueness of the methodology suggests that all four women met their fates at the hands of the same perpetrator. I don't see how the Barringtons could have been involved in the strippers' racket, which was focused on providing sex and silence for a price—that just wasn't their style."

I took a moment of silence to make sure my next statement would have appropriate impact.

"You see, the piece that's missing . . . the key to this whole puzzle . . . is a common denominator . . . You can see that can't you, Mr. Duvalier?"

I paused again to let this concept sink in.

"You wouldn't mind if I dwell on common denominators a moment, would you?"

"Be my guest," Duvalier said but with less ebullience.

"Let's begin with the first victim, Justine Rutledge. Let's assume that she had grown frustrated by a cooling marriage and that she had begun spying on her husband's work for someone—we'll call this person 'Mr. X'—performing surveillance and reporting on her hubby's progress and activities. Then, she became disposable, perhaps when she became disenchanted and threatened to reveal her clandestine role to her husband. Or perhaps when she realized she could get more money by selling her information to another client. Her grotesque death may not only have been a method of disposal, but a way for Mr. X to convince Kevin Rutledge that he meant business.

"Follow me, so far, Mr. Duvalier?"

Duvalier nodded. "Entertaining . . ."

"So, let's turn next to Boom Boom and Wanda, the second and third victims. Let's assume that both were doing some freelance blackmailing, as you've suggested. Perhaps they found out that the work they were doing for Mr. X was child's stuff compared to the bigger spoils available from self-employment. Let's say, in the course of their work, they discovered information regarding Mr. X's real interests and changed the game plan, which pushed him to the point where he had to either capitulate to their demands or silence them.

"Still with me?"

"I find your imagination intriguing . . . "

"Which brings us to the last victim, Jill Barrington. Let's assume that Jill was dating the same Mr. X but, due to changing circumstances, lost her value to him. Perhaps she found out that Mr. X had killed the other three ladies and she tried a little blackmail scheme of her own. Maybe she pushed Mr. X into a corner by placing too high a price on her silence.

"Or . . . perhaps she couldn't take a hint from Mr. X that the relationship was over, and Mr. X felt that the only way to end the romance was via a body bag. Of course, she *could* have been a sacrificial red herring, thrown out to camouflage the purpose of the original murders. But the point is . . . do you see the common thread connecting all these murders? It's quite simple—"

"It's Mr. X," Duvalier jumped in on cue. "Go on . . ."

"Now, we've got Mr. X. But what could be his motive? What is so valuable that it would make Mr. X kill four people to acquire it? Money? No, Mr. X is rolling in filthy lucre. Fame? Not likely. I suspect that due to the nature of his business, Mr. X avoids the limelight. Power? Now *that's* a possibility. It would have to be a *lot* of power, though. Mr. X is no piker, so it would have to be something like the power to rule the world; for example, the power that would be conferred by possession of the XV-1000."

Duvalier frowned and Sal crushed a beer can with one hand.

"You've concocted a marvelous scenario, Mr. McFadden, I'll grant you that." Duvalier was less personable, and his sheen of arrogance was flickering. "If circulated, your theory could possibly start a brush fire here and there, but nothing that couldn't be easily extinguished.

"I don't make many mistakes, Mr. McFadden, but perhaps I should have used better judgment where you're concerned. Maybe I should have consented to Roger's entreaties and turned you over to him after all. Are you going to be a problem for me, Mr. McFadden?"

"Not at all; as I told Del Dotto, I won't furnish evidence to spring Roger unless I can present an ironclad case against the real killer. I do think having Roger behind bars will make the world a safer place."

"Very well, Mr. McFadden. I believe we've reached an understanding."

I was happy beyond words to close the door behind me and beat a quick retreat from that nefarious cast of characters. I don't think I'd ever been exposed in one sitting to evil incarnate masquerading in such disparate and colorful forms. Equally unnerving was the fact that that quintet was probably responsible for more deaths than malaria during the construction of the Panama Canal.

I had surprised myself by taking some verbal risks with Duvalier, but they had fortunately spawned some valuable rewards. For example, despite the suggested links between the four decedents and Duvalier, which I had suggested, I was becoming increasingly skeptical of his involvement. For one thing, if I had been on target with my jibes, he likely would have killed me on the spot; leaving my ghastly remains for Rosarita to throw out with the rest of the empties.

No, the fact that I was still breathing meant that I had some value to him: and that value had to be his anxiousness to find Rutledge. That thought, while initially comforting, soon soured as I wondered what would happen to me if I didn't find Rutledge or if I found Rutledge and he couldn't deliver what Duvalier was after.

I was starting to feel like the proverbial fly trying to climb up the inside of an inverted water glass.

Chapter 23

I returned to the main part of the club and climbed some steps to the runway and the stage. While the curtains were extremely threadbare, I found the backstage area was still darker than the empty house had been. I walked carefully, almost blindly, toward some voices I heard in a wing to the left.

As my eyes grew accustomed to the darkness, I gradually lengthened my stride; my overconfidence, however, soon led me to trip over something on the floor. It seemed to resemble a rolled-up rug, but as I felt the recumbent object while getting back to my feet, I experienced a strange tactile sensation. The object was firm but soft at the same time and had a texture I couldn't identify.

I shrugged, stepped over it, and resumed my walk past some vertical ropes on pulleys and a few props. Not much farther, I located the voices in a room on the other side of a closed door. I knocked and peeked in after a chorus of voices yelled to enter. With an expression I'm sure centered on bug-eyed surprise, I quickly ducked back behind the open door. I'd seen four people sitting in the room, three women and one man—all of them closer to being naked than being dressed.

"Excuse me," I apologized, "I'm sorry. I'll wait outside until you've had a chance to make yourselves presentable."

Before I could withdraw, they giggled in unison, and one of the ladies, a gorgeous redhead, grabbed my arm and pulled me back.

"You must be the guy Sal called about," she said. "It's all right. We're in our work clothes. I'm Jambalaya Bordileaux. That's Trixie Davenport," she said pointing to a brunette sitting on the dressing table, "and the couple on the bench is Eric and Erica."

I recognized Miss Bordileaux, the Queen of the Creole Strippers, from the performance she'd given during my undercover mission—and I must say, she was even more anatomically impressive at arm's length than she had been from a bar stool in the rear of the club. Her chest was easily twice the circumference of her waist, which caused me to marvel, since my own proportions were inversely arranged.

Trixie Davenport was every bit as shapely, except for a bit more stomach than she needed. Her brunette hair was long, and her skin had an olive complexion. Eric and Erica were identical in almost every respect but gender. Their slight but muscular builds were highlighted by platinum blond hair and blue eyes.

The dressing room was nondescript. Two of the three bulbs in the overhead chandelier had burned out, leaving the fluorescent tubes over the mirrors as the main source of illumination. Underneath the mirrors was a long dressing table that sheltered a dozen wooden straight-back chairs. The table was cluttered with containers of all sizes, shapes, and colors, a few wigs, and tissue boxes galore.

"We heard a loud noise outside on the stage. Was that you?" Jambalaya asked as she jerked a hair from her eyebrow with tweezers.

"I'm afraid so. It was dark, and I tripped over a long, cylindrical object on the floor. I couldn't identify it but it felt strange to the touch."

Trixie snickered while rubbing her body with lotion. "That was probably Muhammed Al-Said. He's the boa constrictor I use in my act. He used to belong to Boom Boom, but he adopted me after she was killed. But he hasn't been the same since her death. He used to hold up his end of the act by crawling all over her body and hissing, which really turned the audience on. Now all he does is hang around my neck in a stupor. If he doesn't start picking it up pretty soon, I'm going to give him to the first mongoose I see pass by. He doesn't even keep the club free of mice anymore. I believe he really misses her. "

Playing a sudden hunch, I fished into my pocket and pulled out the gold cigarette lighter inscribed with the initials "JB" and handed it to Miss Bordileaux. "Do you recognize this?" I asked.

"Yes!" she squealed. "Where did you find it? It's been missing for over a month. It was a gift from a boyfriend of mine, and he blew his stack when I told him I'd lost it."

"I found it in Wanda Latouche's apartment when I discovered her body in the bath tub. Any ideas how it got there?"

"Yeah, come to think of it. The thieving bitch must have borrowed it and never given it back. Wanda was like that—always taking stuff from people and never having the courtesy to return it."

I was momentarily taken aback by the plausibility of her explanation. "If the police had found this lighter, they'd have concluded that it was dropped by the killer during the commission of the crime. Care to comment?"

"Wait a minute." Jambalaya said. "Don't try to lay that action on me. I was upset about the missing lighter, but not enough to give Wanda her last curtain call over it. I didn't even know she had it. Besides, Sal told us they caught the killer. What gives?"

"The suspect in custody is, in my opinion, being made the scapegoat for these murders. I'm not convinced he did them. I'm inclined to believe the real killer is still on the loose."

"Oh, great," Trixie sighed. "Just when we were starting to breathe easy again."

"If you're looking for suspects," Jambalaya offered, "Wanda's business is a good place to start. She had a lot of playmates, any one of whom could have dimmed her lights. She always had a scam going and probably got caught dealing off the bottom of the deck. She was a greedy bitch, and didn't know when to ease the squeeze."

"Let's assume I buy your hypothesis about Wanda. How does that relate to Boom Boom?" I asked.

"Both broads could have been shaking down the same trick, and he decided to get out from under once and for all."

"Now tie them in with Jill Barrington and Justine Rutledge. I'm sure you've heard about them. How were the four of them connected, in life or in death?"

"We were rappin' about that when you walked in. The simple fact is, we don't know," Jambalaya said. She looked at Trixie and the Gold Dust Twins, who nodded their assent.

"Jill used to come in the place once in a while with Duvalier. She would sit at the bar and have a couple of drinks while Duvalier conducted business with Sal in his office. I never saw Justine Rutledge in here, though . . . although her husband was in now and then. He and

Boom Boom had a hot thing going, and he used to pick her up after the show."

"Wait a second, Jam," Trixie interrupted. "Rutledge's old lady *was* in here one time. She came in looking for her husband a couple of months ago and found him at the bar. They had a big spat in front of everybody. She even slapped him and threw a drink in his face. That woman had a temper. I never saw her besides that, but once was enough."

"What was Kevin Rutledge like?"

Jambalaya spoke with a trace of wistfulness in her voice. "He was a real gentleman. Treated everyone like a lady. I could have gone for him myself if that bitch, Boom Boom, hadn't lifted her leg and gotten his attention first."

"I get the impression that their demises didn't provoke much in the way of sustained grief at the Glad Gland."

"Only with Sal and Duvalier," Trixie said. "Why should any of us care? They'd been here less time than anyone else, but they got the highest salaries and top billing even though neither one of them could dance."

"There's something else, too," Erica said, breaking her silence. "We're a close-knit group. We share and share alike. But Boom Boom and Wanda weren't like that. They were selfish and didn't care about anyone or anything but themselves. They treated us like dirt. They got special treatment from management and enjoyed rubbing it in our faces. We have mixed emotions about their deaths, but we don't know anything about their murders."

The others looked at me with such sincerity that I retreated. "Back to square one, I guess. Has anybody else been around asking questions?"

"Sal and a couple of his heavies grilled us good but we told them nothing," Trixie said.

Jambalaya added, "We're clueless. At first, we thought it might have been some maniac or sex pervert with a thing for snuffing strippers. When Boom Boom was murdered, we got antsy. When Wanda was killed a few days later, we got scared shitless. We started giving everyone in the club a good look-over. We don't walk out to our cars alone anymore, or even stay in this dressing room by ourselves. We told Sal about our concerns, but the jerk just laughed—told us to start wearing rubber panties to ground the electricity."

"Maybe Sal's our killer," I offered.

There was a brief silence before Trixie put her bottle of lotion down and answered for the group. "It's possible. I wouldn't put anything past the greasy bastard, but I don't think he's your man. For sure he'd do anything for a dishonest buck. But Sal runs the L.A. end of a white slavery railroad—he wouldn't kill a good-looking girl, he'd drug her up and sell her to some pimp in the Far East; I just can't see him burying something that he could have sold for a profit. One of his own nieces is still giving head in Bangkok, thanks to Sal, trying to earn plane fare back to the states."

"Okay, let's change direction a bit. Can any of you recall seeing customers who've been acting strangely in the past few weeks?" I asked, taking another approach.

The quartet looked at each other and shrugged. Trixie appeared to sum up what was on their minds. "Can't help you there either. Strange behavior doesn't exactly stick out like a sore thumb at the Glad Gland."

"Although . . . there was one incident you might be interested in," Jambalaya said. "One night, while I was doing the closing number, Kevin Rutledge came in and sat by the runway. A few minutes later, a redhead came in and parked right beside him. I could tell she was a surprise by the look on his face. Pretty soon, they got up and moved to a booth. Well, I was a little curious, and when my dance was through, I let a guy in the booth behind them buy me a drink."

"What happened then?" I asked eagerly. This was the best lead I'd had on Rutledge all week.

"I could only catch scraps of the conversation. He said something like things would eventually work out for them, but in its own good time. There were big changes at stake, he said, and jumping the gun would screw things up. He told her she shouldn't have followed him to the club. He admitted he liked her, although he realized it wasn't in the same way she liked him. He was nice about it, but it was the old kiss-off."

I got the feeling that Jambalaya, with slight urging, could wax eloquently about Rutledge ad infinitum.

"What was her reaction?"

"Well, that's the part I thought you'd be interested in." She paused, and I leaned forward in my chair.

"She said that she couldn't live without him, and if she couldn't have him, nobody else would. She wasn't hyped up or anything, but she meant it and Rutledge knew it. She got up, kissed him, and said she'd see him the next day—'at work.'"

"Sounds like an associate of Rutledge's that I recently met," I said, referring to Dr. Tubinski. "When did this little vignette occur?"

"A few weeks ago. That was the last time Rutledge was in, and it was a couple of days before his old lady was done in by the vibrator virtuoso."

"Did you ever see Rutledge in here with anyone else?" I asked.

"No," she said, "except for that spat with his old lady."

I felt something rub my instep and looked down to see Muhammed Al-Said sliding across the top of my shoes. In the past, I would have leaped off the ground, but now I just nudged him with my foot, and he slithered over to the corner and wrapped himself around the base of a hat rack.

"You've been most helpful," I said. "Thanks for your time and the information."

"Come back any time," Trixie said. "And good luck. We won't sleep a wink until this nut is caught."

I exited past the deserted orchestra pit and looked down out of curiosity to see what was there. Not surprising, it wasn't much of an orchestra: a piano with several keys missing, one drum with a hole in it, and two guitars with a couple of snapped and curled up strings.

I knew the feeling.

Chapter 24

Jambalaya's information about Dr. Tubinski made it clear that a follow-up visit was in order. Her townhouse was one of two dozen just like it on a street in Encino, a tony suburb south of Ventura Boulevard. As I walked up to her door, I glanced over to an adjacent yard and spotted a slim, elderly man with a shock of white hair and an unlit pipe. He was applying a coat of paint to his mailbox.

I smiled at him with the knowledge that neighbors, especially retirees, can be goldmines of information if approached properly. "Excuse me, can you tell me if this is Dr. Tubinski's residence?" I dangled the bait.

He paused only long enough to shift the pipe between corners of his mouth.

"It's her place. Been pretty busy this morning, too."

"Is that so?" I prompted. He'd taken the bait, plus the sinker and six feet of line.

"About half an hour ago, she got a telegram." He paused to swirl his brush in a jar of paint thinner. "A few minutes after the Western Union guy left, a couple of guys in gray suits drove up in a white Chevy. They went in—only there a couple of minutes—then they walked out with her. She hasn't been back."

"That's very interesting, Mr. . . ."

"Van Horn's the name."

"Mr. Van Horn, did Dr. Tubinski appear to be going of her own free will?"

"She wasn't kicking and screaming, but they did seem to be hurrying her along," the village monitor replied.

"Did you know Dr. Tubinski well?" I asked.

"Van Horn re-lit his pipe and drew deeply a few times to get it started. "Not really. She isn't home very much and keeps to herself a lot.

My wife and I invited her over to dinner a couple of times, but she always found some excuse to cancel out at the last minute."

At that moment, a gray-haired female stuck her head out of the screen door behind him. "Ask him about her sunbathing in the nude. It got so bad I had to take his binoculars away." She ducked back inside the townhouse quickly, missing Van Horn's withering stare.

With that interruption, Van Horn looked at me inquisitively, realizing that my presence was no less suspicious than my predecessors. "You a friend of hers? I don't believe I caught *your* name."

"Bristol, Lester Bristol," I lied. "I'm Dr. Tubinski's stepbrother from Sacramento. I'm here in L.A. on business and borrowed a friend's car to drop in and surprise her. Perhaps I can write her a note and slip it under the door."

Van Horn chewed on this a moment before opening the way. "Seeing as how you're family, you can leave it inside if you want. She left the door open when she left. I closed it for her, but I didn't lock it in case she didn't have her key with her."

I thanked Van Horn and tried the door, which, as he said, was unlocked. I waved my appreciation to the helpful neighbor as I entered. Once inside, I peeked out the window to see what he was doing. He stared at my hostess's door a moment, and then disappeared inside. As I suspected, he was back a few seconds later, making his way to the curb with a pad and pencil to record my license plate number.

I knew I wouldn't have much time before Van Horn became truly suspicious, so I scanned the interior, trying to decide how to most judiciously use my time. I was halfway expecting to find the place ransacked but instead found professionally selected decorations and furnishings that were flattered by immaculate housekeeping.

Dr. Tubinski must have been surprised by her visitors while in the process of preparing lunch—on the kitchen counter was a bowl of freshly made tuna salad, flanked by jars of mayonnaise and pickle relish. A stalk of celery and half an onion lay nearby, and fragments of eggshell were scattered in the garbage disposal side of the sink. Since she probably wouldn't be back any time soon, and since tuna salad doesn't keep very well, I grabbed a fork and dug in.

I was halfway through the refreshing repast when I bit down on something that offered a gentle resistance. I stopped chewing and reached into my mouth to find a tightly wadded piece of paper. I unfolded it and was delighted to find a telegram, presumably the one that had been delivered to Dr. Tubinski just prior to the arrival of her abductors. While ingeniously hidden from her captors, she could not have anticipated my visit or my fondness for tuna salad.

My pulse raced when I saw that the message had been wired from a place called Lancaster, New Hampshire, and was from none other than the elusive Dr. Kevin Rutledge.

> will be leaving country soon stop keep my location secret stop research notes in three briefcases in airport locker 181 stop key under your doormat stop good luck and much success stop kevin

I had the first real lead on Kevin Rutledge, and I had to move quickly. He was preparing to relocate to parts unknown and it sounded like he was severing communications with his former colleague with this wire. I had my doubts that Rutledge was the killer, but I was certain that he could clear up a lot of loose ends.

I headed out of Tubinski's townhouse, locked the door behind me, and checked under the mat; but Dr. Tubinski had already taken the locker key. I then rushed down the sidewalk and hopped into my car; I didn't even take time to wave to Van Horn, who was observing my departure through the dilated space between two slats in a set of Venetian blinds.

I stopped at the library on the way back home and looked up New Hampshire in volume seventeen of the Funk & Wagnalls. Lancaster was in Belknap County, and appeared to be located on the southwest foot of Lake Winnipesauke, in the central part of the state. The closest airport to Lancaster was in Manchester, some thirty-five miles away. With that knowledge, I sped to Jake's and borrowed travel money before calling the airport to make a reservation. The next available flight was scheduled for 10:35 the following morning.

I sat back and decided to call it a victorious day. Since it was already mid-afternoon, I returned to my apartment and tried to read some pulp fiction and work a few crossword puzzles. My mind kept wandering back to Rutledge, however . . . Would I find him? What would he be like? Would he be cooperative or difficult?

I finished packing for the trip before supper and dozed off.

Chapter 25

The plane lifted off from Los Angeles International Airport the customary thirty minutes behind schedule. Even so, I was still struggling with my seat belt extension when the flight attendants descended en masse to take cocktail orders. If air traffic control was as efficient as beverage service, airline departures and arrivals would be as timely as Mussolini's trains.

The takeoff was smooth enough, and we left the runway and Venice Beach behind us as we rose swiftly over the Pacific Ocean with the late morning sun at our backs. I was on the right side of the plane, and watched Santa Monica, Pacific Palisades, and the Malibu communities recede into nothingness as we climbed in altitude.

The flight time was eight and a half hours from L.A. to New York because of the three-hour time change. The trip seemed much longer, however, due to the fact I was seated next to the ubiquitous young mother who spent a large part of the trip changing diapers on her drop-down tray. I still think she must have been weaning the little tyke off strained Limburger cheese.

We touched down around 7:30 p.m., late but in plenty of time to catch my flight to Manchester on Pilgrim Airlines at 9:45. I walked around the waiting area and picked up enough abandoned magazines and newspapers to fill the time.

While slouched in a hard plastic chair, reading an issue of *Time* magazine I had lifted from the weather-beaten face of a sleeping indigent, I was approached by three figures claiming to be Children of the Divine Docetism. They were all bald, slender, in their early twenties and dressed in pale orange robes, so their gender was difficult to determine. One of them brandished a tambourine, the second had a large offering basket, and the third held a bunch of flowers. I was handed a daisy, which I inserted into the lapel of the sleeping vagrant next to me. I then placed a pen in his unconscious hand and wrote an IOU on a slip of paper that I handed to the apparent treasurer of the trio. They muttered something about "cheap Philistine" and walked away after snatching the impromptu boutonniere back from the tramp. The snatch startled the grizzled old swagman, who creaked to his feet and staggered off in hypnotized pursuit of the siren song of his wine goddess, Muscatella.

Just as I thought my boredom would never peak, the loudspeaker finally announced my flight, and we left Kennedy only fifteen minutes late. That put us in Manchester at 11:30—only 8:30 by my body's time. Still, I was too tired to trudge on to Lancaster—nothing tires me more than doing nothing, so I took my cabby's advice and booked a cheap room at O'Rourke's boarding house for what was left of the night. I slept soundly until the landlady's knock the next morning, which was attached to an invitation to a family style breakfast.

I dressed as quickly as possible and hurried downstairs to the large dining room. I had hoped to get the jump on my fellow boarders, but this expectation was not realized. I was greeted by a half-dozen diners with knives and forks already poised in attack position, waiting only for the conclusion of the blessing being given by Mrs. O'Rourke. Her "amen" precipitated a flurry of activity: plates only a moment ago piled high with country biscuits, flapjacks, fried eggs, and slices of cured ham were depleted in the blink of an eye.

I managed to squeeze into a place at the end of one of the benches and had barely tucked my napkin under my chin, before I was startled by a crescendo of burps and a chorus of lips smacking in satisfaction. The race was over.

Mrs. O'Rourke chuckled at my predicament, then rose and wiped her hands on her large apron, picked up my virgin plate, and disappeared into the kitchen to fill it from the reserves. Her serving was generous, and I expressed my appreciation in what was evidently the local fashion—by eating as if it was my last meal.

The dining room cleared as quickly as the feast had disappeared, and Mrs. O'Rourke sat down at the end of the table, sipping from a large mug of steaming black coffee. She grinned at me with a mirthful twinkle in her eyes.

"Sonny, you don't look like you're any stranger to a knife and fork, but I believe you butted heads with some pretty stiff competition this morning."

She was a large woman with an omnipresent smile, whose skin had a ruddy red hue. She had flour on her cheeks from making flapjack batter and large forearms, probably from years of rolling dough. Her salt-and-pepper hair was pulled back and fastened to her head with a large, red plastic comb.

"Madam, I would require a handicap to keep pace with that colorful legion," I replied, wiping crumbs from my mouth.

She sipped spilled coffee from her saucer and slapped her thigh with glee. "If you didn't talk so funny, you'd be the spittin' image of my nephew, Donicus. He's also bald-headed, wears them glasses with thick lenses, and uses the end notch on the biggest belt he can find." She noticed my plate was approaching empty and took it back to the stove to refill it as plentifully as before. "I'll bet my boy Donicus wishes he was eatin' with us this morning," she sighed upon her return.

"Oh?" I replied between bites. "Where is he?"

She shook her head sadly while heaping a mound of strawberry preserves upon the bottom half of a biscuit. "Donicus is serving three to five at the county farm," she said after licking her knife. "He got liquored up one night and stole a truck from the state highway transportation boys—used it to dump a couple thousand cubic feet of horse manure and river rock in the mayor's new swimming pool."

"The penalty appears a bit severe for the offense," I commented.

"I'd agree," she said, "but the mayor was in the pool at the time, cavortin' around naked with his young secretary. When the mayor's wife got back home a week later, she found them under some rocks at the bottom of the pool when she drained it. They'd been dead all that time and stunk to high heaven. They had to be buried nine miles out of town and no one, and I mean no one, followed the hearse. It's been more 'n two years, and to this very day, the mayor's widow can't leave flowers on the grave 'cause of the swarm of flies buzzin' around the headstone." She grew quiet after her revelation, and only my chewing and her breathing stirred the early morning air for a few moments.

"Where you from?" she asked, changing the subject.

"Los Angeles."

"Now, that's a coincidence," she said. "We don't get many people from California through here, but we had another fella staying here a week or two ago from Los Angeles. Don't remember his name, but he was headed toward Lancaster. I remember him because he sat next to a computer salesman at breakfast and dang if he didn't know more about computers than the salesman."

Rutledge! I was on the right track.

"Can you tell me the best way to get to Lancaster?" I asked.

"The bus station's in the next block over. They got a local that leaves at ten on weekdays. You can probably catch it if you get a move on."

New Hampshire, or what I could see of it through the dirty bus windows, was attractive. Once we left the factories of the manufacturing town of Manchester, we crossed the Merrimac River, then drove through forests of birch, beech, elm, and maple, to which were added some spruce, fir, and pine as the trip progressed. We reached Lancaster in an hour and a half, after a number of stops along the way to pick up and drop off passengers and light freight.

Lancaster was a small town of two thousand or so, located in the Lake District southwest of Lake Winnipesauke and east of Lake Winnisquam. The bus station was a corner of a discount drugstore and was populated with in-transit hoi polloi. I found a motel with a vacancy a couple of blocks away whose rates were easy on the wallet and unpacked.

My first attempt to get a lead on Rutledge was to walk down the street to the post office. It was a one-window affair, located in the rear of a dry goods store. "Back in 10 Minutes" was scrawled on a piece of paper and thumbtacked on the wooden wall beneath a permanent sign that read "Fish Bait, Marriage Licenses, Cold Beer."

Norman Rockwell would have loved this place. Two middle-aged men puffed semi-lit pipes and rubbed their beards while playing checkers on top of an upside-down barrel half. A couple of spectators looked on with only mild, distracted interest—one of them whittled a wooden duck decoy, while the other one made trout flies, peering inside a book now and then for guidance.

Not far away, a black potbellied stove—cozy but not really necessary for this time of year—was sitting on a bed of bricks, giving off some warmth from the smoldering remains of an earlier morning fire. A hound of indeterminable lineage with half-opened eyes was curled up on a nearby rug, motionless, except to occasionally swat a fly with his tail.

The postal window opened, and the face of a wrinkled little man with sallow cheeks appeared behind the vertical bars. Black garters on his arms held the cuffs of his long-sleeved shirt above his wrists, while a faded Boston Red Sox cap shielded his eyes from the naked light bulb suspended overhead.

"Can I help you, young fella?" he wheezed, while tapping his chest with a weakly clenched fist. His tongue had a glossy finish to it: no doubt the result of licking a surfeit of stamps and envelopes.

"Thanks. I'm looking for the postmaster," I said.

"You found him. Been opening this window six days a week for fifty-five years. What's it you'd be needing?"

"I'm looking for some information. You impress me as a man of exceptional memory. Do you recall ever seeing this man?"

I handed him the picture of Kevin Rutledge that I'd been given by Judge Barrington.

"He's probably been in town for only a short period of time," I added, "perhaps a couple of weeks. He may have arranged for mail delivery or possibly rented a post office box. His name is Kevin Rutledge, although he may be using an alias."

The old codger rubbed the stubble on his chin as he studied the photograph.

"I know pretty near everybody in these parts and most visitors who are here for any length of time. This face looks sorta familiar, but I can't exactly place it."

I let him examine the picture another minute since he didn't seem to be in any hurry to return it and I wasn't in any hurry to get it back. He put his wrinkled old hand across the lower half of Rutledge's face, and his mouth slowly opened, which turned out to be the nascence of recognition.

"Take this black grease pencil, young fella, and draw a beard on this jasper. Make it a light beard, mind you, just long enough to be past the itchin' and scratchin' stage."

Not being a police artist, I accepted the assignment reluctantly and took hesitant pains to lightly darken the bottom portion of Rutledge's face. When I reached the point where further improvement was unlikely, I slid the altered photograph back to the postmaster for his critique.

The old man held the photo closer to his squinting eyes and chuckled. "Not bad. You musta got your art training practicing on a shithouse wall. I recognize this fella now, though."

Excited by this disclosure, I lurched forward, bumping my pate against the iron grille that separated us. While attempting to rub away the pain and refocus my vision, the old man continued.

"Yep, that's him, all right. Name's not Rutledge, though—least that's not the name he gave me. Calls himself Randolph."

"Do you know where I might find Mr. Randolph?" I asked. I was beginning to sense a goose egg beginning to form.

"Nope, can't tell you that. I believe he's renting a cabin in the woods on the other side of the lake, but I don't figure to know which one it might be. He did rent a box, though."

"That's just as good," I said. "When does he usually come in to pick up his mail?"

"He hasn't been by in a couple of days, so he should be in tomorrow. Sometimes he comes by himself, and other times he has a girl friend with him." The old man squinted at me and asked, "By the way, what might you be seekin' him for?"

"My name's Chauncey McFadden, and I'm from Los Angeles. I work for a firm that locates missing heirs. We think Mr. Randolph may be entitled to a share of a recently settled estate, but I need to talk to him to be sure he's the correct person. This is a delicate matter, and I'd appreciate you keeping this confidential."

I slid the amenable informant a twenty dollar bill in exchange for his silence.

"Keep your city money," he said, pushing it back. "Conversation ought not to have a price tag attached to it."

I thanked him and walked across the street to a thrift shop. I felt conspicuous in my green checked suit and decided that attire more in tune with the locale would help de-emphasize my presence. Accordingly, I purchased a pair of second-hand overalls and a red-and-black plaid shirt, both on sale at a thrift shop. I returned to my room and changed into my new garb before going to the town square to kill some time on a park bench.

It was past six o'clock, and the small downtown area was practically deserted. While basking in the solitude of that bucolic setting, I felt a tap on my shoulder from behind. Startled, I looked up into steel-gray eyes, a tobacco-filled cheek, and the reflection of the last rays of a setting sun upon a silver deputy's badge.

"If you don't mind, son, just take your driver's license out of your wallet and pass it back to me."

"Certainly, officer. Anything to oblige the constabulary." I handed over my license with chagrin, disappointed that I had not achieved the anonymity that I had sought.

He studied the license for a moment and compared the picture to my face. Satisfied, he handed it back.

"Any problem, officer?" I asked.

"I don't mind telling you," he said, sending a stream of brown juice from his stained lips to the crest of an adjacent ant hill. "You look like a boy from over Manchester way—fellow by the name of Donicus O'Rourke. You resemble him so much I thought maybe he'd escaped from the county farm again. I can tell from your soft hands that you're no yardbird, though. Sorry to have troubled you."

He tipped his hat and sauntered across the street, continuing his rounds by tugging at the front doors of closed businesses.

I turned in after four bowls of Brunswick stew at a diner that crouched behind a "Home Cooked Meals" sign and enjoyed ten hours of uninterrupted sleep in a four-poster canopy bed.

After breakfast, I walked to the dry goods store and found a chair behind the checker players with a vantage point which would allow me to observe the postal customers without being noticed by them. As this promised to be a boring stakeout, I ingratiated myself with the locals by buying a round of Royal Crown colas and circulating a tin of snuff. After a while, I passed the time alternating between reading some pulps and watching Archie and Gomer play checkers. They made reading appear strenuous in comparison.

Tick-tock, tick-tock . . . Morning crept on and, having encountered no obstacles in its path, became noon. Time hung heavy, like the dense fog that rolls in from the ocean to blanket San Francisco Bay. The ticking of the grandfather clock was frequently the only sound and the swing of the pendulum the only movement in the store.

By mid-afternoon, I was starting to get sleepy. Postal activity had been slow all day, except for a handful of merchants with commercial business to transact. In fact, I was beginning to doze off, my multiple chins spreading out like a cravat, when I was stirred by two voices. The first was Archie, who, in atypical fervor, had cried out when one of his checkers reached the last row on Gomer's half of the board—"King me!" The second voice, much more subdued, was that of the old postmaster, who was still talking to a gentleman at the window.

"Just sign for it here, Mr. Randolph. Would you be wantin' anythin' else today?"

"No, thank you. I trust these letters will go out in tonight's mail?"

"They should. The bus won't be here for another two hours. I should have 'em sorted and bagged up in time to catch that outgoing express. Have a nice evening."

A handsome man and an attractive girl turned away from the window and strolled hand-in-hand to the door of the dry goods store. I rose to my feet and followed them to the sidewalk, turned so my back was toward them, and watched their reflections in the store window as they crossed the street and entered a coffee shop. I folded the newspaper I had been pretending to read, tucked it under my arm, and firmed the grip on my small camera. Rutledge had never met me, so I knew my initial presence shouldn't create a cause for alarm. I followed the couple inside and watched them sit down in a booth, across the table from each other. Rutledge was just slipping a piece of paper into his shirt pocket when I took a deep breath and approached them. He looked up in surprise when I stopped in front of the table and remained speechless as I told the waitress to give us a few minutes. Surprise changed to astonishment when I sat down beside the young lady, then to shock when I used my body to nudge her toward the wall. Next, his face ran the gamut to irritation and anger when I reached across the table and grabbed his forearm.

"You don't necessarily have to fear me, Dr. Rutledge." I didn't want to anger him to the point of assault or frighten him into bolting, but I did want to establish the upper hand and sustain it.

"Who are you?" he asked in bewilderment.

"My name is McFadden. Chauncey McFadden. I'm a private investigator from L.A. I was hired by your father-in-law to find out who murdered your wife. Since then, as you may know, your sister-in-law and two other women have been similarly dispatched. Time is of the essence if we're to prevent additional atrocities."

"How did you find me?" he asked.

"I'll ask the questions, if you don't mind." This boldness was uncharacteristic of me, but I was beginning to enjoy the role and played it to the hilt.

"First," I started while turning to the young lady, "who are you and what's your relationship with Rutledge, or Randolph?"

She hesitated and looked at Rutledge. He nodded and she responded. "I'm Uva Rehnquist. I met Kevin years ago, when he worked at the Lancaster Lodge and Spa during summer vacations from MIT. We dated and became quite close but went our separate ways after Kevin graduated. We bumped into each other a week ago, here, in town. During a romantic dinner, we discovered that the flame was still there."

Uva was something else at close proximity. She had the body of a Scandinavian Olympic speed skater and it was flattered by a turtleneck sweater that fit like the skin on a grape. Her fathomless Baltic-blue eyes, deep dimples, and blonde shag haircut made her a complete package.

Rutledge was every bit her physical equal. He had a perennially boyish face and the type of slim hips that drove women wild. His nascent beard matched his dishwater-blond hair and added a touch of masculinity to his magnetic profile. It was easy to understand why he was never alone for very long.

"Look here, McFadden," Rutledge snapped angrily, "what right do you have intruding on us like this?"

"Rutledge," I said, "with one phone call, I can have a lot of people here who'd like nothing better than to get their hands on you. For reasons you know as well as I, their methods of extracting information are bizarre and painful. Do I make myself clear?"

"Kevin," Uva implored, "what's he talking about?"

Rutledge slumped in his seat and looked pale. I almost felt sorry for him, but I had a job to do.

"All right," Rutledge sighed with resignation, "what do you want to know?"

"For starters, what do you know about your wife's death? That seems like a good place to start."

Rutledge bit his lip, and I could tell from his eyes that her memory was genuinely painful. "Nothing. I swear it," he said softly. "I came home one night and found her . . . dead . . . in the bathtub. I went to pieces. When I got myself together, I threw a few things in a suitcase and took off. I kept running until I wound up here. I had no particular reason for coming to New Hampshire, other than I knew the area well from family vacations and work during college. Also it's far away; about as much distance as I could put between me and California."

"Why didn't you call the police instead of running?"

"I was afraid they'd arrest me. Justine and I hadn't been getting along, and it was obvious that I'd be a prime suspect. I didn't have a supportable alibi, either, which would only have strengthened their case."

"Did you kill your wife?"

"Of course not," he replied indignantly. "I'm a scientist, not a murderer."

"I wasn't aware that the two were mutually exclusive," I retorted. "Try again, Rutledge. A man comes home and finds his wife murdered—he doesn't run just because he doesn't have a strong alibi and they've been squabbling. Care to run another one past me? If it will lubricate your rusty memory, I'm aware of the supercomputer you were working on and the intense interest it had generated from both worthy and unsavory sources."

Rutledge softened. I could tell I'd have no further trouble with him.

"All right . . . all right," he conceded again. "I was working on a top secret project for the government that focused on the expansion and acceleration of data processing and transmission possibilities. I had received advanced and ongoing funding from them.

"In the first phase of the project, we made excellent progress and I was convinced that a data storage and processing breakthrough was within the realm of possibility. But we hit a wall. We subsequently reached a point where things began to stall, and I couldn't overcome some of the obstacles to laser technology. Uncle Sam became increasingly impatient for results.

"At first, I falsified some test data and progress reports to keep them at bay for a while. But they became suspicious and submitted my reports to computer science consultants of their own. My credibility was suddenly in doubt and they applied pressure for more substantive proof. The government threatened to cancel the grant *and* demand repayment."

"Where does Duvalier fit into this?" I asked.

"I have some big gambling debts and Duvalier wound up with my markers. I couldn't raise the cash and when he found out what I was working on, he demanded repayment in the form of design specifications and test results. He increased my gaming limit at the casino in Gardena, too, and I tried to win the money back to get out from under his control. However, the more I played, the more I lost. I got in deeper and deeper. He and his friends made some not-so-veiled threats against me and those closest to me. When I found Justine dead, I panicked. The way she died—it was terrible. It's the sordid type of thing Duvalier and his cronies might do without a second thought."

"Other than your suspicions, do you have anything concrete that implicates Duvalier?"

"No," he admitted. "Just that you have to have a pretty strong stomach to murder someone in that way. The only person I could think capable of that kind of brutality is that creature who works for Duvalier."

"Roger?" I asked.

"Yeah, that's the one," he said.

"Did anyone else have an interest in your development of the XV-1000? Anyone other than Duvalier and his consortium? I'll assume, and God help us all if I'm wrong, that we can exclude Uncle Sam from Justine's death."

"No, Duvalier and the feds are the ones who kept applying the pressure."

"Had you received any actual threats against your life, family, or associates at any time?"

"Only the little scares that Duvalier dropped on me when the progress of the project stalled, like waking up with my ears sliced off or being thrown into a pit of scorpions. Until I . . . found Justine, I didn't take them seriously. I assumed that intimidation was Duvalier's way of doing business. The bottom line is I got in over my head. I couldn't satisfy the government with results *or* pay Duvalier what I owed him.

"I knew the time of reckoning would come, and I worked frantically to come up with a breakthrough. I was depressed and my marriage continued to fall apart—Justine didn't know how to deal with my despondency and she became critical and frustrated. Finally, she reached the breaking point and I knew a decision had to be made. I was driving around trying to determine what to do the night Justine was killed.

"Finding her like that when I returned home made up my mind. I probably should have stayed and seen the thing through, but it seemed I would be dead one way or the other: either at the hands of Duvalier's hired thugs or a jury's verdict. Neither prospect was attractive, so I made a coward's choice."

Rutledge slumped, defeated, against the back of the booth. "There you have it—the whole sorry story. I'm not proud of myself, but I'm not a murderer. Besides, as you indicated, three more women have been killed in the same manner as Justine, and I do have airtight alibis for those: Uva and a couple of people in town."

"I'll vouch for Kevin, Mr. McFadden. He's been with me every day since he's been here," Uva confirmed.

"If Duvalier had your wife killed as you suspect, what motive would he have for killing the other three?" I asked.

"I don't know," Rutledge replied. "I would guess that the other murders were committed to camouflage Justine's death; or it may be that Justine's murder sent Roger off on a spree."

"I agree that when Roger gets the germ of an idea into his idiopathic mind, the consequences can be tragic. Suffering follows Roger like exhaust behind a tailpipe, but these crimes were too well-planned and coordinated to have been masterminded by Roger," I rebutted.

"How so?"

"For one thing, none of the cadavers had been sexually assaulted, other than by the vibrator penetration. No evidence of semen was ever found. That's not Roger's style. He would have fished the victims out of the tub and romanced them royally. When Roger feels frisky, conscious consent from a living being isn't exactly a prerequisite.

"Another factor is fingerprints. Roger's weren't found at any of the scenes of the crimes, which is unusual. Roger wouldn't think of taking the precaution to mask his digital identification . . . No, these crimes required a little finesse . . . and a little ideation . . . Roger has anything but."

Rutledge nodded. "What you say makes sense, but where does that leave us?"

"Back where we started, I'm afraid. I'm looking for some common thread that connected the four decedents. The Barringtons were sisters to whom you were related by marriage. And, I understand you were keeping company with Cleotha Saperstein, whose roommate was Wanda Latouche. Which brings us back to you, Rutledge."

"Your conclusion is purely circumstantial, but it enables me to see why I'm of interest to you," Rutledge said. "My marriage had reached the point where Justine was leading her own life and I was leading mine. I was introduced to Cleotha at the Glad Gland one night after Duvalier and I had met there to discuss how I planned to settle my account.

"In retrospect, I can see that our meeting and the affair were prearranged by Duvalier. I began seeing Cleotha, but the attraction to her was only physical. I was working long hours at the lab, and Cleotha knew how to make a man relax." As an afterthought he added, "Not that it's an excuse, but I'd previously been made aware of some of Justine's indiscretions."

Rutledge glanced at Uva apprehensively. His disclosures had made an emotional impact on her. "Uva, I'm sorry. I couldn't tell you any of this. I didn't want you to know anything—to keep you from being involved. The danger is too great." She smiled and stroked the back of his hand.

I continued. "Did Cleotha ever ask you questions about your work?"

"Yes, but I was always noncommittal. I figured she was pumping me for information on Duvalier's behalf, but that didn't bother me. It was a small price to pay for the comfort she was providing. I rarely saw Wanda except at the club and once in a while when I was with Cleotha at their place."

"How well did you get along with your father-in-law?" I asked.

"We hit it off okay. He was always cordial but it was never a relationship based upon warmth. I always had the impression that he would have preferred Justine marry one of the city's social elite—someone of his choosing—but I think he eventually adjusted his expectations and was happy just to have her wedded to someone respectable. He thought it might settle her down, but that proved to be wishful thinking."

"Did you ever ask the judge to bail you out?" I asked.

"No. First, his wedding present was quite generous and allowed us to maintain our standard of living. Second, I didn't want to do anything that might tip him off about my gambling problem."

"How often did you see Jill?"

"More often than I cared to. She and Justine had a love-hate relationship. Jill was forever trying to seduce me as a way of getting back at Justine." Rutledge paused and looked into my eyes. "In anticipation of your next question, she didn't succeed."

"Are you worried about Dr. Tubinski's well-being?" I asked. "Couldn't she be in danger as well because of her participation in the project?"

"I'm concerned about Clovis, of course. But her knowledge of the project makes her a valuable commodity, and I expect the government will step in and ask her to pick up where we left off. The research documentation I left should provide her with job security for the foreseeable future. Given enough time, and the right kind of assistance, she may be able to achieve and move beyond what evaded us before."

"Rutledge, I'm afraid I have some bad news. I have reason to believe that Dr. Tubinski may have been kidnapped the day before yesterday. She was seen being escorted from her townhouse by a couple of men. I don't know how much peril she may be in and, unfortunately, I had to leave L.A. before I could pursue the possibility further."

I was surprised when Rutledge smiled wanly and removed a piece of paper from his shirt pocket which he handed to me. "Here's an overnight express letter that Uva and I just picked up from the post office. It's from Clovis."

> Kevin, I hope this letter finds you. This is the only communication I will be able to send since I am being relocated. I have been picked up by the National Investigation Agency and placed in protective custody, sort of like a witness protection program. They are changing my identity and relocating me to Minnesota to continue our work on the XV-1000. I will be working in a high security environment and promoted to director of operations. We picked up the research notes. Thank you so much. They have promised me whatever I need. I pray for your safety and will always think of you. Good luck.

"Do you mind if I keep this?" I asked. "It will allow the missing persons department to stop dragging the bay for her body." I folded the message and placed it inside my pocket. "Now, while it removes Dr. Tubinski from harm's way, *you* still have a problem."

"Duvalier," Rutledge answered with chagrin.

"Exactly. The cops have cancelled their APB on you since it's been arranged to have Roger take the fall for the four homicides. Duvalier's another story. He is relentless. No matter where you go, he will eventually find you. I only got to you first because of my fondness for tuna salad." Uva and Rutledge were clearly puzzled by this reference, but I didn't stop to explain. "Duvalier is probably only a step or two behind. Nobody stiffs him with a marker and leaves this Earth without pain. How did you plan to handle him?"

"I hadn't gotten that far in my thinking, but we're planning on leaving the country," Rutledge admitted.

"May I make a suggestion?" I asked

"You've got my undivided attention," Rutledge said.

"You must have had life insurance on Justine. How much?"

"We each had one million dollar policies," Rutledge recalled. "Judge Barrington's financial advisor encouraged us to take out life insurance when we got married."

"How much do you owe Duvalier?"

"$530,000," Rutledge replied.

"Since Roger's arrest clears you of any implication in your wife's death, send your insurance company a copy of Justine's death certificate. Their settlement will allow you to pay Duvalier off with a money order or cashier's check, plus provide a relocation nest egg for you and Uva."

Rutledge brightened. "Sounds like a plan. Thanks, McFadden."

His face then changed, as if startled by a sudden realization. He asked resignedly, in a tone of mild disgust, "I may have been a little naïve where you're concerned, though. What are you expecting to get out of this?"

"As the locals are fond of saying, 'keep your city money.' I have no intention of blackmailing you, Rutledge." From my overalls, I extracted a couple of sheets of blank motel stationery and a pen. "What I want is very simple and costs you nothing."

"Write a letter to Duvalier telling him that I've found you. Tell him you will honor your gaming debts with insurance proceeds, which will be forthcoming shortly. Explain that since you're no longer connected with the supercomputer project, you have no further value to him. Once he's received your money, I believe he'll call off the hounds."

"If I do as you ask, will *you* forget about Lancaster, as well? I'd rather not give anyone a trail to follow."

"Please, Mr. McFadden," Uva implored, with a look that could have melted the marble penis off the statue of David. "Kevin's sorry for what he's done. We only want a fresh start and a chance to be together in a place where we don't have to constantly look over our shoulders. We've found a place in the Canadian wilderness, and Kevin has gotten a job as director of software development with a remote pulpwood company. We plan on leaving the states tomorrow. Please . . . please . . . promise you won't give us away."

For *Maltese Falcon* fans, I can assure you that Brigid O'Shaughnessy lives on. A tear formed in the lower corner of each eye and raced over her cheeks until they fell on her up-thrust breasts below. *This* was an impromptu emotional tour de force of the highest order.

"The histrionics aren't necessary. I have no intention of turning you in if you comply with my request," I said.

Rutledge overcame his initial reticence and penned his apologia on the cheap paper.

"Wait—don't sign it yet," I instructed as he neared the bottom of the page. "I want to have your signature witnessed and notarized by the bank across the street."

He pushed the sheet across the table to me with a sigh of relief. The act of writing out his transgressions seemed to have served as a sort of secular expiation; he looked more relaxed and at ease with himself now than he had twenty minutes earlier. I scanned his statement and complimented him. "This will do quite nicely."

I handed him the newspaper I had been carrying as part of my cover. "Now," I told him, "hold the front page of this *Boston Globe* under your chin so that I can take a close-up picture of the date and your face. Your notarized signature and the dated picture should provide

Duvalier with adequate proof that I found you." Rutledge did as instructed and I snapped his picture with a flash. "You'll find me as good as my word insofar as this meeting is concerned," I said.

We walked over to the bank and concluded our business, and then I escorted them to a utility vehicle. As I saw them speed away toward the edge of town, I couldn't help but wish Rutledge better luck—in his next venture and his new relationship.

Chapter 26

The return flight to the City of Angels was uneventful, which suited me fine. When I arrived, the Hudson even responded to my fervent prayers by starting up, belching black smoke, and wheezing spasmodically in the airport's long-term parking lot. Before heading to my apartment, I dropped by the office to check on the mail and feed the mice. The telephone started ringing just as I opened the door.

I recognized the voice of Rubella Saperstein, though I had to apply some audible strain to understand her sentences, which were interrupted by sniffles and sobs. She disclosed that she and Montrose were at the hospital—Roger had tried to commit suicide in his jail cell and come about as close as one can get without crossing over the river Jordan. He wasn't expected to live for more than a few hours, and Rubella asked if I would join them. I agreed.

The intensive care unit was on the third floor, and Roger's room was easy to locate because a police guard was sitting outside in a chair propped against the wall reading a racing form. He barely looked up when I tapped lightly on the door and was admitted by Mrs. Saperstein.

Montrose was sitting on the edge of a chair, polishing a bed pan with his handkerchief.

Roger lay in supination, his enormous head swathed in a turban of white bandages. In repose, with the upper half of his head covered, he looked almost human instead of pongid, but even an inert Roger was menacing enough to send chills down my spine.

"Hello, Montrose," I greeted. "I'm sorry to hear about Roger."

"Hear, sir?" Montrose said, looking up. "Roger can't hear anything with all those bandages wrapped around his head."

"I meant to say that I was sorry to learn that Roger had tried to take his own life."

"Oh, that," Montrose said. "I'm afraid Roger has an unenviable track record when it comes to botching things up. Time will tell whether or not a successful suicide will end his string of failures."

Montrose was handling his grief very well. "How's the hospital treating him?" I asked.

Montrose shook his head. "They haven't been particularly responsive, sir, but perhaps it's because he's been in a coma and can't press the buzzer."

"Buzzard, Montrose? Those scavengers won't show up until he's dead."

Touché.

I motioned for Mrs. Saperstein to follow me outside, and I took hold of her upper arm to provide support. I led her a few paces down the hall where I treated us to some vending machine coffee. She eased into a nearby chair, and I offered her a handkerchief, which she used to dab her eyes.

"Thank you," she said. Her voice was barely a whisper. "Thank you for coming. Montrose and I have only been here an hour ourselves."

"How did it happen, Mrs. Saperstein?" I asked.

"They say he tried to take his own life by banging his head against the wall of his cell. He's lost a lot of blood. They don't expect him to last the afternoon."

"I wouldn't have thought Roger would inflict pain upon himself . . ." I was trying to be kind in consideration of a mother's love, but it wasn't easy. I still harbored visions of Roger staring at me with undisguised ferality in his one good eye. "Has he been conscious at all? Has he said anything to anyone?"

"He comes to every now and then, stirs slightly, and then drops back into unconsciousness."

"Mrs. Saperstein, I'll be glad to be of any assistance I can, but I'm uncertain why you asked me to join you here."

"I'm convinced that Roger couldn't have done those horrible things," she began. "He knows more than he's telling, but he's keeping it to himself. This may be our last chance to find out the truth. I was hoping he'd regain consciousness so you could question him and get to the bottom of this. People don't lie on their death beds, do they? I can't bear the thought of Roger going to his grave carrying this terrible secret with him. My niece, Cleotha, is still not avenged and I owe it to her dead parents to identify the murderer and see that he goes to the gallows. Will you stay by Roger's bedside in case he comes to and try to get his last confession?"

I acceded to her request, which seemed to comfort the distraught woman. To be frank, I really didn't want to be around if Roger regained consciousness. He was only minimally intelligent to begin with and who knew what state of mindlessness he might be in after having left what little gray matter he did have splattered against the jailhouse wall. I was ultimately swayed by the facts that Rubella had, after all, paid for my professional services and that I had, after all, accomplished little in return.

We walked back to Roger's room where I was greeted outside the door by the decaying grin of Lieutenant Del Dotto.

"Well, well, McFadden, what're you doing here? If you're planning to donate your fat ass to medical science, they'll have to accept it under the installment plan. They ain't got the facilities to handle all your bloated organs at once."

"Good afternoon, lieutenant. Why are you here? Trying to close a case by planting some evidence on a convenient corpse?"

"Very funny, but you're not far from being right. I just stopped by to check on Roger's condition. I've got eight deputies standing by with a reinforced stretcher to haul that big son-of-a-bitch down to the maggot-mobile. I hope he cashes in soon. We ain't got all day."

"You've got quite a bedside manner there, lieutenant. You must be a riot at funeral parlors. Do the next-of-kin ever invite you back for an encore?"

"It's a job," he shrugged, spitting a toothpick out of his mouth and onto a tray that was being carried by a passing nurse. "What's your angle? Waiting for somebody to die so you can steal their fruit cocktail and hamburger patty?"

"I'm here in case Roger is up to doing some last-minute talking."

"I brought a plainclothes dick here to do that. You're wasting your time—not that you have anything to do with it anyway."

"It shouldn't come as a surprise to you, lieutenant, but Roger's mother doesn't have a great deal of confidence in the police. She'd rather get anything Roger has to say straight from his mouth, not after it's been ghostwritten by the city hall grifters who yank your chain. Incidentally, Roger's mother asked if a priest had been requested to give Roger his last rites."

"Roger don't need a priest, he needs an exorcist. Father Houlihan was here but he took off like a purse snatcher after his crucifix melted at Roger's bedside. Besides, absolution is going to be a little hard to come by for our friend if his rap sheet is any indication. If St. Peter is keeping an evil deeds book on Roger, he ran out of ink years ago. I suspect that within fifteen minutes of death, Roger will be buggering Satan and running hell as if it was his own personal playground."

"In that same vein, you'd better hope that St. Peter's vigilance has been lax where the Magic Fingers Motel is concerned. If he's been casing the joint with any regularity, you might as well drop your pants, grab your ankles, and get ready for Roger's charge as well."

Del Dotto's jaw dropped a foot, and his eyes looked murderous as he snapped, "Listen peeper, your license and tubby little ass exist at my pleasure. Both can be cancelled at any time and don't forget it. Confine your snooping to what you're being paid for and stay outta my personal affairs." Then, in a hushed voice, he looked around and asked, "Where'd you hear that anyway?"

"Why you're the talk of junior high, Del Dotto. Thanks to you, there's not a virgin in the ninth grade—all the fourteen-year-olds are limping around campus with battered vaginas, marveling at your sexual gymnastics. They like the way you whip them with their training bras and force them to perform fellatio without bending their braces."

Del Dotto exploded in a rage and attempted to pull his service revolver from his holster. It took a bear hug by the deputy guarding the door to keep him from firing it. I was looking around for a safe place to scamper when the door to Roger's room opened and Rubella stuck her head out.

"Mr. McFadden, come quick. Roger's coming to."

I didn't need a second invitation. I dashed into the hospital room, locking the door behind me. Inspired by genius, I yelled through the door, loudly enough to be heard in the hallway, "Help! Roger's on his feet and walking around. Look out!"

The other side of the door grew silent as a stampede of footsteps faded down the hall. Congratulating myself on my quick thinking, I approached Roger's bed.

He appeared to be aware of visitors in the room. His face had grown pale; almost the color of the bandages, and his one functioning eye was open. Rubella pulled me closer to the other side of the bed.

"Roger," she whispered, pushing the bandages above her son's ear, "this is Mr. McFadden. You remember him, don't you? He's here to help. *Please* tell him what you know about the murders."

Roger turned his head slowly in my direction and gazed at my face. He seemed to nod, indicating his recognition. We couldn't know how long he would be conscious, so despite his weakened condition, I pressed for information.

"Roger," I pleaded, "you're standing on the edge of eternity. You don't have long to live. If you weren't responsible for the murders, please tell us who was. Get this weight off your chest before it's too late." He appeared to be digesting the words and running the idea through his rudimentary thought processes.

Outside, the sunset had given way to twilight, and the faint light of the expiring day crept through the sheer fabric of the curtains to bathe the room in an eerily subdued glow. The only sounds were Roger's labored breathing and an occasional gurgle from a suspended bottle of clear fluid that was providing intravenous nourishment.

Roger licked the perimeter of his mouth and motioned for me to lean closer with a slight jerk of his head. My heart was pounding so loudly, and the tinnitus in my ears was so deafening, I was fearful that Roger's expiratory comments would be lost. Still, I took a deep breath and placed my ear as close to Roger's mouth as possible, straining to catch any emission. He began to whisper, haltingly, and my eyes and mouth widened with each passing word. I was completely stunned. I slumped into a chair, shaking my head . . .

Now that I had the answer, I could see in retrospect where the questions should have taken me.

Roger's last gurgle interrupted my thoughts, and I rose to stand behind his parents. At that moment, his head slumped on his pillow and his breathing stopped.

With my thumb, I lowered his eyelid and crept from the room, leaving the odd couple to mourn their loss in privacy.

Chapter 27

After loading my pockets with some tools of the trade, I once again sputtered onto the Ventura Freeway and drove northwest from L.A. through the San Fernando Valley. As I twisted through the hilly terrain of the Conejo Valley thirty minutes later, heavy clouds rushed inland from the coast, dropping the temperature and casting a gray shadow over the area. Some freeway construction beyond Thousand Oaks funneled northbound traffic into one lane, which prevented me from reaching the Camino Real Sanitarium until after dark.

Once I arrived, I inched around the near-deserted streets of the grounds at five miles an hour, pulling over when I spotted a familiar figure beneath a street light stepping off a curb.

"Rudy," I yelled, while braking. "Do you have a minute?"

Rudy Williams, the institutional attendant I had met during my previous visit, approached the car warily, but broke into a grin as he realized who I was.

"Chaun-cey, what's happening, my man? What brings you to reality's alter ego this time of evening?"

"I need to locate Calvin Nately. I tried to look him up in the telephone directory, but was unsuccessful. Do you know where he lives?"

"Calvin has an apartment in Oxnard, but he may be unlisted. He's still here on the grounds, though, if you want to see him. I saw his van parked in front of Bernice Barrington's cottage a little while ago."

"Thanks, Rudy. I'd like to surprise him. Where's her cottage?"

Rudy looked around before answering. "It's after visiting hours, actually. If one of the regular staff sees you driving around, they might run you off. Better park your car here and walk over to her place since it's so close. It's the second street over and a block to the right. Her cottage sits off by itself under a couple of big oak trees. Calvin's white van is out in front. You won't miss it."

I thanked Rudy and squeezed out from behind the steering wheel, shut the car door quietly, and walked in the direction he had indicated. A couple of other pedestrians were out, taking slow, aimless strolls, but none of them paid me any particular attention. It was a moonless night and the only two sources of illumination were the yellow nimbus surrounding each street lamp, and some slivers of light that spilled out upon the sidewalks from beneath drawn window shades.

An evening fog from the ocean had managed to cross the coastal mountain range and was creeping inland like giant shadowy fingers; with it, the air became distinctly cooler. Combined with the spreading fog and dampness, the chill permeated my clothing as if it were cheesecloth. In response, I turned up my collar, buttoned my jacket as much as my girth would permit, and quickened my pace.

The sidewalk ended abruptly—transformed to a gravel path that crunched under my feet. To avoid the noisy broadcast of my approach, I crossed over the grass median and resumed my advance on the asphalt street. Ahead, as promised, in front of a cottage with two overhanging oaks, I found Calvin's van without difficulty. I tried its two rear doors and those on the driver's and the passenger's sides, but they were all locked. The fog had now evolved into a mist of suspended droplets and, while it was uncomfortable, it did provide a welcomed camouflage.

I crept up to the cottage and cautiously circled its perimeter, searching for an opening that would enable me to peer inside. At the rear of the cottage, I discovered an open window whose vertical curtains were separated by a six-inch gap.

I kept my head low, barely above the sill, and peeked inside. The interior was well lit and from this vantage point, I could make out the furnishings of a living room. The room was deserted but a portable radio on a bookcase was softly playing some easy-listening music. On an adjacent table were a Grand Marnier bottle and two aperitif glasses.

Laughing voices from another part of the small cottage drew my attention, and I could also hear what sounded like a shower running. Assuming that a shower was the source of the noise, I deducted that one or both of the occupants were in the bathroom. I needed to confirm the identities of those inside, so I continued around to the front door, found it unlocked, and cautiously stepped inside.

Through the first open door, which turned out to be the bedroom, I saw a pile of clothes on the floor—a white ensemble of shoes, socks, pants, underwear, and a short-sleeved shirt, in that order. On the dresser were a woman's nightgown and the same housecoat I'd seen on Bernice Barrington during my previous visit—*both neatly folded.* As if that wasn't enough of a shocker, in a corner, I saw something equally chilling: *Mrs. Barrington's empty wheelchair*.

I tiptoed to the bathroom door, which was opened just a crack and carefully expanded the space to a couple of inches so I could see in. Steam started to roll out of the room, and I stepped back so as not to fog up the lenses on my glasses. A moment passed and I peered around the door again to see a tub that had been converted to an enclosed shower; through the sliding glass doors were discernible the nude silhouettes of a man and a woman locked in a passionate embrace.

I pulled the door back, retraced my steps to the pile of Calvin's clothes, and rifled through his pants until I found a ring of assorted keys. I grasped them tightly to stifle any noise and headed outside to the van.

The damp, thickening mist was playing havoc with my glasses, and it took me several tense minutes of trial-and-error to match the lock with the correct key. Finally, I got the back door of the van unlocked, opened it, and crawled inside. Fortunately, the interior dome light was not activated which allowed me to feel less exposed. I relaxed for a second and removed my glasses to wipe the lenses with my handkerchief before I pulled out my pen flashlight. I clicked it on, and gasped.

The beam of my flashlight was weak, but I felt as though I'd stumbled across the viper's nest after weeks of searching for the serpent responsible for a series of snakebite victims.

Scattered around the floor of the vehicle behind the two forward bucket seats were numerous accessories of death. Two pairs of rubber loafers with crepe soles caught my attention, as did some needle-nosed pliers, rolls of electrical tape, electric cords, a bottle of chloroform—and a couple of vibrators. I retrieved my camera from my pocket, inserted a flash cube, and took several pictures to record the evidence. I stopped after a dozen exposures and replaced the camera in my pocket. I had gotten what I came for and was grateful I wouldn't have to search Calvin's apartment as well.

Being on all fours wasn't a comfortable position, but the excitement and anxiety of this discovery had temporarily displaced any realizations of pain caused by the direct contact of my knees with the iron floor of the van. I was now feeling the pain, however, and backed slowly out of the van, using the rear bumper to lower myself to the ground. I stretched, arched my back, and paused a moment to catch my breath. How long I had been near the point of hyperventilation, I couldn't remember, but as the physical exertion redistributed itself throughout my body and the psychological impact of my discovery started to sink in, my breathing returned to normal—

Until I felt a sharp jab in my back and heard what sounded like a revolver being cocked. I raised my shaking hands without prompting, and prayed for the best.

"Well, well, it's Dr. McFadden, ain't it? Breaking and entering is a serious crime. In fact, it just became a capital offense. What've you got to say for yourself before I carry out the sentence?" My captor took the key ring out of my hand and increased the pressure of the gun barrel against my spine. The squeaky voice and the smell of fresh soap identified my captor as Calvin Nately.

"Oh, hello, Nately. I was just admiring your van. I've been thinking about buying something like this. Would you recommend the dealership where you bought it?"

"A thirty-minute lease would be *your* best bet since you'll be dead long before you get the title papers. Did you find what you were looking for?"

"Quite possibly. I've been investigating a string of vibrator-related murders. And, it may be nothing more than a coincidence, but your van seems to contain all the components of the murder weapons that were used."

"It's no coincidence," Nately said with a chuckle. "I've been helping Bernice with her mission to end the sinful lives of her two daughters. Along the way, we were forced to throw in a couple of others of questionable virtue for good measure."

I stalled for time, though I wasn't sure why. "I commend you both for your sense of civic responsibility in attacking the vice problem in our city. I'll be sure to nominate you for the mayor's Community Improvement Award."

"That won't be necessary. We're modest about our accomplishments. If it's all the same to you, we'll step aside and let some other deserving citizen get the glory."

"You may feel differently later on, though. If you'll allow me to lower my hands, I'll get the tape recorder from my car and record your confession. You might want credit some day."

"You're a riot, McFadden. I don't even know if I'll be able to keep a straight face when I dump your body in a hole. Got any last words?"

"For starters, how about, what's a little pip-squeak like you doing out on a night like this—" I had follow-up questions in mind, but that was all I managed to stammer before I felt a hard blow on the back of my head . . . sharp pain shooting through my skull . . . spasms traveling down the base of my neck . . . and my face dragging along the cold, wet door of the van . . . down . . .down . . . down . . .

Chapter 28

I'm not sure what stirred me back to consciousness. Perhaps it was the intense throbbing in my head, because every pulsation was amplified into an explosion. Or, perhaps it was the discomfort caused by having my hands tied behind my back and lying on my side. Or, maybe it was the roar coming from the van's untuned engine, or even the hard rock music that was blasting from the eight-track tape player. No, I suspected it was the bumpy road, whose jolts tossed me back and forth between the sides of the van.

I knew I wasn't dead because I hurt too much. I was also starting to acquiesce with my current circumstances, which strangely had a relaxing effect that led me to start drifting back into unconsciousness until a pothole of crater-like dimensions jarred me up into a sitting position.

It was then that reality swept back over me. I was the prisoner of a madman being driven to my death. I didn't know where we were or our ultimate destination, but I decided I had better start using what time I had left as if my life depended on it—because I had a feeling it did. Somehow I had to free myself . . .

Since I'd been bounced into a sitting position, it was easy for me to brace myself against the side of the van. It was still dark, and everything was blurry, which I attributed more to the fact that my glasses were missing than the pain in my head. Squinting helped to sharpen my focus, so I was able to look around to make an assessment. With a forward glance, I saw the back of my abductor's head and noted that he was alone. The winding road and a steady drizzle required his undivided attention, which hopefully meant he would rarely look back over his shoulder to check my status. I guessed us to be on one of those twisting roads that meander through the Santa Monica Mountains, tenuously connecting Ventura Highway 101 with the Pacific Coast Highway. These roads were seldom traveled, and with tonight's conditions, I was as sure as my captor that we would encounter few, if any, highway companions—an observation that added to my uneasiness.

I frantically examined my environment for tools of emancipation. I ruled myself out as a likely source, since I had obviously been searched by Nately—the pockets of my pants and coat were all pulled inside out so they resembled the ears of a dejected beagle. The only items Nately hadn't confiscated were my belt and wallet, but neither the buckle nor my overcharged credit cards would be sharp enough to saw through the ropes binding my wrists, even if I could have grasped them. Nately had also taken the precaution of removing any sharp instruments from the back of the van, which was disappointing, since they might have provided aid.

I battled to resist despair and suppress the panic that was welling up inside me by focusing on my search. Without thinking, I shifted my legs to a more comfortable position and experienced a sharp sting in the back of my right calf. I twisted my leg slightly, and barely made out a tear in my trousers and a small gash from which a glisten of blood trickled.

A closer look disclosed the source of my injury to be a small piece of jagged metal that was sticking up from the floor of the van like a ferrous stalagmite. In a pique, I raised my foot to flatten the tetanus-spawning tormentor, but then I stopped—if this piece of metal could rip clothes and flesh, it could also work against a length of rope . . .

I slid my ample buttocks across the floor of the van and faced forward, placing my body between my kidnapper and the working area in order to shield my subterfuge. As soon as I located the jagged edge, I began the laborious process of sawing the rope that bound my wrists against it. I paused every minute or so to apply stress to the fibers, and to catch my breath. Several minutes later, Nately turned the music down and I looked up to see him looking back over his shoulder.

"Well, McFadden, glad you could rejoin the living, brief as that's gonna be. You're probably uncomfortable back there, but I'll put you out of your misery shortly."

"Where are we going?" I asked.

"If I told you, I'd have to kill you." He chortled at his own wit—another Del Dotto. He turned the music back up and increased the speed of his windshield wipers and the van.

The sound of Nately's voice had infused me with renewed incentive, and I redoubled my efforts at liberation. I continued to saw away without knowing how much, if any, progress, was being made. This absence of feedback was nerve-racking. Suddenly the van screeched to a halt, precipitating an almost identical coronary reaction on my part. Nately turned the engine off and stepped out of the van.

Was this it? Was this to be the site of my execution? Was I to be unceremoniously dumped over the edge of the road? Was I to rest at the bottom of some arroyo until the wild coyotes left nothing but bones to be found by hikers in the months or years ahead?

I went berserk. I sawed like a fiend possessed. I strained with every ounce of strength to pull my wrists apart and snap the rope that bound them. Any second now, I knew the back doors of the van would swing open, and Nately's pale, ghoulish face and sardonic smile would beckon.

I worked in a frenzy, disregarding any fatigue or soreness that engulfed my body. If I had been in shape, attempting escape would have been a lot easier. I cursed myself for years of sloth and physical deterioration. I sawed away and strained all the more.

But the back doors didn't open.

I stopped breathing for a second and heard Nately swearing and grunting—but the sounds were coming from in front of the van. I opened my eyes, which had been tightly shut to focus my concentration, and blinked the sweat out of them. Struggling to one knee, I looked through the windshield and saw the reason for the interruption of our journey. Several dozen rocks the size of basketballs had become detached from the canyon wall and rolled onto the road. They couldn't be driven around or over, which meant enough of them had to be moved to permit passage.

In relief, I collapsed back to the floor of the van; however, I quickly repositioned myself to continue my attempted extrication—this stay of execution was only temporary. Following more grunts and more expletives, Nately reentered the van, restarted it, and jerked it back into gear. I stopped only momentarily to keep my balance, then alternated between sawing and pulling and sawing and pulling until I finally felt some fibers give way; finally, the rope began to slacken. Minutes later, a hard tug completed my task. I was free! I hadn't escaped yet, but at least I could present a defense. My life might not have been worth much as lives go, but a couple of people took more than a passing interest in its preservation—myself included.

Moving with the motion of the van, I fell back down on my side, returned my hands to their criss-cross position, and feigned a relapse into unconsciousness. In that "unconscious" state, I plotted my next move. I outweighed Nately by more than a hundred pounds, but that would only work to my advantage if I could get on top of him. That would require that I have the element of surprise on my side. Since he had a gun, the surprise had to occur at a strategic point in time, when the weapon wasn't in his hand.

I entertained the thought of jumping him now, but was dissuaded by the probability of several outcomes—all bad. The first was that the van could go off the road, killing us both. The second was that he might see me rise into an attack position—either with a backwards glance or a reflection in the window—and stop me in my tracks with a well-placed shot. The third was that he might elude my pounce, stop the van, exit, and come around to shoot me through the rear door of the van while I was cornered. Due deliberation led to the adoption of another plan, one that required I do nothing for the time being but roll with the van.

I didn't have to wait long before the van eased to a stop. The knowledge that I was in a more opportune position than I had been ten minutes earlier did not help much in quelling my anxiety. As soon as I heard the driver's door slam shut, I closed my eyes and rolled over on my back to keep my free hands out of view.

I heard the rear door open. "Okay, McFadden. Get your fat ass out here."

I didn't budge.

Nately reached in and slapped my feet with his open palm. "C'mon, man, let's go. It's wet out here."

I still didn't budge.

"Aw, for Christ's sake," I heard him complain, "the fat bastard's passed out again."

He grabbed my ankles and pulled desperately to move me toward the back door of the van. My weight was a problem for him, fortunately, as evidenced by his testimonial grunts and groans.

He finally got me to a point where I was lying on my back with my legs dangling out of the van at a ninety degree angle. Following a brief break, he leaned over, pressed a shoulder against my chest and stomach, put his slender arms around me in a hug, and pulled with all his might to lift me to a sitting position.

This was the moment I had been waiting for! I clenched my fists and swept them around in opposing arcs, pounding Nately in his temples with my knuckles. With my thumbs, I then gouged his eyes as deeply as his sockets would allow, stopping only when he jerked his head to the side. Before he know what was happening, I next clasped my hands around this throat and fell out of the van on top of him, pinning him to the road; I brought my knee up into his groin several times for good measure, but my grip on his windpipe was quite secure. I locked my arms and used my upper body weight to push down and squeeze, easily cutting off his flow of oxygen.

He flailed away, scratching my face and bruising my ribs, but I continued to push down and squeeze . . . and squeeze . . . and squeeze.

I'm not sure how long I held Nately in that position. Probably long after his arms had fallen limply to his sides. I didn't know what else to do. I only knew I couldn't let him up. It never dawned on me that I was extinguishing a life; only that I was battling the paralysis of fear to protect my own.

I eventually struggled to my feet and looked down at Nately's face. His eyes were open and filled with the same terror that had filled mine earlier. His mouth was agape, frozen in his last futile attempt to suck air into his body.

My own lungs burned as I struggled to catch my breath. I was wet from the drizzle, sore, dirty, tired, drenched with perspiration. I slumped back against the rear bumper to regain my strength.

After ten minutes or so, I recovered enough to struggle to my feet. I loaded Nately's body aboard the van, locating my glasses in the process, and closed the doors. I found a spot to turn the van around and headed back to Camino Real.

It was only ten thirty, the clock on the dash said, when I pulled up in front of Bernice Barrington's cottage. As soon as she saw the lights of the van through her window, she rushed to the front door to welcome Nately back. The look on her face said it all when I stepped out instead.

"It's all over, Mrs. Barrington. Calvin won't be coming back. Now, let's say you tell me why you killed four women."

She took a deep breath of resignation, turned abjectly, and stepped back inside the cottage, allowing me to follow her in for the rest of the story.

Chapter 29

By the time I turned Bernice and her story over to the police and got back to my apartment, it was three in the morning. The police assured me that, based upon a preliminary review of the facts, my dispatch of Calvin Nately would be deemed justifiable homicide. The past few days had taken their toll, but after a good night's sleep and a long shower, I found myself able to get back into some slacks I hadn't used in ten pounds. I was anxious to see Jake and Girtha, but there were a couple of other matters that had higher priority.

First, I stepped across the hall to Melkoff's office because I wanted to be the first to tell him that Roger's trial would be cancelled, due to his untimely death. Melkoff was visibly annoyed at my news since he was expecting a healthy fee for providing little in the way of a legal defense for Roger.

He quickly recovered, however, when I told him how Roger had incurred his fatal injury while in custody. He frantically scribbled notes and mumbled something about filing a wrongful death suit on behalf of Roger's parents—a much more lucrative opportunity.

After returning to my office, I called Del Dotto—a personal visit being ill-advised since he may not have recovered from my earlier threatened disclosure of his pedophilia—and brought him up to date on my trip to New Hampshire, specifically my encounter with Rutledge and the information I'd gathered regarding Clovis Tubinski's disappearance. I also filled him in on the arrest of Bernice Barrington and the death of Calvin Nately.

Del Dotto was not overly happy; while this information would allow him to close the missing persons cases on Rutledge and Tubinski and the murder files of the sisters Barrington, Boom Boom, and Wanda, he now needed to reopen those two dozen old, weird homicides he had planned to pin on Roger.

I next called Rubella Saperstein to inform her that the death of Nately and the arrest of Bernice Barrington had exonerated Roger, and that his spirit—at least as far as these four murders were concerned—could rest in piece. I refused further compensation, telling her that her $99.90 deposit was sufficient.

Finally, I was able to hit the street. At noon, I was on my way to my first stop, Halcyon Hills to see Judge Barrington. Montrose opened the door and admitted me. He was holding a silver tray that contained six condoms.

"Montrose, it appears your reconciliation with your ex-wife is going well. Congratulations." I complimented.

"Oh, these are not for me, sir. I'm taking them to the cemetery to leave at the graves of Jill and Justine."

"Do they need them at this point?" I asked.

Montrose looked surprised at my question. "Sir, the afterlife is full of such despicable characters that I want to make sure the girls are protected against sexually transmitted diseases. Like Egyptian royalty, they should be provided with earthly artifacts to serve them in the hereafter."

Good old Montrose: he was as loyal to his mistresses in death as he had been in life. "That's very considerate, Montrose. Is Judge Barrington in?"

Montrose dutifully escorted me to the judge, who was in his library, reading a stock ticker. I recounted the events of the night before, and he listened to me in stunned disbelief, struggling to accept his wife's complicity in the murders. A simple call to the Ventura County police confirmed that Mrs. Barrington had been taken into custody and charged with all four homicides.

With that part of his case file cleared, I informed him that I had located his son-in-law in New Hampshire and showed him the statement Kevin had written at my instruction along with the picture I'd taken at the coffee shop. After pledging to get Bernice the worst attorney possible, he summoned Montrose to fetch his checkbook. I recommended Melkoff to earn a finder's fee—income opportunities are where you find them—and eagerly pocketed the check for $10,000. On the way out, I sweetened my payday by swiping one of the condoms off the silver tray.

My next stop was the Century City office of Armand Duvalier. Since I didn't have an appointment, his receptionist informed me that Mr. Duvalier was in conference and couldn't be disturbed. Unabashed, I wrote a note, handed it to her, and insisted that it be delivered to Duvalier at once. She accepted it begrudgingly and, after checking her lipstick and make-up in her compact's mirror, swished down the hall and passed it to Duvalier's private secretary.

A few moments later, an interoffice buzzer sounded on the receptionist's console, and I was directed back to the secretary's desk. A couple of goons frisked me thoroughly, stopping just short of a cavity search, and waited while the secretary opened the door to Duvalier's chambers.

Duvalier listened attentively as I described my meeting with Rutledge and the events of the previous evening. I gave him the dated picture from the coffee shop as well as Rutledge's statement with its notarized signature and its promise that Rutledge would make his markers good from the proceeds of his deceased wife's life insurance policy—but only if the bounty on his head was rescinded and the future of his physical safety was guaranteed. Ever suspicious, Duvalier went to his wall safe and withdrew Rutledge's gambling markers to compare the signatures.

After completing my report, I encountered resistance from Duvalier obtaining my fee. Duvalier initially balked at paying me since I could not confide Rutledge's current location. However, I reminded him that I had only been hired to find Rutledge, which I had done. I further convinced him that Rutledge had ceased to have any commercial value to him or to his consortium. Primarily, I told him that the research on the XV-1000 had not been completed and that it would not be available to him now that Uncle Sam had seized control of the project's documentation and lead scientist.

Duvalier finally agreed that little more would be gained from the pursuit of Rutledge, and he promised to remove the bounty as soon as the $530,000 check was received in good order. He then dismissed me with a wave of his hand and instructed his secretary to prepare me a check for $10,000—plus $1,654.21 in expenses.

By the time I left my bank and leaned on the counter of Jake's kiosk, it was mid-afternoon. I arrived just as he was finishing a late lunch, evidenced by the familiar remains of *taramosalata, avgolemono soup*, *souvlaki*, *fresca fasolia*, and *tiropitakia*, which Jake ate as dessert. When he caught sight of me, he wiped his mouth on his sleeve, scattering bits of feta cheese on top of a stack of *True Detective* magazines.

"Chauncey, you corpulent conqueror of conundrums; you—" He stopped mid-sentence when he saw the bruises on my face and the patch of purple flesh cresting my bald head. "Sweet Jesus," he said. "You look terrible. What happened? Are you okay?"

"I'll live. Good news, Jake. I've solved the case."

"Well done, my friend. Whodunit?" Jake asked.

"Bernice Barrington and her personal attendant at the mental hospital, Calvin Nately."

Jake gasped. "How could that be? She's in a wheelchair, and confined to an institution!"

I answered while Jake went back to serving customers. "The wheelchair was a ruse. She can walk as well as you can. As far as the Camino Real Sanitarium is concerned, there's virtually no security over patients who are not under a legal restraint, especially when they are attended by a privately paid health care professional. For all practical purposes, she was in an assisted living facility and could come and go as she pleased. The murders always took place after dark, so their departures and returns would be inconspicuous. Mrs. Barrington had her own private cottage, took her meals in private, and never participated in sanitarium activities, so the staff was accustomed to her absences."

"Okay, they had the opportunity, but what was the motive?" Jake asked. "Why did they murder four people, and why did they kill them the way they did?"

"Bernice originally intended to kill only her two daughters. She was emotionally racked by their promiscuity, and it eventually drove her to borderline insanity. She felt an acute sense of guilt and came to the conclusion that the only way to cure herself of madness, and atone for her sin of bringing them into the world, was to kill them. She also hated her husband for having her committed and viewed the deaths of his daughters, whom he loved deeply, as a way of getting back at him. She chose vibrators to give their deaths an ironic symbolism. She wanted them to die the same way they had lived. She was also intrigued by the idea of giving her husband a couple of doses of public humiliation."

"Okay, then, what were her reasons for killing Boom Boom and Wanda? I'll bet she killed them to cover up her real motive, right?"

"Not really. She killed them as acts of self-preservation. Bernice was being blackmailed by Boom Boom, who learned the fine art of extortion from working in that capacity for Duvalier and Valentinuzzi. Boom Boom drove over to Rutledge's home one night, when she knew he'd be working, to have it out with Justine for possession of Kevin. But she spotted Bernice and Nately leaving the premises after the murder.

"Boom Boom's curiosity was aroused by Bernice's presence at the Rutledge house, because Kevin had told Boom Boom of his mother-in-law's confinement in Camino Real and of her inability to walk. Boom Boom waited until they left, and then walked in to discover Justine's body in the tub. She knew Bernice had money of her own, or could get it, and she couldn't pass up the opportunity to do a little freelance blackmailing of her own.

"So, she went to the sanitarium to see Bernice and demand money for her silence. I had seen her name on the visitor's register during my first visit there, but I hadn't been able to make a connection. Bernice promised to get the hush money together and have Nately deliver it in a few days.

"Instead, she and Nately showed up that night at Boom Boom's house with a bottle of chloroform and a vibrator to induce her silence. They did the deed and were in the van, across the street getting ready to leave, when they saw Wanda come home and pull into the driveway. They stayed around a few minutes and saw Wanda flee from the house after discovering her roommate's body.

"They then followed her to a Hilton where she checked in for the night. The hotel didn't afford the homicidal privacy they required, so Nately took Bernice back to Camino Real and then returned to the hotel lobby to stake out Wanda. He followed her the next morning when she stopped by my office before fleeing to Long Beach. Once Nately learned where she had settled, he returned to Camino Real. He and Bernice paid Wanda a visit a couple of nights later."

"Why did they kill Wanda?" Jake asked.

"They perceived Wanda to be a threat to them. Two things made them nervous about her. First, the fact that she had stopped by the office of a private detective—they had no idea we hadn't spoken. Second, in an attempt to enhance her safety, Boom Boom had told Bernice at the sanitarium that she had shared Bernice's secret with another person who would inform the police should anything happen to her.

"While that was probably a bluff to help insure her personal safety, Wanda's behavior made them suspect she was that confidante. Bernice was reluctant to risk it and decided that Wanda must share the same fate as the others. The fact that both women exhibited the same loose sexual lifestyle as the Barrington sisters made it logical—at least in Bernice's mind—that they be dispatched in the same way. Besides, if you can regain your sanity and ease your conscience by killing two tramps, it stands to reason that killing four tramps is even better."

"This Wanda—why did she stop by your office?"

"We'll never know. Possibly a cry for help. My office is only a couple of miles from the Glad Gland and her home, so she may have picked me for reasons of convenience. She could have then bolted for a number of reasons.

"She may have sought bodyguard protection or wanted me to find Boom Boom's killer but had second thoughts and changed her mind. Or she may have seen Rubella Saperstein pulling up to the curb from my office window and got frightened. She may have even seen Nately's van although she would not have known that he was tailing her. I didn't recognize my visitor had been Wanda until I found her body and the blond wig in her apartment."

"I been following this thing in the papers, so I gotta ask, why was Roger arrested?" Jake asked.

"To understand that, you have to appreciate Bernice's problem of accessibility to her daughters. Justine and Kevin lived in a house so it was just a matter of arranging an evening when Justine was home and Kevin wasn't. Jill was harder to get to. She either spent her time in Halcyon Hills or at Duvalier's various love nests.

"Bernice had to avoid Halcyon Hills because she ran the risk of being recognized by the private security force in town, as well as the problem of her husband and domestic staff members being in residence at the Barrington estate.

"Duvalier's places were no better, since they are perpetually guarded by professional henchmen. Bernice solved the problem by calling Jill, under the pretense of revealing something about Justine's murder, and asking to meet her at a seedy motel where people come and go in anonymity. A motel room gave Bernice the perfect trap she needed to carry out her execution: privacy, a tub of water, and a convenient electrical outlet.

"Armand was curious about Jill's secret rendezvous that night, so he had Roger follow her. Roger tailed her to the Magic Fingers Motel and from his car watched her go into room fifteen. A half hour later he saw Nately and Bernice leave room fifteen. Roger was excited when he saw the couple leaving the room because he recognized one of them—Calvin Nately.

"Although they had not seen each other in several years, Nately and Roger were old friends from the Happyvale State Hospital in Oregon. Nately worked there as a male nurse while Roger was serving time for various and sundry offenses against the citizenry. When Nately would perform euthanasia on some of the older patients, he would allow Roger to perform necrophilia on the warm corpses. Roger, in turn, would terrorize the younger female patients into submitting to Nately's sexual whims without registering a complaint. It was a mutually satisfying relationship until the sanitarium burned to the ground.

"I should have seen this connection long ago. In Roger's police dossier, it mentioned his stretch in Oregon, and Nately had told me of his previous employment there during our chat at Camino Real.

"In any event, Roger was confused. Duvalier had told him to only observe, and not to intervene, in whatever Jill was up to. However, when Jill didn't come out of the room after Bernice and Nately left, Roger went in to check on her. Now normally, Roger would have dropped trou', fished the cadaver out of the water, and humped like hell before rigor mortis set in. However, since his old pal Nately was obviously involved in Jill's death, and since Jill was the paramour of Roger's boss whom Roger obeyed like a faithful dog, Roger had a problem. He was sitting in the motel room pondering his options when he was discovered by the maid."

"What will happen to Mrs. Barrington?" Jake asked.

"It depends on the finding of the court. She will either be found legally competent to stand trial or adjudicated not guilty by reason of insanity. I suspect she'll be spared the poison pellets, but she'll probably spend the rest of her life at the Correctional Institution at Tehachapi."

"How about Nately?"

"He's dead, I'm afraid." I then related the events of that fateful evening, beginning with Roger's deathbed confession and ending with the arrival of the Ventura County police at Bernice's cottage. Jake was visibly shaken at how close I had come to death and excoriated me at length for taking such a chance.

"How did Mrs. Barrington get Nately to do those things for her?" Jake asked.

"I think it was one of those *Harold and Maude* affairs. I suspect they loved each other in their own way. Nately had a self-image problem and probably enjoyed the attention of someone from the upper crust. He may also have hoped to get a share of the Barrington estate if the judge predeceased his wife. Mrs. Barrington, in turn, had in Nately a devoted servant who was eager to do her bidding. Since Nately was wrapped a little too tightly in the first place, her requests were seeds dropped on fertile soil."

"Then Rutledge wasn't involved in the case at all, except for being made a widower. And the supercomputer design never played no part in the murders."

"That's about the size of it. Rutledge turns out to be a red herring. His computer project and Bernice's tragic attempts to win atonement are like double helixes, wound closely around each other, but not related.

"Well, I've got to be going, my friend. I've got to run over to Girtha's. By the way, here's the plane fare I borrowed from you and a small contribution to your foundation." I pressed an envelope into Jake's hand and then walked across the street to Cosmo's.

It was a shame to leave such a beautiful afternoon to step inside the diner. The rain of the previous night had finally cleared the air and bequeathed to the following day a bright sun in a cloudless sky.

I immediately spotted Girtha who had backed through the swinging doors of the kitchen balancing several plates of ordered fare in each hand. She turned and spotted me, stopping in her tracks and gasping at the bumps and bruises on my head. She almost dropped the plates but regained her composure in time to transport them to their destination without further incident. After raking some tips from a couple of vacant table tops into her uniform pocket, she returned and collapsed at the counter. I relayed the previous night's events—minimizing the actual peril which had actually existed—for the umpteenth time while Girtha listened in wide-eyed in amazement.

Girtha, and the other regular lunch patrons, raised their eyebrows when I ordered a diet plate and low-calorie beverage. Their shock was later doubled when I broke precedent and settled my outstanding tab.

"You know, Girtha," I said, toying with the remains of my cottage cheese and pineapple, "there's a romantic movie playing at the Bijou this evening. How would you like to go?" I paused for a breath and to raise my eyebrows. "Afterwards, we could stop by Spago's for a little repast . . . And after that . . ." I discreetly flashed the purloined condom, "it's anybody's guess. Whaddoya say?"

A smile flashed on her cherubic face. Then, in surprising animation she hustled to the time clock, punched herself out, and tossed her apron under the counter.

"There's no time like the present, lover," she said, laughing as she grabbed my arm and led me hopping to the door.

THE END

LaVergne, TN USA
20 August 2009
155414LV00007B/199/P